W9-AAY-985

GAME CHANGERS

BY JOHN FEINSTEIN

THE SPORTS BEAT SERIES

Last Shot: Mystery at the Final Four

Vanishing Act: Mystery at the U.S. Open

Cover-Up: Mystery at the Super Bowl

Change-Up: Mystery at the World Series

The Rivalry: Mystery at the Army-Navy Game

Rush for the Gold: Mystery at the Olympics

THE TRIPLE THREAT SERIES

The Walk On

The Sixth Man

The DH

THE BENCHWARMERS SERIES

Benchwarmers

Game Changers

OTHER NOVELS

Foul Trouble

Backfield Boys

The Prodigy

GAME CHANGERS

JOHN FEINSTEIN

FARRAR STRAUS GIROUX · NEW YORK

Farrar Straus Giroux Books for Young Readers
An imprint of Macmillan Publishing Group, LLC
120 Broadway, New York, NY 10271
Copyright © 2020 by John Feinstein
All rights reserved
Printed in the United States of America
Designed by Michelle Gengaro-Kokmen
First edition, 2020
1 3 5 7 9 10 8 6 4 2

mackids.com

Library of Congress Cataloging-in-Publication Data

Names: Feinstein, John, author.
Title: Game changers / John Feinstein.
Description: First edition. | New York : Farrar Straus Giroux Books for
    Young Readers, 2020. | Series: Benchwarmers ; [2] | Audience:
    Ages 8-12. | Audience: Grades 4-6. | Summary: A new coach's flagrant
    racism, a teammate's endless sabotage, and local media interest make it
    difficult for Andi Carillo and Jeff Michaels to keep both of their basketball
    teams on track.
Identifiers: LCCN 2020007201 | ISBN 9780374312053 (hardcover)
Subjects: CYAC: Basketball—Fiction. | Racism—Fiction. |
    Sportsmanship—Fiction. | Middle schools—Fiction. | Schools—Fiction.
Classification: LCC PZ7.F3343 Gam 2020 | DDC [Fic]—dc23
LC record available at https://lccn.loc.gov/2020007201

Our books may be purchased in bulk for promotional, educational,
or business use. Please contact your local bookseller or the Macmillan
Corporate and Premium Sales Department at (800) 221-7945, ext. 5442,
or by email at MacmillanSpecialMarkets@macmillan.com.

This is for my friend Jackson Diehl, who helped me survive my early days at the Washington Post *and has been both an inspiration and a sounding board for more than (gasp!) forty years . . .*

1

ANDI CARILLO HAD BEEN LOOKING FORWARD TO THIS DAY
since early fall.

She'd spent the soccer season proving to her coach
and many of her teammates that a sixth-grade girl
could not only compete against boys but could thrive.
She had gone from getting cut from the team for com-
mitting the crime of being born female—and then being
virtually nailed to the bench for the same issue—to
being one of the leaders in the Merion Middle School
Mustangs' run to the conference championship.

She'd won over her coach and her teammates, but
it hadn't been easy. In fact, it had been an emotional
roller coaster for most of two months.

Throughout the soccer season, her mind had often
wandered to basketball season for the simple reason that, unlike soccer, Merion Middle had a *girls'*

basketball team. That meant she'd be competing against and alongside other girls. It wasn't that she hadn't been able to hold her own against boys—just the opposite, in fact—but she wouldn't be dealing with a skeptical coach and a group of teammates who would always see her as an interloper.

"You could have been Megan Rapinoe and some of those guys would never accept you," her friend and teammate Jeff Michaels had said to her, referencing the world's greatest female soccer player. "It's their problem, not yours."

Andi knew Jeff was right, and it had been gratifying to see many of her teammates—most—come around as the season progressed and she finally got the chance to prove herself as a player. Now, though, she wouldn't have to deal with any of that. She would actually have teammates to share a locker room with and she wouldn't be an outsider. She'd be, as Jeff liked to say, "one of the guys."

Andi was nearly five foot six, which made her tall for an eleven-year-old girl, but not tall for an eleven-year-old basketball player. She knew there would be at least four girls who were taller than her at tryouts. Debbie Lee was close to six feet, not surprising because her father, who had played on the Chinese national team, was six-ten (Andi had looked it up), and her mother, who had played college ball at Villanova, was six-two.

Andi didn't mind that at all. She liked handling the ball and knew her three-point shot was the strength of her game. With plenty of taller kids on the team, she'd be free to play outside.

Most important, though, today was the first day she would be judged like everybody else—for good or for bad. She couldn't wait.

Jeff was just as excited as she was about the first day of basketball season and the start of tryouts for the sixth-grade team.

He'd played very little soccer prior to the fall and had zero experience playing it on an organized level, so he'd wondered if he could make the team. But he had made it, only to spend the early part of the season sitting right next to Andi on the bench. His crime was different: He'd gotten his dad, who worked for NBC Sports–Philadelphia, to do a story about how a misogynist coach named Hal Johnston was refusing to give Andi a spot on the team even though she was clearly one of the best players during tryouts.

The story had embarrassed Principal Arthur Block enough that he had ordered Coach Johnston to reverse himself and add Andi to the team. It had taken a while for both Andi and Jeff to get a fair chance, but when they finally did, both had performed well. Andi had become a star striker, Jeff a solid contributor at mid-field.

All along—for different reasons—Jeff had looked forward to basketball because he *knew* he was good at the sport, having played it a lot as a kid on playgrounds and in gyms. He had always been one of the best players, whether he was playing pickup ball or organized age-group ball.

Which was why he wasn't nearly as nervous about three days of tryouts in early December as he had been during soccer tryouts in early September. He'd played enough with his competition in gym classes and in after-school pickup games to be confident he was one of the twelve best players in the sixth grade. Truth be told, he was convinced he was one of the two or three best even though he knew he hadn't seen everybody play.

On top of that, Jason Crist was the sixth-grade basketball coach, and Jeff knew and liked him—both as his history teacher and as the assistant coach during soccer season. For much of the fall, Mr. Crist—Coach C on the soccer field—had been the voice of reason when Coach Johnston had been completely unreasonable. Jeff was looking forward to playing on a team with Coach C as the boss.

Jeff walked from the locker room to the gym with his friend Danny Diskin, who he knew was going to be one of the team's best players. Danny wasn't that tall, probably about five foot six or five foot seven, but he was built like a Mack truck, and with his strength and quickness he would be an ideal power forward.

Jeff was a point guard, there was no doubt about that. At five-four, he might not have been the shortest of the kids walking onto the floor, but he was certainly among them. More important, he knew he was as quick as any of them and was willing to bet he could dribble with his off hand—his left—as well as or better than anyone. That was the result of his dad insisting he learn to handle the ball with both hands when they had first started playing on the hoop in their driveway.

It was exactly three fifteen when they all walked to the center jump circle, where Coach C and his assistant coach, Al Benyak—who taught seventh-grade chemistry in real life—were waiting. They had the gym for an hour. The girls would get the court at four fifteen. The two teams would alternate day to day, boys going early one day, girls the next.

Coach C had a big smile on his face as they formed a circle around him and Mr. Benyak.

"I think it's a promising start to see everyone here on time," he said. "It's even more promising I didn't have to blow the whistle to get you over here." He smiled again. "Probably helps that there are no basketballs out here yet to distract you."

Everyone laughed.

He introduced Mr. Benyak, noting that most of them didn't know him because he taught seventh grade, but that he'd played college ball at nearby Drexel. Both coaches would go by initials: Coach C and Coach B.

"We've got nineteen guys here," Coach C said after he'd finished the introductions. "We've only got twelve uniforms. So, unfortunately, we're going to have to cut seven guys after we finish three days of tryouts. We're going to give you all plenty of opportunity to show us what you've got. Don't make any judgments on what we think of you based on who you're playing with. We're going to mix it up every day."

He went on to explain that the boys would start out divided into four teams, playing half-court ball, four-on-four. This would leave three players on the sidelines, waiting to be rotated in and for three others to take their places. "And just so you don't think we've made any judgments, the three guys not starting today are the last three guys alphabetically. Tomorrow, it will be the first three in the alphabet. Friday, we'll take the remaining thirteen names and put 'em in a hat and pick three. In the end, everyone will get the same playing time."

He began calling out names for each team. Then he gave everyone ten minutes to warm up. Basketballs had magically appeared.

Jeff was pleased to see he and Danny were on the

same team, designated Blue One. There would also be Blue Two and White One and Two. Each practice jersey was blue on one side, white on the other.

"Okay," Coach C said after everyone had warmed up. "Blue One ball at midcourt. Michaels, get your guys started."

Jeff eagerly grabbed a ball and looked at Tommy Mayer, the other guard on his team. He was *so* ready for this.

Then he looked and saw who was lining up to guard him for White One.

It was Ron Arlow, who had been his—and Andi's—nemesis for much of the soccer season. Arlow had seemed to come around by season's end.

Now, he was in a defensive stance, glaring at Jeff.

"Here we go again," Jeff murmured, returning Arlow's glare.

He passed the ball to Diskin and basketball season began. Finally.

2

ANDI HAD WALKED INTO THE GYM AND JOINED HER POTENTIAL teammates at the baseline nearest the locker rooms while the boys finished. She glanced at the digital clock on the scoreboard and saw it was 4:14.

The boys were huddled around the two coaches at midcourt for a few final words. She saw them all put their hands up with Coach C in the middle and say, "Get better!" That was the slogan of the day.

As the boys came off the court, some jogging, some walking, she spotted Jeff. There was no sign of his usual smile, which was surprising because they had talked about how much they were both looking forward to basketball season getting started.

"How'd it go?" she said as Jeff came into earshot.

"Don't ask," he said—and just kept walking.

Andi was confused and wanted to find out what

had happened, but at that moment she heard a sharp whistle coming from center court. Amy Josephson, the coach for the girls' team, was standing there, hands on hips, pointing at the clock, which now read four fifteen.

Everyone hustled to the jump circle.

"Good," she said, pointing again at the clock, which had just clicked to 4:16. "First thing I want everyone to understand is when the clock hits sixteen, whether we're practicing first or second, you're late."

She smiled. "This is the first time I've been a coach, so I'm going to be learning as I go. But I *did* read up on coaching this summer, and there's a quote from a famous coach that goes like this: 'To be early is to be on time. To be on time is to be late. To be late is to be forgotten.'"

Coach Josephson was in her midforties. She was of medium height, with short brown hair and brown eyes. She was clearly all business about being a coach for the first time.

She looked around for a second, then continued. "You can't be early when we have the late start time, I get that. But I'd recommend you not be late—because you *will* be forgotten."

Andi's head was already spinning. Coach Josephson sounded a little bit like Coach Johnston had at the start of the soccer season—and that was no compliment. Andi wondered why she had decided to coach *now*, for the first time in her life.

She introduced her assistant coach, Joan Axelson, who was also a first-time coach but had played college basketball on the West Coast.

"Believe it or not, they play decent basketball out there, too," Coach Axelson said. "But, like Coach Josephson said, we're all here to learn together."

Andi liked her. She was a first-year teacher and taught sixth-grade earth science, or, as the kids called it, "rocks for jocks." Actually, everyone in the sixth grade had to take it—jock or not—but it was pretty easy. All you had to do was memorize the names of a bunch of rocks. Coach Josephson was a gym teacher. Andi hadn't been in her class, so she didn't know her.

Coach Josephson noted that there were twenty girls trying out for twelve spots on the team. They would play three-on-three half-court basketball some of the time and five-on-five full-court some of the time. Before that, though, they would do drills—dribbling, passing, setting, what Coach Josephson called *picks*.

Andi was pretty certain Coach Josephson had read about the importance of drills in a book. She also knew from her brothers and from watching basketball on TV that a pick was generally called a *screen* nowadays. She suspected Coach Josephson's book was a little out-of-date.

Before anyone was allowed to touch a basketball, they went through ten minutes of calisthenics, the kind they were often asked to do in gym class. Andi was beginning to wonder if they would actually play basketball at any point.

After calisthenics, they went through their drills. It was four forty-five by the time they did anything involving a basketball.

"Okay," Coach Josephson said. "Everyone line up for free throws. I want five of you on each basket."

The sides of the court where bleachers were rolled down during games had baskets to go with the ones at each end, so they were able to break into four groups.

"Everyone shoots five," Coach Josephson said. "If you miss three, you run."

Andi knew that, without any shooting warm-ups at all, there were going to be girls who would miss three or more. This wasn't, in her opinion, the way to start a practice—or a tryout. Making free throws didn't prove you could play.

The assignments, read off by Coach Axelson, were alphabetical. Andi was the fifth name called in the first group. By the time it was her turn to shoot, three of the four girls who had gone ahead of her had missed at least three times and had walked to the baseline to wait until everyone was finished. Only then would they run.

When it was Andi's turn, she made her first three—which took the pressure off. She'd always been a good free-throw shooter. When she had been allowed by her two older brothers to play with them, she had *always* beaten them in free-throw shooting contests and in HORSE.

Andi wondered if she was supposed to keep shooting after she made three. Kara Bishop, the only other girl in the group to make three, had gotten to the number on her final shot.

Kara was the only one in their group not standing on the baseline. When she tossed the ball back to Andi and Andi hesitated, she hissed, "Shoot already, Carillo, before she makes us all run."

Andi spun the ball quickly in her hands and shot. She missed. She took her time on the fifth one and made it. Four out of five.

There were only six girls out of the twenty who had made three. The other fourteen were lined up on the baseline.

"Okay, just so everyone's equal on the first day, let's have everyone run," Coach Josephson said. "All I need is this: Run to the foul line—and back; to the midcourt line—and back; to the far foul line—and back. And then the length of the court and back."

Andi knew from her brothers, who had both played in high school, that this was known as a suicide. It didn't sound bad until you actually did one. Or had to do more than one.

"Okay," Coach Josephson said. "On Coach Axelson's whistle. And I'd advise running hard. Those who finish in the back of the pack aren't going to be happy."

Most of the players moaned.

"No one has to be here," Coach Josephson said. "This is strictly voluntary. Coach Axelson, let's get 'em going."

Andi took off at the sound of the whistle.

When Jeff and Andi got together via text that night to compare notes on their first day of tryouts, they had trouble agreeing on who had the worst day.

Andi was convinced she was playing for a coach better-suited to being a drill sergeant than a basketball coach.

We NEVER scrimmaged. Not for ONE minute. We drilled, shot free throws, ran, shot more free throws, ran AGAIN! How do you decide who can play THAT WAY?

Jeff had to admit that sounded pretty gruesome and, clearly, she was right. At least the boys had actually played some basketball.

The problem was the continuing migraine headache in his life, Ron Arlow.

As soon as he saw Arlow lining up against him as White One's point guard, he knew he had problems.

It wasn't that he was intimidated by Arlow or didn't think he could compete with him. This was basketball, not soccer. Arlow had been the star of the soccer team—until Andi had stepped forward late in the season to be at least the costar—and Jeff *had* been intimidated by him for a while on the soccer field.

Arlow was the classic bully. He always acted like he was ready to pick a fight until someone like Danny Diskin, who was almost as tall as Arlow but more muscular, stepped in. Then Arlow suddenly had to go someplace.

It had never occurred to Jeff that he might compete with Arlow for the point guard spot. Arlow was a good four inches taller than he was, but in basketball that hardly made him tall. As Jeff looked over the other players that afternoon, he put Arlow somewhere in the middle in terms of height. If he had given any thought to Arlow as a basketball player, he probably would have figured him to be a small forward. Maybe a shooting guard. But a point guard? No way.

Still, Arlow was a good athlete and clearly could handle the ball—though not as well as Jeff. He could shoot well enough, but Jeff was convinced he was the better shooter.

They weren't matched up against each other long enough for anyone to make any decisions on who was the better player, but on one occasion, boxing out for a rebound, Arlow had intentionally backed into Jeff much harder than necessary, sending Jeff sprawling.

The coaches were officiating and Jeff waited to hear a whistle for the obvious foul. There was none. Coach B was reffing that end of the floor, which was unfortunate. Coach C had seen Arlow's act all fall and would have known exactly what was going on. But he was at the other end of the floor.

Jeff jumped up and, just to make sure Arlow understood this was a different season and a different team, got right in his face. "Don't start, Arlow," he said.

"Why not?" Arlow sneered. "Or are you going to send Diskin after me?"

Play had stopped because the ball had gone out-of-bounds during the scramble for the rebound. Fortunately, Danny didn't hear what Arlow said, because if he had he would have put Arlow through the floor. Which would have been deserved.

Instead, Jeff pointed a finger in Arlow's face and said, "I don't need help to handle you."

By now, Coach B was stepping between them, and Coach C had blown his whistle to stop play and had come running. Danny came up behind Jeff and pulled him back. Someone else grabbed Arlow, who was clearly pleased that he'd gotten to Jeff so quickly.

Coach C arrived and angrily pointed at both of them. "I am not going to put up with the kind of garbage that happened during soccer season," he said. "I swear, I don't care how good either one of you is, you start this stuff again, I'll cut you both. If you think I'm kidding, try me."

He stared at Jeff. "You got me, Michaels?"

Jeff knew it took a lot to get Coach C angry. "Got you, Coach," he said quietly. "Sorry."

The coach turned to Arlow. "Arlow, you understand?"

"But, Coach, I was just boxing out—"

Coach C's hand came up. "I don't care!" he said. "Last chance, Arlow. You got me?"

"Yes, Coach," Arlow finally said.

"Oh, and by the way, you guys continue this in the locker room, I'll hear about it and you won't be here tomorrow," Coach C added. "Okay, let's play. We've wasted enough time."

Arlow and Jeff exchanged glares for another moment. *So much for the end-of-soccer-season truce,* Jeff thought. Then Coach B's whistle got their attention and Jeff went to inbound the ball.

His text describing the scene to Andi that night left out most of the details.

Arlow's still a bully. Almost got into fight. Coach C threatened to cut us both. Nice start, huh?

Andi texted back.

OK. U win. Least I didn't get in any trouble.

She paused then sent one last text for the night.

Yet.

3

IT WASN'T EXACTLY TYPICAL FOR A SIXTH-GRADE BOY AND girl to be best friends, but that was the way Andi looked at her friendship with Jeff. She suspected that Jeff had a bit of a crush on her, but she just didn't like him *that way*.

The two of them had gone to the school's Halloween dance together, but Andi had looked at that as a celebration of what they had accomplished as soccer teammates. And, if she was going to go to the dance, Jeff was definitely the person she felt most comfortable with that evening. A number of other boys had asked her, but she knew that Jeff wanted to go with her, and so she held out until she finally more or less told Jeff they were going together.

Andi was comfortable with Jeff, enjoyed his company,

and knew he would never take the friendship any further than she wanted it to go.

When they'd said good night after the dance, he'd looked around as if afraid he was being watched by somebody, then leaned up to kiss her on the cheek. She'd smiled, said, "Thanks for a fun night," and went to greet her parents, who had come to pick her up.

Their friendship was such that after her miserable first day of tryouts—if you could even call it that— Jeff had been the first person she'd thought to contact. There had been very little talk in the locker room about the non-playing.

The only person who had said anything to her at all, after they'd finally been told to remember they had the early session the next day, was Karen Joyce. As they walked into the locker room, she'd said: "Guess you think you're already the star in basketball, too, don't you, Carillo?"

Andi had been baffled by the comment. How could anyone possibly tell who the star was or would be after that wasted hour?

"What are you talking about?" she'd answered.

"You made some free throws. Big deal," Joyce said before walking away.

Andi had been one of three girls who had made at least three free throws in both rounds of foul shooting.

She'd again made four the second time around and, in truth, was a little annoyed when she missed her third one on the second set.

Maybe that had shown in her face?

Or maybe this had nothing to do with making free throws.

The next day, she sat down at lunch with Jeff and they began trading details of what had gone on the day before.

"Hey, Michaels, you trying to talk her into trying out for the boys' team again so she can save your butt?"

Andi looked up. It was—of course—Ron Arlow.

Before Jeff could respond, she did. "Arlow, why don't you go crawl back under your rock."

That, she realized, wasn't exactly an original comment either.

Arlow—naturally—smirked.

"One thing I know for sure, Carillo," he said. "No one will miss *your* act during basketball season."

"We'd have never won conference without her and you know it," Jeff said, wading in.

"And we'd have won that city championship game if you hadn't taken that guy down in the penalty box," Arlow said, reaching quickly for his trump card.

It was true. In the city championship game against West Philadelphia Middle, Jeff had lost his balance pursuing one of the West Philly players and piled into him in the box, leading to what turned out to be the game-winning penalty kick. What Arlow didn't mention was that Jeff was trying to cover for Arlow, who had been faked out of his shoes near midfield by the same guy.

Andi started to say something, but Jeff reached out and grabbed her arm.

"Forget it," he said.

She took a bite out of her sandwich and said nothing.

Arlow, feeling as if he'd had the last word, turned and walked away.

"And I thought basketball season would be a breeze," Jeff said.

"Never easy when you're a benchwarmer," Andi said.

They had dubbed themselves that early in soccer season. Neither had any intention of riding the bench during basketball. But things were definitely off to a rocky start.

The girls went first that afternoon.

Andi was relieved that, once the drills were over, they actually started to play basketball. The three-on-three half-court game was a little frustrating because it seemed as if everyone just wanted to show the coaches that they could shoot the ball. No one seemed interested in playing much defense.

At one point, when Andi got screened around the foul line, she instinctively yelled, "Switch," to tell her two teammates that someone needed to get to the shooter she couldn't reach because of the screen. No one made a move.

A moment later, it occurred to Andi that there were probably girls on the court who didn't know what *switch* meant. She had played age-group basketball for three years, so she knew the term, which is why she'd yelled it out.

Left open, the shooter made a fifteen-foot jump shot. As luck would have it, Coach Josephson was reffing that end of the court. After the shot went in, she blew her whistle to stop play and walked over to Andi.

"You're Carillo, right?" she said.

"Yes, Coach."

"The soccer star."

"I played on the soccer team."

Coach Josephson nodded.

"And you are apparently such a basketball maven that you know what it means to switch while playing defense, right?"

Andi wasn't completely sure what a maven was, but the coach's sarcastic tone made it clear she wasn't using it to compliment her.

"I've played some basketball and—"

"And have we had any conversations yet about making a switch to get around a pick?"

"No, ma'am, we haven't."

"It's Coach."

"Sorry, Coach."

By now, everyone on the floor was standing and staring at the top of the key, where the conversation—*lecture, humiliation?* Andi thought—was taking place.

Coach Josephson turned to Carolyn McCormick, who had set the screen, and said, "Nice job with that pick." Then she added, "Okay, let's get some water and then we'll play some full-court."

As Andi walked with the others in the direction of the water, Jamie Bronson, the girl Andi had yelled at to switch, walked over next to her. Andi was expecting her to say something like, "Hey, don't worry about it."

Wrong again.

Quietly, she leaned into Andi and said, "You ever show me up like that again, I don't care how many goals you scored in soccer or how much the boys all love you, I'll take you down."

Bronson was several inches taller than Andi and several inches wider. There was no doubt she could take Andi down in a heartbeat.

"I wasn't trying to show you up," Andi answered. "It was just a gut reaction when I saw the screen."

She was about to apologize, but Bronson cut her off.

"I don't care what you were doing," she said. "Don't do it again."

She walked away, lingering just long enough in front of Andi to make sure Andi was last in line to grab water. Andi actually smiled for a moment. Bronson had just set a pretty good screen.

Jeff's second day went better than Andi's.

Understanding that it was probably better for everybody to keep Jeff and Arlow apart, Coach C kept them at opposite ends of the court once scrimmaging began. When they went full-court, Jeff and Arlow weren't on the court at the same time—until the last few minutes.

There was part of Jeff that wanted to take Arlow on, to show the coaches that he was a better player. But he was content to know he was playing well and was going to make the team comfortably. Once the tryouts were over, he would worry about competing with Arlow for playing time.

In the final segment of the day, Jeff finally got his chance to go head-to-head with Arlow.

Coach C ordered four minutes put on the clock and selected two teams of five players each, calling out names—telling the first five to put on white, the next five to put on blue.

Looking around at who had been chosen, Jeff

guessed the coaches had decided these were the ten best players and wanted to see what they looked like going against one another.

He was the point guard for the white team, Arlow for the blues.

"Team that wins doesn't run," Coach C said. "Team that loses runs. The rest of you—he pointed to the nine boys watching forlornly from the sidelines—have the option to run or not run." Clearly, he was testing the remaining nine, perhaps to help decide who would fill the last two spots on the team.

They started with a jump ball, like in a real game, and Camden James, playing center for the blues, out-jumped the whites' Tate Matthew for the ball.

Arlow brought the ball up, passed it to Jonathan Andrews, got it back, and instantly shot—with Jeff in his face.

He missed and Tate rebounded.

The coaches didn't want to call fouls, but they had to call one when Jeff shot-faked Arlow out of his shoes and Arlow almost fell on top of him as Jeff went up to shoot.

There were no free throws on fouls, just inbounding the ball. *Too bad*, Jeff thought.

It was 9–9 when Arlow took a three-point shot with about twenty-five seconds left—and missed again. By Jeff's mental count, he'd made one of four. Arlow reminded him a little of JJ Redick, who had played for the 76ers. Someone had once said, "He only shoots when he actually has the ball in his hands."

That was Arlow.

Now Jeff came downcourt with the ball, calling out, "One shot." In a real game, you'd never do that, but the team had no actual plays and everyone knew they were going to hold for one shot anyway.

Jeff dribbled near midcourt until the clock was under ten seconds. Then he drove at Arlow as Matthew, who Jeff had played a fair amount of pickup ball with, came out to set a screen to the right of the key. Arlow had no idea how to get around the screen, and Jeff was able to pick his dribble up with two seconds left and shoot a wide-open fifteen-foot jumper.

It swished as the clock hit zero.

His teammates rushed to high-five him while Arlow whined that Matthew had been moving when he set the screen—which would have been an offensive foul.

Coach C ignored him and called them all to midcourt. "Okay, I liked what I saw today," he said. "Game was too close for one team to have to run."

A cheer went up from the blues. Jeff wasn't cheering. *Heck*, he thought, *I just drilled Arlow at the buzzer, I should be able to stand and watch him run.* Then again, drilling Arlow the way he had was probably enough satisfaction for one day.

"One more day of tryouts," Coach C said. "After tomorrow, Coach B and I will sit down and talk, and we'll post the twelve names online by eight o'clock tomorrow night so you all don't have to wait until Monday. We'll put a link to the final roster on the school website.

"Michaels, you hit the winning shot today, why don't you lead the cheer?"

Jeff had never been asked to do anything like this during soccer season. He thought for a second, walked to the middle of the jump circle, put his hand in the air, and said, "Just win, baby! On three." That had been the mantra of Al Davis when he had owned the Oakland Raiders. Jeff's dad like to quote it.

Everyone walked into the circle, hands in the air, and on Jeff's three-count said, "Just win, baby!"

One player, Jeff noticed, had said nothing. Arlow. *Figures,* Jeff thought, *since his theme for the day had been, "Just shoot, baby."*

Jeff walked in the direction of the locker room with a smile on his face. Arlow had jogged ahead. For once, it seemed, he had nothing to say.

4

ANDI MANAGED TO MAKE IT THROUGH THE THIRD DAY OF tryouts without upsetting her coach or any of her future teammates.

After Jeff told her that the boys' team was going to be posted online on Friday night, she figured the same would be true for the girls' team. She thought wrong.

"If you go to the gym offices on Monday morning, we'll have posted the team there," Coach Josephson said after Friday's final day of tryouts.

Andi wasn't worried. She was pretty convinced that she and Eleanor Dove had been the best players among the twenty, and Eleanor was clearly destined to play center. She was taller and stronger than anyone else and had a real feel for the game. On the couple of occasions when she and Andi were on the same team, they got one easy basket after another, setting each other up.

At one point, after they had run a pick-and-roll, a play that led to a wide-open layup for Eleanor, she ran over to Andi, high-fived her, and said, "Stockton and Malone!"

Eleanor clearly knew her hoops. When John Stockton and Karl Malone played together for the Utah Jazz in the 1990s, they had more or less invented the pick-and-roll. It was a simple play: the guard—Stockton—would dribble behind a screen from the big man—Malone. When Malone's defender came up to defend a possible shot, Malone would roll to the basket, catch the ball wide open, and dunk. It seemed simple to defend, but if the defenders didn't attack Stockton, he'd have a wide-open three-point shot. It was a pick-your-poison sort of thing. Now every team at every level of basketball ran some form of the pick-and-roll and it was still very difficult to guard.

Andi and Eleanor ran it without any discussion. It made sense for Eleanor to screen for Andi, and both knew the game well enough to know that if Eleanor's defender came up at all, she could roll to the basket and look up to see Andi's pass arriving.

Andi was prepared for Coach Josephson to tell the two of them to stop showing off, but she said nothing. In fact, both coaches said little—good or bad—during the Friday tryout. Andi sensed they were trying to make final decisions on who to cut and who to keep. In her mind there were five players who were automatics.

Unfortunately, Jamie Bronson was clearly one of them. She could shoot and, next to Eleanor, was probably the best rebounder on the floor. Maybe once they were officially teammates, Bronson would cool her act.

Andi walked off the court with Eleanor and Maria Medley after Coach Josephson thanked everyone for coming to the tryouts. Eleanor and Maria were the only two African American kids who had come out for the team. Maria was as petite as Eleanor was big and, to Andi's thinking anyway, would be the team's point guard.

They were good friends with each other, and it was clear that they felt none of the resentment toward Andi that Bronson and some of her pals seemed to feel.

"You know, I gotta say, you're pretty good for a white girl," Maria said with a wide smile as they headed for the locker room.

"And I gotta say you're pretty good for a shrimp," Andi answered. If Maria was five foot one, it was a lot.

All three of them laughed. This was the sort of banter Andi had missed during soccer season. She knew that the boys' locker room had been infested with cliques, but she also knew that some of them had a healthy give-and-take. It wasn't so much about talking

dirty or using profanities as it was about never missing the chance to get off a good joke at the expense of
a teammate.

Andi's experience with her brothers and their
friends had taught her that much.

"I'll tell you what, though," Eleanor said. "Some of
those other white girls need to loosen up on the atti-
tude. There are no Sue Birds out there."

"Or Larry Birds, either," Andi said.

Sue Bird was the legendary Seattle Storm star
who had won two national championships in college,
three WNBA championships, and *four* Olympic gold
medals. She was, in many ways, the role model for
any aspiring female basketball player. Larry Bird was
equally legendary—in fact, his nickname was "Larry
Legend"—having revived a moribund Boston Celtics
franchise and led the team to three NBA titles.

Andi liked hanging out with Eleanor and Maria.
They knew their hoops. And they could play.

"Be a long wait till Monday," Maria said.

"Seriously?" Andi said. "You worried?"

Maria grinned. "No," she said. "I may not be Sue
Bird, but I know there aren't any guards out there who
can guard me."

She was right. Andi knew the three of them were a
lock to be on the list Monday morning. Coach Josephson shouldn't need to consult a book to figure that out.

Jeff wasn't worried, either. And unlike Andi, he didn't have to worry about whether his coach understood basketball.

Coach C was clearly a lot more comfortable in charge on the basketball court than he had been as an assistant on the soccer field.

It was apparent to Jeff on Friday that he was pretty certain who was going to make the team—with the exception, perhaps, of the last one or two spots.

Even so, he was online at eight o'clock and found himself squirming a little when there was no sign of the link.

He sat and stared at the screen for about a minute and then went to a sports website and tried to read a story about Villanova's chances to have a successful basketball season. He was a fan of all six of Philly's Division I basketball teams—the Big Five plus Drexel—but Villanova had been the dominant team in the city recently, winning two national championships in three years.

He got halfway through the story and, at 8:04, having vowed to wait until 8:05, went back on the Merion Middle School website. And there it was: *Boys' Basketball Team Roster.*

Finally.

He hit the link and there were the twelve names.

The list was alphabetical. *Jeff Michaels* was the ninth name. The second name—sadly—was *Ron Arlow*. Jeff had known that was coming but had held out a tiny bit of hope that Coach C and Coach B might decide Arlow's talent was outweighed by his ability to divide the locker room.

> Jonathan Andrews
> Ron Arlow
> Eric Billings
> Marco Bonventre
> Danny Diskin
> Manny Friedman
> Camden James
> Tate Matthew
> Jeff Michaels
> Crew Tayler
> Mike Roth
> Tavon Washington

Of course, the truth was, the locker room wasn't divided—he and Arlow were divided.

Jeff sighed, then started to text Andi. Before he could hit Send, his phone pinged and there was a text from her.

Just saw it. Know it wasn't in doubt, but congrats. I have to wait till Monday.

Jeff wiped out the text he had started and wrote back: *No worries, you know you'll make it.*

The reply came right back: *I guess. But I think I'm stuck with another coach who is going to be tough to deal with—just for different reasons. I wish Coach Axelson was in charge. She knows hoops and seems nice.*

Sort of like soccer with Coach J and Coach C.

EXACTLY!

Well, at least you've been through this before ☺

Easy for you to say ☹

See you Monday, he responded.

Easy for you to say, she answered. This time, she added a smiley face.

First period at Merion Middle each morning was at eight thirty. At eight fifteen, Andi, trying to look casual, made her way to the gym office and found several girls who had been part of the tryouts standing in front of what appeared to be a blank bulletin board.

"Don't bother looking," Lisa Carmichael said as Andi walked up. "It's not there yet."

"Any idea *when* they're going to let us know?" she asked.

Carmichael shook her head. "None at all," she said.

Carly O'Hara was also staring at the blank board. Now she turned on Andi.

"Come on, Carillo, what are you worrying about? You know you're on the team. You and your two *soul sisters*. You're the big soccer star and there's no way the coaches could get away with cutting *them*."

Andi felt some heat rise in her neck. She knew that O'Hara was one of Jamie Bronson's pals, so she wasn't surprised by her hostility. She was surprised by how ugly her words were—not so much the whole jealousy thing directed at her, but the racial comments directed at Maria and Eleanor.

Her parents talked often at the dinner table about how divisive the issue of race continued to be, so Andi certainly wasn't blind to it, but she'd never really experienced it at school.

"Maria and Eleanor will be on the team because they can play," she said, knowing she had raised her voice. She didn't care. She was angry. "Why don't you get over yourself."

She turned and walked away without waiting for a response. She knew there was a decent chance O'Hara would say something that would lead to an actual fight, and that was not a good idea. Not on a Monday morning. Not any time, for that matter.

Lisa Carmichael chased her down as she made her way back to the main part of the building.

"Don't pay any attention to her," she said. "She and Jamie and a couple of others are just jealous of you."

"I know that," Andi said. "But what about what she said about Maria and Eleanor?"

Lisa smiled. "They're jealous of them, too. So they make it about race. Easiest cop-out in the world."

Andi stopped and looked at Lisa. She barely knew her—it was a big school—but now she wanted to know her better. She was about five-eight, strawberry blonde, and very pretty. Chances were good, she guessed, that Bronson, O'Hara, and her crowd would be jealous of her, too. She was also a good player—clearly one of the twelve who would be on the team.

The five-minute bell rang.

She put a hand on the taller girl's shoulder. "Thanks," she said. "I feel better."

They turned in opposite directions to head for their first-period classes. Lisa had made Andi feel better.

But Andi knew there was more trouble ahead.

5

IT WAS NOON BEFORE THE GIRLS' ROSTER FINALLY GOT posted.

Andi had walked back to the gym office at the start of lunch break and found a note pinned up that said, *The girls basketball team roster will be posted at noon. Sorry for the delay. —Coach Josephson and Coach Axelson*

"Well, at least they apologized," said a voice behind Andi.

It was Jeff.

"Since we can't use our phones during the day, I figured I'd come down and see if they'd posted it yet. I know you just want it over with."

"You aren't just kidding," she answered.

They went to the cafeteria and got their lunches. Andi filled Jeff in on what had happened earlier that morning.

"Sounds like you've got some Arlow wannabes on the team," he said.

She smiled and looked up at the clock on the cafeteria wall. It was almost noon.

"Should we go look?" she said.

"Wait a few more minutes," Jeff said. "My guess is they won't be right on time."

He was right. When they reached the gym office's door at 12:05 p.m., there was a crowd of girls standing around Coach Axelson, who was just putting the list up.

Jeff felt a little embarrassed because he was the only boy in the hallway. He felt worse when one of the girls—who he didn't recognize—turned to Andi and said, "Did you bring your boyfriend for support, Carillo?"

Wow, Jeff thought, *Arlow could learn a lesson from these girls*.

Coach Axelson, who Jeff thought was strikingly pretty and looked young enough—at least to him—to still be in college, held her hands up for a moment once she had the list up.

"Girls, we're really sorry this took so long, but the fact is, we had some tough decisions to make. You all worked so hard last week, we hated to cut anybody. But, it's done."

She turned and more or less fled up the hallway,

probably not wanting to hear the anguished wails from those who were cut.

Andi and Jeff stood back, letting the other girls look at the list first. There were shrieks of pain and of joy—the shrieks of joy coming from girls who had no doubt been on the bubble and had made it. Girls, Jeff noticed, were a lot more willing than boys to wear their emotions on their sleeves.

One girl was sobbing, and as she walked past Jeff and Andi, she shot Andi a look of true hatred.

"You and your buddies made it, Carillo," she said venomously. "Big surprise."

"Who's that?" Jeff whispered as the girl kept going.

"Carly O'Hara," Andi whispered back. "She's the one I told you about from this morning."

"So, good news she's not on the team then, huh?" Jeff said.

It was good news. But even before she actually looked at the list, Andi knew that several members of Jamie Bronson's crowd would be there.

She was right. Once she found her name, she looked up and down the list:

Hope Allison
Ronnie Bonilla
Jamie Bronson
Andi Carillo

Lisa Carmichael
Eleanor Dove
Randi Eisen
Brooke Jensen
Alayne Jolie
Debbie Lee
Jenny Mearns
Maria Medley

So Eleanor and Maria were there, too. She smiled seeing that Lisa was also there. She had expected nothing different but was glad to see their spots confirmed.

Also on the list, though, were Jamie Bronson and her pals Hope Allison, Alayne Jolie, and Jenny Mearns. But at least O'Hara wouldn't be there, too. *You take your victories where you find them*, she thought. Something her mom liked to say.

The five-minute bell to start afternoon classes was chiming.

"Good luck at practice," Jeff said.

"I guess I'll need it," she said, with a laugh that was probably more of a sigh.

6

TROUBLE STARTED EVEN BEFORE PRACTICE.

"Great way to become a team," she said under her breath as Jamie Bronson pushed past her in the locker room prior to their first real practice as a team.

Bronson stopped and turned.

"Problem, Carillo?" she said, as if hoping Andi would challenge her.

"Haven't got a problem in the world, Bronson," Andi answered, and turned back to tying her sneakers.

She had plenty of time and decided to take a minute to relax before heading out for practice.

But instead of relaxing she found herself fretting about her grades.

Her parents were both successful lawyers who expected a lot from their three kids. Her oldest brother, Todd, was a junior at Penn and played on the soccer team there. Her second brother, Drew, was a sophomore at Columbia and played varsity tennis and intramural basketball.

Both her parents had always encouraged their children to take part in sports, but there was no doubt what the priority was in the Carillo home: school. Good grades were a given; great grades were preferable.

Andi knew if her grades slipped, she'd no longer have to worry about Coach Josephson or the mean girls on the basketball team because she wouldn't be playing. Where that line would be drawn exactly, she didn't know, and she had no desire to find out.

Her midsemester report card had four As and a B on it. The B was in math and it was because she had trouble staying awake in class. Her interest in numbers was limited to baseball box scores, football quarterback ratings, and basketball stats. Soccer stats were pretty simple to follow but Andi also knew who the leading scorers were in the National Women's Soccer League, Major League Soccer, and the English Premier League.

Algebra? Not so much.

She was shaking her head, thinking about algebra homework, when she realized she was alone in the locker room. Everyone else was on the court, warming up. The girls had the three-fifteen practice, and as Andi jogged onto the court from the locker room, she heard Coach Josephson's whistle calling everyone to the jump circle.

She breathed a sigh of relief that her daydreaming hadn't made her late. The feeling of relief didn't last long.

"Well, Ms. Carillo, I see we don't feel the need to warm up like everybody else," Coach Josephson said as Andi joined the circle.

"Coach, I'm sorry . . ."

Coach Josephson held up a hand. "No, no, it's perfectly okay. You probably don't need to stretch, either. Soccer season undoubtedly left you in better shape than everyone else. So, while your teammates stretch, why don't you give me a couple suicides. Just two is fine. Shouldn't tire you out too much."

Andi had about a dozen answers for the snide tone and the crack about playing soccer, but she knew any of them would only make things worse. So she walked to the baseline, put her hands on her hips, and waited for Coach Josephson to start her.

"Is there something you want to say to your teammates?" Coach Josephson said.

She clearly wasn't letting this go.

"I'm sorry I was on time," she said. "I know that means I was late."

"Okay, line up for stretching," Coach Josephson

said. "Coach Axelson, please make sure Ms. Carillo hustles through those suicides."

Coach Axelson nodded, walked to where Andi was standing, and said, very softly, "Sorry."

Then she said, "Take your mark," and blew her whistle.

Jeff's first practice as a full-fledged member of the boys' sixth-grade team was a cakewalk—as he would learn later—compared to Andi's.

The two coaches spent a good deal of the workout putting in plays, talking about how to set legal screens on the offensive end of the floor and how to get around them on defense. They would play both man-to-man defense and zone defense.

They then split into two six-man teams to scrimmage. It was pretty apparent to Jeff that Mike Roth and Eric Billings—the two players who began the scrimmage watching—were going to be the last two players on the bench. It was also apparent that the coaches hadn't yet decided who the five starters would be. It seemed they had divided the two teams up evenly, and as the scrimmage went on, they had players flipping their shirts from white to blue and blue to white in order to see who played well with whom.

When play began, Jeff was the point guard for the

blue team; Ron Arlow was the point guard for the whites. Later, Arlow was moved to the blue team to play next to Jeff, who had mixed emotions about that: He preferred playing against Arlow, especially because he was convinced he was the better player and wanted to prove it. Beyond that, he wasn't in love with the idea of teaming up with Arlow.

Then again, when the season started, they'd be on the same side whether Jeff liked it or not. So, just as in soccer, he had to accept the fact that they needed to get along on the court, if not off it.

For the final phase of the day, Coach C had Jeff and Arlow switch spots—Arlow taking the point, Jeff moving to the shooting guard spot. At first, Jeff wondered why. But when he thought about it, it occurred to him that the coaches had been moving everyone around throughout the afternoon. That's what preseason practice was for, especially with a brand-new team.

When they finished, the coaches called them together and Coach C told them how pleased he was with the way they'd worked.

"This is what we're going to do most of the week," he said. "We want to put all of you into different situations, playing with different guys. Don't read anything into whether you're in blue or white right now. I'm sure most of you noticed that just about everyone spent time wearing each color."

He smiled. "I know coaches always say before the season starts that there are no starters, that every spot is up for grabs. Well, in this case, it's true. Coach B and I are both still learning about you. We have six practices to decide who should start and where each of you should play. We open next Tuesday playing over in New Jersey against Camden Middle. If you go to the school website tonight, you can see our whole schedule. We'll play two non-conference games and two conference games before winter recess and then play ten conference games after the New Year. We'll play four conference teams twice and the other four once each. There's not enough time to play everybody twice, so it's just luck of the draw who we play once and who we play twice.

"Oh, one other thing, on Monday before practice we'll give each of you a piece of paper and ask you to vote for one captain." He smiled. "Everybody good?"

"Yes, Coach," they all responded. A simple nod of the head wasn't good enough when your coach asked a question. Jeff had learned that during soccer season.

"Okay, Ron, bring 'em in."

He nodded at Arlow, who got a grin on his face that told Jeff he thought being picked meant that Coach C was somehow endorsing him for captain. He'd been the captain of the soccer team because Coach J had made him the captain. Basketball would be different.

Jeff had no idea who would be chosen. But he felt confident it wouldn't be Arlow.

Arlow walked to the middle of the jump circle and put up his hand. Everyone surrounded him, one hand in the air. "Hard work!" he said.

That was harmless enough. Jeff and the others repeated "Hard work!" and they headed for the locker room.

This, Jeff thought, *should be fun.*

7

ANDI MANAGED TO GET THROUGH THE REST OF THE WEEK
without any more run-ins with her coach.

As she had expected, the team quickly divided
into cliques. Hers was Eleanor, Maria, and Lisa. At
the opposite end of the pole was Jamie Bronson's fan
club, which included Alayne, Jenny, and Hope. Stuck
squarely in the middle were the other four players—
Debbie Lee, Brooke Jensen, Randi Eisen, and Ronnie
Bonilla—who didn't really side with either group.

Over the summer Andi had watched the old movie
West Side Story. It was a musical based on the story
of Romeo and Juliet, who had fallen in love with each
other even though their families were sworn enemies.

In *West Side Story*, Tony and Maria fell in love.
It wasn't their families who fought one another but
rival gangs: Tony was white and a member of the Jets.

Maria was Hispanic and her brother was the leader of the Sharks.

Eleanor, Maria, and Lisa had started sitting with Andi and Jeff at lunch, and Andi brought up the movie one day, explaining the basic plot.

"So what happens to me in the end?" Maria asked.

"Well," Andi said, "Maria lives, but Tony dies."

"Gee, not exactly a happy ending," Jeff said.

"No," Andi said. "The story is supposed to make a point about what hate can do to people."

"Well," Eleanor said after a long sip of lemonade, "I guess the good news is, no one's going to die on our basketball team."

"Yeah, I guess," Andi said. "But it could kill our basketball season."

"Not exactly tragic," Jeff put in.

Andi smiled. "Easy for you to say."

Jeff wasn't exactly thrilled with the presence of Eleanor, Maria, and Lisa at lunch. It wasn't that he didn't like them—he did, although he did his best to avoid standing next to Eleanor when they all went through the line to pick up food. For some reason being towered over by a girl felt worse than being towered over by a boy.

What bothered him was losing his alone time with

Andi. Lunch was always the part of the day when they caught up with each other and shared gossip and stories. Now it was a group conversation, and since the four girls were on the same team, there was a lot more talk about that team than about Jeff's team or life.

Not surprisingly, it didn't take Andi long to pick up on his discomfort.

Their one afternoon class together was earth science—last period. That usually gave them a couple minutes to talk before one of them had to head to practice.

"You were quiet at lunch today," Andi said after class on Thursday.

Jeff smiled. "Not a lot of room for me to talk," he said.

She nodded. "I get it. You're used to just you and me going back and forth. This is different."

"A *lot* different," Jeff said, with more emphasis on *lot* than he had intended.

She shot him a look. "They're really nice, you know," she said.

"I know they are," Jeff said. "But it's just . . ."

"Different, l know," she said after he paused.

"Yeah," he said. "And since there are four of you and one of me, it isn't like a lot of the conversation's going to focus on me or on the boys' team. I mean, I get it . . ."

She gave him her dazzling smile. "But you'd rather have me all to yourself."

"Well, yeah," Jeff admitted, feeling his cheeks heat up.

"Let's see how it goes for a little while longer at least," she said, glancing at the clock above the doorway they were passing through. "I have to get to study hall and you have to get to practice. Let's talk later."

Jeff didn't really think there was much to talk about. He understood why she would want to have the other three girls join them at lunch. Suddenly, an idea flashed through his head, and before he had the time to lose his courage, he heard himself talking.

"Maybe we can find some other time to talk, you know, just us," he said.

She patted him on the shoulder. "Let's talk about it later."

And she was gone.

Easy for you to say, Jeff thought.

Jeff and Andi texted periodically throughout the weekend, but there was no further discussion of finding another time to hang out together.

Jeff and his dad went to the Palestra on Saturday afternoon to see Temple play Penn. Jeff's dad didn't often go to games as a spectator—unless he was with Jeff. Sometimes his dad would get a media credential for Jeff so he could sit with him on press row. That didn't happen often, though, and it wasn't going to happen for a Big Five game where every seat on press row would be occupied.

Still, they had very good seats—actually, there were *no* bad seats in the Palestra—about ten rows up from the Penn bench.

"So how come you aren't working today?" Jeff asked his dad as they sat down, each with a Philadelphia pretzel and a soda in hand.

"Have the Eagles tomorrow," his dad reminded him. "Truth is, I'd rather work this game, but not working the Eagles isn't an option."

Jeff understood this. He knew that Philadelphia was pretty much like every NFL town—only more so. The Eagles weren't so much a passion for people as an obsession. This had become even truer a few years back when they had finally won the Super Bowl for the first time.

Tom Michaels had worked at NBC Sports–Philadelphia for twelve years. That meant he'd been there Jeff's entire life. Before that, he'd worked at the *Philadelphia Daily News*, but seeing the downward trend in the newspaper business, he'd accepted the offer to go work on television for the local sports station and had been their lead reporter on everything—but most important the Eagles—ever since.

Jeff had been in the press box at Lincoln Financial Field—aka "the Linc," to everyone in Philadelphia—prior to Eagles games in the past. He couldn't sit there during a game because NFL rules said you had to be at least eighteen to sit in the press box during a game.

But he'd always been amazed at the number of media members who showed up to cover the Eagles and how seriously they all seemed to take the idea of covering football.

Jeff knew his dad didn't take it nearly as seriously. He'd often said he enjoyed stories that most people didn't want to cover more than those that everyone was covering. That was why Jeff had been able to convince him to do a story on Andi when she was being denied a spot on the soccer team. His father's story had led to something of a media frenzy. When Andi got a chance to play—and play well—he and several other reporters had returned to follow up.

"So, we haven't had much time to talk this week," his dad said. "How's your team shaping up?"

"Hard to tell," Jeff answered, "since we're playing against each other right now. We'll learn a lot, I think, playing against Camden. Their high school teams are always really good, so I'd guess their middle school teams are good too."

"Nationally ranked good," his dad said. "Of course, who knows about a sixth-grade team?"

The game tipped off and they talked less, both focused on the court.

During the first TV time-out, his dad asked, "You think you'll start?"

"I think so," Jeff answered. "I *should*. The only issue is, Ron Arlow wants to be the point guard, too. I'm guessing Coach C will start both of us, but I hope he doesn't play me off the ball. I'm better at point than Arlow is."

"Arlow behaving any better than he did in the fall?" his dad asked.

"Not really," Jeff said. "But this is different. In soccer he was the best player, so we had to put up with him. He's good in basketball, but not the best player. So I don't feel intimidated by him the way I did in soccer."

"He was the second-best player," his dad said. "Andi was the best player. And you know what? By the end of the season, I'm not sure he was the second-best player. Might have been you, the way you improved."

Jeff smiled. "Dad, I thought reporters were supposed to be unbiased."

His dad smiled back. "Not when their son's involved. Or his best friend." He paused and then added, "And I'm not *that* biased."

Jeff just smiled. He wanted another pretzel.

Before Monday's practice began, Coach C told the players he and Coach B had decided on the starters for the Camden game.

"This is all subject to change," he said. "It could change for the game Friday or it could change in January. Or, it might not change at all—though that's unlikely. We're going to judge you from game to game, at least for right now. We think we have twelve guys on this team who can play and play well, so we're going to make sure everybody plays—certainly tomorrow afternoon.

"So, for now, here are the starters: James, Tayler, Matthew, Arlow, and Michaels."

To Jeff, there were no surprises in that group, except for Tavon Washington not being the starter at center. He was a better shooter than Camden James, but James was the tallest player on the team at six-two. Tate Matthew and Crew Tayler would be the forwards. Crew was about five-eight and had the skills to play guard. Arlow and Jeff were clearly the two best guards.

Jeff glanced at Danny Diskin, whose look of disappointment was easy to see. Danny's problem was that he was what coaches called a tweener. He wasn't a good enough ball handler or shooter to play outside, but he also wasn't tall enough to be really effective inside, although his strength certainly helped him as a rebounder.

Arlow had his hand up. "Coach, which of us has the point?" he asked.

"To start the game, Michaels," Coach C said. "But you'll both see time there."

Clearly that wasn't the answer Arlow wanted to hear. He put his hands on his hips and stared at the ceiling. Coach C looked at him for a second, then moved on.

"Al, you're up," he said, turning to Coach B.

From the clipboard he was carrying, the assistant coach took out slips of paper. He walked around the circle, handing one to each player.

"Go sit for a minute and use the bleachers to back up your voting slips. Write *one* name down for captain and hand the slips back to me."

They all did as instructed.

"We'll let you know at the end of practice who's going to be captain," Coach C said. "Okay, let's stretch."

The next fifty-five minutes took about four hours to pass. Jeff thought he had a decent chance to be elected captain. He was glad the coaches weren't simply going to appoint Arlow—or anyone else—the captain. However it worked out, Jeff was comfortable with it being decided by a fair vote.

The only thing noteworthy about the practice was how evenly matched the starters and subs seemed to be. Tavon Washington, clearly unhappy about not starting, outplayed Cam James most of the day. Danny Diskin could also compete with the starters. Mike Roth, who played the off-guard spot for the second team, could shoot, although he usually needed a good screen or pass to get his shot off.

At 4:13 p.m., with the girls ringing the court for their practice, Coach C blew his whistle—which he didn't do very often—and brought them all to the center jump circle.

"Gentlemen, we have a tie in the vote for captain," he said. "No need to break it. We'll just have cocaptains."

He paused for a second and smiled while everyone waited in suspense.

"Congratulations," he finally said, "to Jeff Michaels and Ron Arlow."

Jeff's heart leaped and fell with a thud, all in about two seconds. Everyone was clapping. Arlow was clearly just as unhappy as he was.

"Captains," Coach C said. "Bring 'em in. Let's hear 'one and oh,' on three."

Jeff and Arlow moved to the middle of the circle,

looking more like wrestlers circling each other than newly named cocaptains.

"Ready?" Jeff asked Arlow as he raised his hand in the air and everyone moved in around them.

Arlow didn't answer. Instead, he threw his hand up and said, "On three, one and oh!" Everyone responded with, "One, two, three, one and oh!"

Everyone except Jeff. His arm still in the air, he was glaring at Arlow. Their cocaptaincy was off to a great start.

As everyone headed for the locker room, Jeff had one thought: *Who the heck had voted for Arlow?*

ANDI KNEW SOMETHING WAS WRONG WHEN JEFF SPRINTED
past her—and the rest of the girls' team—as soon
as the boys had done their post-practice cheer. She
guessed that he hadn't been elected captain and was
disappointed by the vote.

She had no illusions about whether Coach Josephson was going to pick her as captain. She didn't even
know at that moment if she would be starting, although
she couldn't see any way that she, Maria, and Eleanor
wouldn't start. It was clear to everyone that they were
the three best players on the team.

The other spots were—or should be—up for grabs,
although Andi guessed that Jamie Bronson would
start, if only because she was the most physical
player on the team. Bronson had hands of stone,
which made her an offensive liability, but her sheer

strength made her a good rebounder and someone who, when she *did* catch the ball cleanly, was tough to stop inside. Lisa Carmichael should also start. At least if Andi were picking the lineup—which she wasn't.

There were no clues on Monday who the starters would be. Coach Josephson continued to use different combinations throughout practice—which made no sense to Andi. The starters—whoever they were— needed to work together to begin to get some feel for one another. Apparently that notion didn't appear in any of the coaching books their coach had read.

At five fifteen on the dot, Coach Josephson blew her whistle sharply. Everyone had been shooting free throws without threat of running suicides for a change. The players ran to the jump circle.

"Good practice today, girls," Coach J said. "We play here tomorrow at four o'clock. I want everyone in the locker room by three thirty. We'll let you know then who will be starting. Coach Axelson and I will make our final decisions tonight."

Andi found herself wondering why those decisions couldn't have been made at least a day earlier to give the starters some time to work together as a unit. She glanced at Eleanor, who gave a little eye roll as if to say, "What is going on here?"

Fortunately, the coach didn't see her.

"One thing we have decided on is who is going to be our captain," Coach Josephson added. "I think we have several excellent leaders on this team, but I think you'll all agree there's one girl who has stood out since the first day of tryouts."

She paused as if she were about to announce who had been thrown off the island on one of those reality shows.

"So, congratulations to our team captain"—another pause . . . *seriously?*—"Jamie Bronson!"

Bronson's clique cheered; the non-clique four clapped politely. Andi, Eleanor, Maria, and Lisa almost got their hands together but didn't quite make it there. Coach J had to notice but chose not to comment.

Instead, she asked Bronson if she wanted to say anything to her teammates.

Bronson, showing what kind of leader she would be, said, "Let's go out and win tomorrow!"

Great speech, Andi thought.

Then Coach Josephson suggested everyone come together for a cheer. "On three," she said, "win!"

The response to that was mixed.

As they walked off the court, Andi said quietly to Eleanor, Maria, and Lisa, "No wonder she picked Bronson. They're equally articulate."

"Hey, they both think winning's a good idea," Maria said with a grin.

They left it at that.

Jeff was as aware as any sixth grader that the preferred method of communicating among his peers was texting. But he wanted to talk directly to Andi that night, so after dinner, he texted her to see if it was okay to call.

Finishing homework, she texted back. *Give me fifteen minutes.*

He patiently waited sixteen minutes and then called.

"You looked upset after your practice," she said. "Who got elected captain?"

"I did," Jeff said. Then, before she got the wrong idea, he added, "And Arlow did. The vote was a tie. We're cocaptains."

Andi understood. "Not exactly ideal," she said. "Who do you think voted for him? None of his posse from soccer's on the team."

"I know," Jeff said. "I can't figure it out. I kinda wish Coach C had just named a captain the way Coach J did in soccer. I'm pretty sure he would have picked me."

"Well, having the coach pick a captain didn't work out so well for us," Andi said.

Jeff realized he hadn't given any thought at all to

what Andi was dealing with on the girls team. He felt embarrassed.

"I forgot she was naming a captain today. How bad?"

"Bad as it gets," Andi answered. "Bronson."

Jeff was up to date to on Bronson and the mean-girl faction of Andi's team.

"Jeez, I'm sorry about that," he said.

"It gets better," Andi said. "She didn't even name the starters for tomorrow. Said she'd let us know before the game. Whoever the starters are, they haven't practiced together at all."

"I guess having your starters work together isn't in any of the books your coach read," Jeff said.

Andi laughed. It was amazing how often she and Jeff thought exactly alike.

"Camden's a jock school, in every sport from what I've heard," she said. "And they've had sixth-grade teams in New Jersey for years before they started them here. I suspect they might kill us."

The way the schedule worked, the boys and girls teams played the same school on a given day. When the boys traveled, the girls played at home. When the girls traveled, the boys played at home. The same was true for the varsity teams—they played after the sixth-grade games. The only difference was that the varsity teams played thirty-two minutes—four eight-minute quarters—the way high school teams did. The sixth graders only played twenty-four minutes—four six-minute quarters.

"Well, I'm not exactly optimistic about our game, either," Jeff said. "I mean, Coach C and Coach B know what they're doing, but we aren't exactly a close-knit team right now."

"You guys are lifelong friends compared to us," Andi said. She had a positive thought. "Hey, we got off to a terrible start in soccer and ended up winning the conference. Maybe that'll happen in basketball, too. Slow start, then get better."

"We got better in soccer because Coach J finally started playing you," Jeff said.

"And you," Andi said quickly.

"Yeah, true," Jeff said. "Maybe we should suggest to our coaches that we start the season on the bench."

"Benchwarmers forever!" Andi said.

They both laughed. At least, Jeff thought, they both seemed to feel a little bit better.

Any good feelings Andi might have had quickly vanished soon after she walked into the locker room the next afternoon.

On the whiteboard in the corner of the room, in bright red marker, was the word *Starters*.

Below it, in the same red marker, were five names:

Bronson

Dove

Jolie

Mearns

Medley

Andi gasped. It had never occurred to her that she wouldn't start. Coach J was starting Bronson and two of her pals—Alayne Jolie and Jenny Mearns. Eleanor Dove and Maria Medley clearly deserved to start, but so did Andi and Lisa Carmichael.

She felt an arm go around her shoulder. "She's crazy," Eleanor said. "Unless she's planning to sub you and Lisa after about thirty seconds."

"I doubt that's the plan," Andi said. "I know she can't stand me, but what the heck did Lisa do wrong?"

"I'd say being friends with you, but then why are Maria and I starting?"

"Maybe because she'd rather not lose by fifty," Andi said.

Before Eleanor could answer, the door opened and the two coaches walked in.

"Okay, everyone," Coach Josephson said. "You see the starters. I would expect all of you who aren't starting to play—at some point. How much will probably depend on how the game's going or foul trouble. It will also depend on how much support you show for your teammates from the bench."

She looked directly at Andi. "Those of you not dressed yet, you've got five minutes. I want everyone on the floor for warm-ups at three forty. Bronson, make sure they're all ready to go by then. Got that?"

"Sure, Coach," Bronson said. "You bet."

The coaches walked out. Bronson whirled and pointed a finger at Andi. "If you're not in uniform in five, Carillo, I'm going to suggest you not suit up."

It was Maria who answered. "Just take care of yourself, Bronson," she said. "Let the coach pick on Andi. She doesn't need your help."

Bronson took a step in Maria's direction, but Eleanor stepped in between them. Bronson was wider than Eleanor, but Eleanor was probably four inches taller.

Bronson stopped. "Oh yeah, I forgot you come equipped with a bodyguard," she said, staring straight at Eleanor. "That's the way you people work, huh?"

If Bronson was looking to start a fight, she'd picked the right words. It wasn't Eleanor who charged at her; it was Lisa Carmichael. Andi was half a step behind. It seemed as if everyone in the room was pushing and shoving: Bronson and her crew squaring off with Andi and her friends while the four neutral parties tried to pull them apart. Andi and Jenny Mearns wrestled each other to the ground before they all heard a whistle—which, in the small locker room, sounded more like ten whistles blasting at once.

They all looked up and there were the two coaches.

"What in the world is going on here?" Coach Josephson yelled. "Who started this?"

Before the finger pointing could get going, Coach Axelson stepped in.

For the first time since tryouts had started, she blew her whistle. Andi hadn't even known she *had* a whistle until that moment.

The sound of the second whistle—especially given its source—got everybody's attention.

"Girls!" she shouted. "We are on the *same* team— that includes everyone in this locker room. If you have issues with someone, stow it. Camden is the opponent today, not anyone in here. So just *stop!*"

There was dead silence. Finally, Coach Josephson said, "Everyone on the court in two minutes. Any more fighting, no questions asked, the people involved don't play today."

She turned and walked out. Andi pulled free from Mearns and ran to her locker to get dressed. No one said anything. Andi waited to see if Bronson was going to apologize to Eleanor and Maria.

The only thing she said was, "Everyone, hustle up. We've got a game to get ready for."

Maybe so, Andi thought, but this wasn't the end of

this by any stretch of the imagination. This team was no longer just divided by cliques.

It was also divided by race. It could have been the Jets and the Sharks. Andi couldn't think of anything worse.

9

ON THE OTHER SIDE OF THE BENJAMIN FRANKLIN BRIDGE, the boys' team didn't have any pregame locker room fights or anyone screaming at one another. Even the two team captains managed to remain civil to each other.

The trouble began after they left the locker room. It came in the form of their opponent.

Jeff was hardly surprised by this. His father had briefed him on some of Camden's history before the bus trip across the Delaware River. Camden High School, which Camden Middle fed into, had been known for its athletics for years. In the 1980s, University of Louisville basketball coach Denny Crum had recruited so many Camden players that other coaches talked about his "Camden connection." The high school had won numerous state championships and had produced players who had gone on to the NBA—most notably Milt Wagner, a star on Louisville's 1986 national championship team. More recently, his son Dajuan had starred at Camden before going on to play at Memphis, where—by sheer coincidence—his father had been an assistant coach.

It was clear pretty quickly that the Camden Middle School team was on a different level than the kids from Merion. On the first play of the game, one of Camden's players, who looked to be about five-seven, stepped in front of a pass Jeff was attempting to throw to Camden James and took off down the court with no one between him and the basket.

Jeff, racing back to try to get into position, was two steps behind when the kid leaped, seemed to hang in the air—and dunked. The tiny gym, which might have seated two hundred people, exploded. *With good reason*, Jeff thought. He knew there were little guys in the NBA who could dunk, but this was a sixth grader.

As soon as Arlow inbounded the ball to him, he was double-teamed. He tried to dribble through it, lost the ball, and watched as another Camden kid went in for an uncontested layup. It was uncontested because Arlow, standing right there, had zero interest in trying to take a charge.

Before Arlow even picked the ball up to inbound it again, Coach C called time-out. The game had started thirty-nine seconds earlier. Jeff had only one thought walking to the bench: *This is going to be a long afternoon.*

Coach C's message during the time-out was simple: Calm down. He looked at Jeff and added, "Don't try to dribble through double-teams. You have to ball-fake and then pass."

It was a simple concept: Pretend to pass the ball in one direction, hold onto the ball, and then throw it someplace else. They had worked on the art of ball-faking and shot-faking in practice. Coach C had actually quoted the famous basketball coach Bob Knight at one point: "Knight liked to say, 'Is there anything better in life than a good shot-fake?' The answer is there are lots of things better, but when playing basketball, a good ball-fake or shot-fake is a very good thing."

Jeff and the rest of the Mustangs did calm down after the time-out and did better against the pressure defense. Jeff even found Arlow streaking to the basket behind the defense at one point for an open layup.

That was the good news. The bad news was the basket made the score 14–4.

It was 18–6 after one quarter and 32–14 at half-time. It wasn't so much that Merion was playing badly; Camden was just better. The Little Wildcats—the high school was the Wildcats—were bigger, faster, and better shooters.

"Other than that," as Jeff said to Danny Diskin after the game, "we were pretty evenly matched."

Danny shook his head. "They were smarter than us, too."

He was right.

Everyone from both teams got to play. Coach C took Jeff out of the game when he put Arlow at the point and then rested Arlow when Jeff went back in to run the offense. They didn't play together at all after the first quarter. Jeff wasn't exactly sure why, but he didn't mind. He understood Coach C wanting to see as many guys as possible in a game that couldn't possibly be won.

The final score was 57–33. Camden didn't press at all in the second half, which was a relief. For all the ball-faking Jeff did when double-teamed, his pass-completion percentage wasn't much higher than 50 percent. That wasn't great for a football quarterback and it certainly wasn't good for a point guard.

When they got back to the locker room, Coach C was direct.

"That's almost certainly the best team we'll play this season," he said. He smiled. "If it's not, then we're in a lot of trouble. I'll be honest with you, I don't think

I've ever seen a sixth grader dunk before. I doubt if we'll see that again.

"If nothing else, we learned a lot about ourselves and what we need to work on today. Okay, let's get into sweats and get back on the bus." There was one shower in the locker room, so they'd known beforehand they wouldn't be showering at Camden. "Michaels, Arlow, get 'em in."

Jeff moved to the center of the room. Arlow took his time getting there even though he was about four steps away. It was clear to Jeff he was sulking—not so much because the team had lost but because he'd only scored four points. Jeff knew him well enough to know his first concern was almost always *his* statistics.

So, when Arlow was slow joining him, he didn't wait. He put up his hand and said, "Get better, on three."

The others came to the center of the room—Arlow, too—finally. The hands went up. "One, two, three," Jeff said.

They all said, "Get better!"

Everyone turned to take their things from their lockers and put on their sweats. All except for Arlow, who was glaring at Jeff.

"Did someone make you captain?" he asked. "Did I miss something?"

Jeff shook his head.

"Can we get through one day without an argument, Arlow?" he said. "We *are* teammates. You were sulking. Our job is to show life and lead the team, win or lose, regardless of how many points we score."

For once, Arlow didn't come back at him. He'd noticed, no doubt, that everyone in the room was staring at the two of them. Jeff's comment made too much sense to fire back. He just shook his head and walked to his locker.

Diskin leaned into Jeff and said softly, "Well, pal, you won that round."

"That's about all we won today," Jeff said.

He hoped Coach C was right about Camden being the best team they would play. He wondered how the girls were doing playing the Camden girls back at school.

The answer was: not very well. Sadly for Andi, that wasn't close to being her biggest problem as the afternoon wore on.

She knew she was in trouble as soon as they walked onto the court after the locker room fight had been broken up.

Right away, she noticed the camera crew set up at the far end of the court. She saw the NBC Sports–Philadephia logo on the camera and she instantly recognized Michael Barkann, usually a studio host but someone who had said on-air during soccer season, "This might be the best story in our town this fall," as Andi had progressed from being cut to benchwarmer to starter to star.

"What in the world are they doing here?" she whispered to Lisa Carmichael.

Lisa smiled. "Following up on the best story of the fall?"

Andi groaned. She was almost certainly right. There was absolutely no reason for a TV crew to be at a sixth-grade basketball game. Maybe Camden had a star they were there to see? Not likely. How could anyone possibly know if a sixth grader was a future star before a single game had been played?

Then, as she went through the pregame layup line with everyone else, Andi spotted another familiar face: Stevie Thomas, the star kid reporter who was now a freshman at Penn. He had also followed her story during soccer season. He did most of his work for the *Washington Herald* and had brought a lot of attention to Andi's story outside of Philadelphia. He certainly wasn't here to check on anyone playing for Camden.

He was here for Andi.

The media had played an important role in getting Andi on the team and on the field during soccer season. Now, though, the last thing she needed was any attention at all from the media.

A basketball whizzed past Andi's head.

"Hey, Carillo, get your head up," Jamie Bronson barked.

She'd thrown a pass to Andi in the layup line and it had gone right past Andi because she wasn't paying attention. She'd been lucky not to get hit in the face by the ball.

"What're you doing, Carillo, posing for the camera?"

It was Alayne Jolie, right behind her in the layup line.

Andi didn't answer. She had no answer.

Things didn't get any better when the game started. The Camden girls, Andi would learn later, were every bit as good as the Camden boys. About the only Merion player who was able to score with any consistency was Eleanor Dove. When she got the ball around the basket, she was almost impossible to stop.

Even though Camden had two players who were taller than she was, she was quicker and a better leaper. There were two problems: first, it wasn't easy to get the ball to her since she was frequently double-teamed. Second, none of the other Merion players could score—at all.

Even Maria Medley, who was so much quicker than the rest of her teammates, struggled because it seemed as if all of Camden's guards were as quick as she was. At the end of the first quarter, the score was Camden 14, Eleanor Dove 6. No one else had scored for Merion.

Coach Josephson hadn't subbed at all in the first six minutes. At the start of the second quarter she sent five new players into the game. Andi wasn't one of them. She found herself sitting on the end of the bench next to Lisa Carmichael.

"I know she can't stand me," she whispered to Lisa. "But what in the world did you do?"

Lisa smiled. "Became friends with you?"

She was joking, or at least half joking, but there was a ring of truth to it. Andi guessed the only reason Eleanor and Maria had started was because they were the team's two best players. Or, at least two of the three best. Andi honestly believed she was the best shooting guard the team had. It was tough to prove that sitting on the bench.

Three minutes into the second quarter, Andi heard Coach Axelson say to Coach Josephson, "Amy, we've got to call time and get some subs in."

Coach Josephson shot her a withering look but stood up and put her hands together in a T-signal to get a time-out.

The score was now 22–6. Debbie Lee, subbing for

Eleanor, was a little taller but not nearly as quick or agile. With Eleanor out, Merion was struggling to get a shot off, much less score.

"Dove, Medley, go for Lee and Eisen," she said.

Coach Axelson was pointing at Andi and Lisa. "Coach, we need to get them in," she said.

Andi could see Coach Josephson scowl. Then, finally, she said, "Okay, fine. Carillo, Carmichael, get in."

"For who?" Andi asked.

Coach Josephson looked at her as if she were too stupid to live. Then she looked at Coach Axelson. "Go for Allison and Mearns," she said.

Andi and Lisa raced to the scorer's table to report in to the game. The horn blew. There had been no discussion of tactics at all.

Still, walking onto the court, Andi felt better. She was playing—finally—and that, she decided, was a start.

10

IT WAS QUICKLY APPARENT THAT–PERHAPS BY ACCIDENT–
Merion now had its best team on the floor. Ronnie
Bonilla, who was the only player left in the game after
the subs came in, was a perfect fifth wheel, willing
to screen when she had a chance and a hardworking
defender.

On Merion's first possession after the time-out,
Medley got a solid screen at the foul line from Jolie and
was able to squeeze through for a layup—becoming the
first player not named Dove to score for Merion.

Camden's point guard, who Andi found out later
was named DeShea Watson, got careless with a pass
inside, throwing it over everyone's head, for a turn-
over. Then, Eleanor recognized a double-team when
the girl guarding Andi left her for a moment. She
pitched the ball quickly to Andi, who was wide-open

at the three-point line, and Andi swished the first shot of her career. That cut the margin to 22–11 and Camden's coach called a quick time-out.

The Little Wildcats put in some subs at that point and righted themselves, but the last two minutes of the half were played evenly: It was 26–15 at the break.

Halftime was ten minutes long, so the players only had a couple of minutes to relax before heading back to the court.

Coach Josephson had very little to say, except for one sentence that surprised everyone: "We'll go back with the five that started the game."

The five who had been on the floor the last 3:12 of the half looked at one another as if to say, *Whaaa?* Even the starters looked surprised.

It wasn't as if the starters weren't trying; they were. Eleanor continued to play effectively inside, and the defense seemed better adjusted to the speed of the game than it had been at the start.

But the first four minutes pretty much guaranteed the home team wasn't going to stage any sort of miracle rally. It was 35–19 before Coach Axelson was able to convince Coach Josephson to go to the bench again. This time, she kept Eleanor, Maria, and Bronson on the court and subbed Eisen and Carmichael. Andi remained nailed to the bench.

She finally got back in at the start of the fourth

quarter, but by then it was 39–22. She made another three-pointer—sinking the three after getting a solid screen from Eleanor—and twice found Lisa open on cuts to the basket. As in the second quarter, Merion staged a mini-rally with its best players on the court, slicing the margin to 42–30 with two minutes remaining.

They weren't going to win, but they were making the score respectable. Then Coach Josephson went back to the three starters who were sitting and even took Eleanor and Maria out. Merion didn't score again. The final was 48–30.

Going through the handshake line, DeShea Watson introduced herself to Andi. "You're the soccer player, right?" she said.

"I played soccer, yeah," Andi said.

"Well, you got game here, too. What the heck is your coach doing not playing you and that tall blonde girl more?"

Andi smiled. "You'd have to ask her," she said.

Watson patted her on the back. "Well, she should only play you two if she wants to win games. When you guys were in with the two sisters you were pretty good."

They both moved on. When Andi had shaken the final hand, she headed in the direction of the locker room, only to find Michael Barkann blocking her way.

He put out his hand. "Andi, Michael Barkann," he said. Andi liked the fact that he didn't assume she knew who he was. Jeff had told her that his father often joked about TV people who thought they were "famous for being famous."

"Nice to see you, Mr. Barkann," she said.

"It's Michael," he said. "Can I grab you for a minute?"

Andi's teammates were all walking or jogging past her, giving her "what's going on?" glances.

"Well, I have to go to the locker room right now . . ."

"Understand. We can wait. How about when you're done in there?"

"Why do you want to talk to me?" Andi said, baffled.

"Just following up on the stuff we did on you during soccer. We get a lot of tweets and e-mails asking how you're doing."

Given that it was NBC–Philly's initial story on her that had allowed her to play soccer, Andi thought it would be rude to say no. She wished, though, that her parents, who were both working, or Jeff, who was in New Jersey, were around to talk it over with. She was pretty certain Coach Josephson wouldn't be thrilled with seeing her on TV.

Still . . . she was already on the end of the bench . . .

"Sure," she said. "Give me a few minutes."

Fortunately, she wasn't the last person to enter the

locker room. Her friends—Eleanor, Maria, and Lisa— had lingered waiting for her.

"What was that about?" Maria asked.

"Tell you later," Andi answered as they walked inside.

If Coach Josephson had noticed her talking to Barkann, she chose not to comment on it.

"Okay," she said, when everyone had sat down on stools in front of their lockers. "Disappointing start, but that was a good team. I thought all of you had some good moments and we learned a lot about what we need to work on today.

"We're off tomorrow, give you a chance to catch up on schoolwork if you need to, and back to practice on Thursday. Quick turnaround, though; we play at Chester Heights on Friday."

She turned to Bronson. "Jamie, get everyone in."

Bronson led a quick cheer: "Beat the Lions!" and they all headed to the showers as Coach Josephson went to the door. Once she was gone, Coach Axelson asked to see Andi and Lisa Carmichael before they hit the showers.

They walked to a corner of the locker room, next to the water fountain.

The young assistant looked around as if there might be a microphone hidden in the wall.

"Look, you two," she said quietly. "I know you're frustrated you didn't play earlier and didn't play more.

Be patient. Remember what Coach said the first day: She's learning as she goes. We all are."

She looked directly at Andi. "I saw you talking to the TV guy out there. I'm not telling you not to talk to him, but be very careful what you say. Don't give Coach an excuse not to play you."

Andi said nothing.

"You understand me, Andi?"

"I do, Coach."

"Good. Now hit the showers, both of you."

Michael Barkann and his crew were waiting in a corner of the gym when Andi came out of the locker room. The varsity teams were now warming up for their game and Andi saw there were eight minutes on the pregame clock. She assumed her interview wouldn't last more than a minute or two.

"Thanks for doing this," Barkann said, as Andi walked over to where he was standing.

"No problem."

"The anchor will introduce the piece, reminding people about your soccer season, and then come right to me, so I'll just start asking you questions, okay?" Barkann said.

"Sure, but aren't you usually an anchor?" Andi asked.

Barkann nodded. "Usually, but every once in a while, I like to get out and do some reporting. By the way, your coach refused to talk to me. You have any idea why? This isn't like soccer where your coach tried to cut you for being a girl."

Andi had a lot of answers to the question but decided to keep her mouth shut—even off camera.

"No clue," she said. She glanced at the clock, now under six minutes. "We better get going."

"Right," he said, and signaled his cameraman, who pointed a finger to let him know he was ready.

"Andi, basketball season didn't get off to a great start for you and your teammates today, but how does it feel to be on a girls' team?"

Andi smiled. "Great, actually. I mean, I enjoyed being part of the boys' soccer team, especially because we did so well when all was said and done. But it's fun to not be alone in the locker room."

She figured that was a good, upbeat answer.

Barkann nodded. "Watching the game today, I was surprised you didn't play more. You certainly did well when you got a chance."

"I think our coach is still trying to figure out our best combinations," Andi said. "Everyone played today, so I think she learned a lot. We only had a few days of preseason practice."

"You expect to play more in your next game?"

"I hope so," Andi said. "Beyond that, though, I just hope we play better on Friday than we did today." Barkann started to pull the mic back, but Andi quickly added: "We lost our first couple soccer games and turned it around. I hope we do the same in basketball—only get going in the right direction a little quicker."

"Thanks, Andi. Good luck the rest of the season."

The light on the camera went off.

"Terrific as always," Barkann said. "You're an old pro at this."

They shook hands again. Andi breathed a sigh of relief and turned to go. She hadn't taken two steps before she almost bumped right into Stevie Thomas.

"I have a few questions of my own," he said. "Got another couple minutes?"

Andi knew Thomas's questions wouldn't be as easy to dance around.

She remembered Jeff's dad explaining to the two of them the difference between a TV interview and a print interview: "You duck a question on TV or give a politically correct answer, the interviewer almost certainly won't call you out on camera," he said. "That would be rude and could make him look bad for badgering.

"Print is different," he continued. "You give a

nonanswer, a good reporter will call you on it or ask the same question another way."

Andi remembered that Thomas had made Coach Johnston look pretty bad when he'd interviewed him at the height of the soccer controversy. She had no desire to start any sort of controversy now.

"Why don't we sit down over there?" Thomas said, nodding in the direction of an empty section of bleachers on the baseline.

"My mom's going to be outside to pick me up in about five minutes," Andi said. She wasn't lying. If only the game had lasted a little longer, her mom would already be here.

"Won't take five minutes," he said.

They walked over and sat down.

"I asked your coach to talk to me, too," he began. "She was pretty rude. Said, 'I don't talk to the media.' I said, 'You're a sixth-grade basketball coach and you don't talk to the media?'

"She said, 'You're all the same. Nothing but fake news.' Sounded just like our president."

Andi rolled her eyes. She wasn't surprised.

"So, has she got a problem in general or a problem with you? Or both?"

The honest answer was both. Andi went for a duck. "What makes you think either of those things is true?" she asked.

Thomas laughed. "I know I'm young, but I've met a lot of people the last few years," he said. "I'm guessing Barkann is the first person to ever ask her for an interview and I'm the second. People like that don't stalk off unless they have something to hide or are afraid what the questions might be."

Andi liked Stevie Thomas. He'd been good to her in the fall. Now, though, she felt trapped. "We just lost our first game convincingly," she said finally. "This is the first time she's coached. I think she's struggling with it a little bit."

Thomas nodded. "She didn't make things any easier by not having her best players out there for most of the day."

Andi knew that was true. "We're sixth graders," she said. "It's our first game." She had a sudden thought: "Tom Brady was a sixth-round draft pick. If experts in the NFL can mess up like that, why can't a sixth-grade gym teacher need some time to figure out who her best players are?"

Now Thomas was grinning. "You're a really smart kid, Andi. That's a good answer."

Andi felt better. "Can I ask you a question?" she asked.

"Sure," Thomas said.

"Why are you here? Don't you write for the

Washington Herald most of the time? How am I a story in any way in Washington?"

"Remember, I do some writing for your friend Jeff's dad's old paper, too—the *Daily News*," Thomas said. "But I'd also argue that what you went through in the fall wasn't just a Philadelphia story."

"But soccer season's over."

Thomas grinned. "And basketball season's just starting."

11

THE BUS RIDE BACK TO SCHOOL FROM CAMDEN DIDN'T TAKE very long since they were going against rush-hour traffic.

Jeff sat near the back of the bus with Danny Diskin, Tavon Washington, and Mike Roth. Ron Arlow was up front, surprisingly surrounded by about half the team. Arlow's posse had gradually pulled away from him as soccer season wore on; even his friends had grown weary of his "me, me, me" approach to soccer—and life.

But Arlow clearly wasn't disliked on the basketball team.

The bus pulled up to school at five forty-five. Jeff had told his parents to pick him up at six and it was raining outside. He'd texted his mom when it was clear they were going to be back at school early, but she'd written back that she couldn't make it before six and his dad was working.

Danny, whose mom was waiting when they pulled up, offered him a ride, but he knew that was way out of their way, so he said no thanks. "I've got plenty of homework," he said. "I'll just get started."

His plan was to walk into the gym and sit on the bleachers, but then he remembered that the girls' varsity game was going on. He walked in anyway, figuring he'd see how they were doing and maybe find out how Andi's team had done.

Instead, he almost bumped smack into Andi, who was on her way out, walking with someone who looked familiar. It took Jeff a second to recognize him. It was Stevie Thomas, the star kid reporter they had both met during soccer season. What the heck was he doing here?

"Hey, how'd you guys do?" Andi asked.

"Got killed. You?"

Andi smiled. "Same. Jeff, you remember Stevie Thomas?"

"I do," Jeff said, shaking hands.

"How's your dad, Jeff?" Thomas asked.

He had an easy smile and, Jeff remembered, a girlfriend who had been an Olympic swimmer.

"He's fine, thanks," Jeff answered. "He's at Drexel tonight."

Thomas nodded. "Yup. They're playing LaSalle. Big game for both schools. I'm on my way there right now."

"Don't you ever have schoolwork?" Jeff asked.

Thomas laughed. "Oh yeah, I do. But college is different. Lot more flexibility. I only have one class tomorrow and it's not until eleven o'clock."

Wow, Jeff thought, *that's a pretty good deal.*

Thomas shook hands with Andi and said, "Thanks for the time, Andi. Nothing to worry about, I'm not going to write anything—at least for now."

He headed for the door.

"What was *that* about?" Jeff asked.

"Walk me to the door," she said. "My dad's five minutes away. I'll tell you."

Andi walked Jeff through a shorthand version of the events of the afternoon: beginning with the starting lineup, then the locker room fight, Coach Axelson practically forcing Coach Josephson to put her and Lisa into the game, and, finally, the presence of Barkann and the NBC Sports–Philadelphia crew and Stevie Thomas.

"I guess the only good news is that Stevie says he's not going to write anything."

"For now," Jeff added.

"Yeah, for now. But I'm pretty sure Barkann will air the interview I did with him."

"But you said you didn't say anything."

"I didn't. But that doesn't mean *he* won't say something about Josephson not talking to him."

"You're probably right. You want me to ask my dad if he can get Barkann to go easy—or not use the interview?"

Andi shook her head. "Your dad's done enough for me and I don't think it's fair to ask him to do that."

Jeff smiled. "You're probably right. But I thought I'd offer."

Andi's phone pinged. Her mom was outside.

"See you tomorrow." Then, without thinking, she kissed him on the cheek. "You're a great friend," she said as she ran for the door.

She pulled the hoodie on her sweatshirt over her head and headed into the rain. The weather, she thought, was appropriate.

Jeff stood stock-still for a moment, rubbing the spot where Andi had kissed him. For a moment, a tingle had gone through him, but then he thought about her words as she went out the door: "You're a great friend."

Was that just the first thing that came into her

head? Or was she trying to make a point? You are my friend—period.

Probably neither, he thought. The kiss was certainly a friendly kiss, a quick peck on the cheek. He was over-thinking it, he thought. As usual.

His phone pinged again. It was his mom, saying she was pulling up to the back door of the school—which was where the gym entrance was located.

Coach C had insisted that everyone dress neatly to travel to another school—no jacket and tie, but a collared shirt and pants. Jeff was grateful that he'd worn the Eagles jacket his parents had gotten him for his birthday, but he wished he had a hoodie to cover his head. It was raining hard and, since it was two weeks before the shortest day of the year, it was pitch dark and cold outside.

He hustled to the car, his mind still on Andi's kiss.

"Sorry about the game," his mom said as he climbed in.

"No big deal," he said. "They were just better than us. A lot better."

"Who do you play Friday?"

"Chester Heights."

"Are they good, too?"

"No idea."

Jeff really had no interest in talking basketball. His

mom wasn't a big sports fan but was always interested in how her son was doing.

"Mom, can I ask you something?" he said.

"Of course," she said.

"It's about girls."

Even in the dark, Jeff could see enough of his mom's face to know she was surprised.

"Ask away," she said.

"How can you tell if a girl likes you?"

His mom laughed.

"You mean likes you as a friend or . . ."

"*Likes* you," Jeff interrupted. "As more than a friend."

His mom was silent for a moment.

"You know, the honest answer is, more often than not you *can't* tell." She was smiling. "When I was a girl and I liked a boy, the last thing in the world I wanted to do was let him know I liked him."

"Was that when you were in sixth grade?"

"Sixth grade, seventh grade, and all the way through college," she said. "At least. I never let your father know I liked him."

Jeff knew his parents had met as seniors in college.

"So how did he know he should ask you out?"

"He didn't. He took a chance. Of course, if he hadn't asked me out when he did, I'd have probably asked him."

That was interesting. Andi had, more or less, asked him to the Halloween dance. Maybe she thought it was now his turn. Or maybe not. He might have to take a chance.

His mom broke the silence. "Honey, is this about Andi?"

The question surprised him—although there was no reason why it should. He *had* gone to the dance with Andi and they talked all the time. Not to mention how pretty she was.

Still, it wasn't a Mom question. It was more of a Dad question.

"Yeah," he said finally. "I guess so."

"Jeff, you're both only eleven years old. Give it time."

"But what if one of the older guys asks her out?" he said. "They're *not* eleven."

She laughed at that one. "Jeff, if there's one thing I'm almost sure of, it's that she's already been asked out by older boys. And I'd imagine if she's gone out with them, you'd know about it. I'm guessing that Andi's mainly into her schoolwork and sports right now."

That actually made sense to Jeff. It wasn't like Andi spent a lot of time sitting with a bunch of girls in a corner of the lunchroom giggling and talking about boys.

He felt better.

"Jeff," his mom said, pulling him out of his daydreaming.

"Yeah?"

"You'll know when the time is right."

They pulled into the driveway. Jeff felt better. At least he *thought* he felt better.

12

ANDI KNEW SHE WAS IN TROUBLE WHEN SHE WOKE UP ON Wednesday morning and found text messages from her friends on the team.

Eleanor's started: *Hey media star. You looked great!* The one from Maria said: *Last one off the bench, first one on TV!* And Lisa's said: *Must have been those threes you made . . .*

Andi smiled at those because she knew her friends were just having fun. She hadn't even thought to stay up to see if NBC Sports–Philly had aired the interview. Her dad had suggested calling Tom Michaels to find out if it was going to air on Tuesday or at a later date or at all. Andi had been kind of rooting for not at all and thought it possible since her answers had been so benign—or so she imagined.

The text just below Lisa's quickly wiped the smile

from her face. *Please come see me at the gym office at the start of your lunch period.* It was from Coach Josephson.

Andi was guessing she didn't want to see her to compliment her on how good she looked on camera.

She showed the message to her mom while she was pouring milk onto her cereal. Her mom suggested they look at the piece to see what it said before leaving for school. Andi thought that was a good idea. Her mom's computer was sitting on the kitchen island, so she went to the NBC Sports–Philly website. Just below the lead story on the Eagles was a photo of her talking to Barkann with a link to the story.

"Oh boy," she murmured.

She hit the link and watched it, with her mom looking over her shoulder.

It began with anchor Dei Lynam in the studio and a photo of Andi in her soccer uniform over her shoulder.

"Andrea Carillo became something of an overnight star here in Philadelphia this fall, when she fought her way onto Merion Middle School's sixth-grade boys' soccer team over the objections of her coach and some of her teammates," she began. "She was able to bridge the gender gap by performing so well that she played a key role in Merion winning its conference championship, all the while winning over her coach and her teammates."

Lynam paused and turned to look at a different camera. "Now it's basketball season, and Andi—as everyone calls her—is playing on Merion's sixth-grade girls' team. Based on yesterday's opening loss to Camden, life hasn't gotten any easier for her. Michael Barkann has a report."

The shot switched to Barkann, standing outside in front of the Merion Middle School sign.

"We came here today to update an uplifting story," he said. "We got the update, but the uplifting part got lost somewhere."

Barkann disappeared and tape from the game appeared. First, there was a shot of Andi and Lisa sitting together at the end of the bench. Then there was Andi making a three and finally a shot of the scoreboard at game's end.

Barkann narrated.

"Although it seemed apparent that Carillo was one of Merion's best players, she didn't start the game. Nor did she come in at the start of the second quarter when Coach Amy Josephson put in an entire second unit. When she and Lisa Carmichael finally did get in, the team played noticeably better. The same happened when they got in during the final quarter, when the game was out of reach.

"Andi Carillo is too nice a kid to criticize her coach—especially after just one game."

Andi was next up on camera, giving her carefully worded answers, especially the one about Coach Josephson trying to use different combinations in the season's opening game.

"I don't see anything wrong there," her mom said.

Just as she finished, Lisa Carmichael was on camera and Barkann was saying off camera, "At least one of Andi's teammates admitted to being baffled."

"I don't know why Andi didn't play more," Lisa said. "You'd have to ask Coach Josephson that question."

Barkann was back on camera now. "I wanted to ask Coach Josephson that question, Dei, but she refused to stop and talk. Shades of Andi's soccer coach in September. Must be something in the water in the faculty room here at Merion Middle. Back to you."

Lynam was shaking her head and laughing at Barkann's tag. "Maybe they should bring in some bottled water for the uptight coaches," she said. Then, looking into the camera, she said, "It's sixth grade, Coach Josephson. Lighten up!"

Andi groaned. She had tried so hard not to say anything that might upset her coach, and it had all been blown up by Lisa's one-liner and then by Barkann and Lynam—not that they were wrong; they just hadn't made her life any easier.

"That's a long piece for sixth-grade girls' basketball,"

Andi's mom said, pointing at a little bug above the story that gave the run time as 2:42.

Andi shrugged. "It's midweek. There's not much to say about the Eagles, and the Flyers and the Sixers were both off last night. There was Drexel–LaSalle and not much else."

"When did you become such an expert?" her mom asked.

Andi sighed. "Talking to Mr. Michaels while all the soccer stuff was going on."

"Well, I'd suggest you point out to Coach Josephson that you didn't criticize her in any way."

"I have a feeling," Andi said, "that's not going to be good enough."

Jeff had also watched the NBC Sports–Philly piece before leaving for school. His dad, who was still sleeping when he came downstairs, had left him a note telling him he should check it out before he left.

He found the link quickly, watched the piece, and knew Andi was going to be in a world of trouble with her coach.

En route to school, he texted Andi to see if she'd seen it.

Oh yeah, came the reply. *And so did Coach Josephson. Wants to see me at lunch.*

That, Jeff knew, was not good. *Want me to go with you?* he said, kidding but wanting her to know he'd throw himself on a grenade for her if need be.

NO! came the answer. *She probably thinks I got you to get your dad to do it!*

Jeff hadn't thought of that. He sent a quick reply. *Sorry. Was just kidding.*

Not funny, she answered. *But thanks. Know you meant well.*

Having whiffed on how the coach might react to his potential involvement, Jeff whiffed again on how other students might react.

He was opening his locker when Ron Arlow—who else?—came strutting up to him with that obnoxious smirk creasing his face.

"So, Michaels, still trying to be Andi's knight in shining armor?" he said. Jeff noticed Mike Roth and Steve Reilly, two of the guys on the team who hung out with Arlow, standing right behind him.

"What are you talking about, Arlow?" Jeff said, even though he knew the answer.

"Come on," Reilly said. "We all saw that story with Andi whining about not playing more. Tell us you didn't get your dad to set that up."

"Nope!" Jeff said angrily. "I didn't even know about it until we got back from Camden."

"Yeah, right," Roth threw in, while Arlow continued to smirk.

"Hell with you guys," Jeff said, slamming his locker shut while using a word his parents had told him repeatedly not to use. At that moment he didn't care. His parents weren't there.

"Well, we all know the truth and so does everybody on the girls' team," Arlow said. "If she's smart, she just quits now because no one's going to want to talk to her after this."

Jeff started to answer, but the three of them had turned to walk away.

"She didn't whine!" Jeff shouted at their backs, causing several people in the hallway to give him a funny look.

The five-minute bell rang. It was going to be a long day.

Unfortunately for Andi, Arlow had been right about the other girls on the team—some of them, anyway.

Andi didn't see any of her teammates, other than Lisa Carmichael, on her way to first period. Lisa went pale when Andi showed her the text from Coach Josephson. "But you didn't say anything bad," she said. "I didn't, either. I just told Mr. Barkann he should ask the coach about playing time, not me."

"I know," Andi said. "Don't worry about it. It's not a big deal."

Except that it was. Jamie Bronson and Jenny Mearns were both in her first-period math class.

"Oh, look," Bronson said, "here comes the TV star from that famous show *Whines of Our Lives*."

"Nah," Mearns said. "She's on *Survivor: Whiner Island*."

They both laughed as if they were the two funniest people alive.

Lisa stepped in. "She didn't whine about anything," she said. "You two are just trying to cause trouble."

"*She* caused the trouble because she never met a camera she didn't like."

The comment came from across the room. It was from Alayne Jolie—another member of the Bronson entourage.

Before Andi could even think of a response, Mr. Andrews, the math teacher, walked in as the bell rang to start class.

Andi had only one thought as she found a seat: Was there anyone in this school who hadn't seen it?

The morning crawled by in slow motion. As much as Andi was dreading the meeting with Coach Joseph-son, she was eager to get it over with. She wondered if maybe, when the coach heard her side of the story, everything would be okay.

That, Andi thought, *was about as likely as the sun rising in the west tomorrow morning.*

As soon as the fourth-period bell rang, she walked out of English class and found Jeff waiting for her. This was one time when he was about the last person she wanted to see—or be seen with.

Jeff read her mind. "I know, I know," he said. "I just wanted to tell you to not be scared and I'll see you at lunch."

"If I'm not expelled," Andi said.

That, she knew, was what her parents called gallows humor.

She made her way through the throngs of kids, most headed in the other direction from her—the cafeteria being at the opposite end of the building from the gym.

She went down the steps, across the causeway between the main building and the gym, and almost walked smack into Coach Axelson when she opened the door.

She gave Andi a smile. "Just trying to calm the waters for you a little bit," she said. "Don't worry. You'll be fine."

"Thanks, Coach," Andi said, not feeling the least bit reassured.

She found Coach Josephson sitting at her desk, a bowl of soup and some crackers in front of her.

"Have a seat," she said, waving to an empty chair.

She parked her spoon in the soup, wiped her mouth with a napkin, and pushed her lunch aside.

"I assume you know why you're here," she said.

"My parents always tell me to never assume anything," Andi said. "But I'm guessing it has something to do with the TV piece."

"Good guess," the coach said, her voice dripping with sarcasm. "You have any guesses *why* I would want to talk to you about it?"

"Honestly, no," Andi said. "I didn't think I said anything that would bother you. In fact, I think I told the truth—that you're still trying to figure out our best combinations and yesterday was only our first game."

She didn't believe that was true for a second, but it was what she'd said.

"Did it ever occur to you that just by talking to them you gave them an excuse to attack me?" Coach Josephson said.

Andi shook her head. "No, it didn't. Mr. Barkann did tell me that you wouldn't talk to him and I thought that was a little bit surprising."

"Some people aren't in love with seeing themselves on camera the way you are, Miss Carillo," she said. The sarcastic tone had turned bitter. "I know you are close friends with Jeffrey Michaels, and so I'm guessing you did what you did during soccer season and got his father involved."

It was now Andi's turn to be angry. "I did no such thing," she said. "Mr. Barkann told me it was his idea to come to our first game because they had followed our team closely during soccer season. Jeff"—she emphasized saying *Jeff*, not *Jeffrey*—"didn't know a thing about it until the guys team got back from Camden."

She had one more thought. "And I'm not in love with seeing myself on camera. Mr. Barkann was very nice to me, to all of us in fact, during soccer season. I thought it would be rude to turn him down."

Coach Josephson sat silently for a moment. Then she said, "Since you didn't say anything especially critical, I'm going to let you off—this time. But I had better not catch you talking to the media again."

She pulled her soup back and dropped some crackers into it. Clearly, Andi was dismissed.

She thought for a moment about saying something, maybe asking the coach if she'd ever heard of the First Amendment or asking her what she'd done that had caused her to be in the doghouse since *before* the first practice had even started.

She decided to say nothing . . . for now.

13

JEFF WAS ALMOST FINISHED WITH HIS LUNCH WHEN HE saw Andi walking in his direction, tray in hand. She had a glum look on her face but seemed to brighten a little when she saw that Eleanor, Maria, and Lisa were all sitting at the table where she and Jeff normally sat.

The three of them had arrived together, Eleanor announcing, "We know Andi usually sits with you and we figure she's going to need some support today."

They had heard about Andi being summoned to Josephson's office.

If Jeff had 100 percent disagreed with Eleanor, he wouldn't have argued with her. She was, he guessed, close to six feet tall. Plus, he'd seen her playing pickup in the gym enough to know she'd probably kill him one-on-one. She wasn't just tall, she could play.

For once, Jeff was thrilled to have the three girls

sitting with him. For one thing, he didn't like sitting alone—especially since he never knew when Ron Arlow and friends might wander over. He knew that wouldn't happen with the three girls sitting with him.

He kept quiet while they all waited for their mutual friend—who appeared a few minutes later.

Andi plopped down in the table's empty chair, picked up a fork, and began picking at her pasta. Clearly, she was waiting for someone to ask her what had happened.

It was Eleanor who finally said, "Well?"

"Thought you'd never ask," Andi said, forcing a bright but unconvincing smile. "Basically, she's mad because, even though I didn't say anything bad about her to Barkann, I set them up to make fun of her by talking to him at all."

"Did it ever occur to her that they might not have made fun of her if she'd talked to them?" Jeff said.

"No, I honestly don't think that thought ever crossed her mind," Andi said. "I'm a bad guy, you're a bad guy because she thinks I asked you to get your dad involved, and she's cutting me a break 'this time.'"

"Why in the world would you have wanted Jeff's dad involved?" Maria asked. "Heck, you didn't even know her ridiculous starting lineup until we walked in the locker room yesterday."

"Or her even more ridiculous second five until the second quarter started," Eleanor added.

Andi put up a hand. "You are all making reasonable arguments. Problem is, we're not dealing with a reasonable person here."

Jeff knew she was right. He had an idea—which had nothing to do with his dad. He decided not to voice it at that moment because he knew—*knew*—Andi would shout him down. But he thought it made sense. Beyond that, at this point, he figured Andi had nothing to lose.

There were no practices for either team on Wednesday and the girls practiced first on Thursday since they were traveling on Friday. Now that the season was underway, the team that was traveling would practice first the day before in order to get an earlier start on homework, the theory being that homework time would be lost due to travel. Why that mattered for Friday games, no one understood, but that was the rule.

So, the girls were out there at three fifteen on Thursday. The thought of just quitting, sitting out the winter season, and waiting for tennis in the spring crossed Andi's mind a couple of times, but she decided against it, if only because she thought she'd be punishing herself more than Coach Josephson if she walked away. The *only* good thing about it might be putting in a call to Michael Barkann to see if he wanted to know the full story on why she'd decided not to play.

She never brought that notion up to anyone, not even her parents. Instead, she was in the gym by 3:10 Thursday afternoon, ready to go. When the whistle blew, she was the first one to the jump circle. If Coach Josephson noticed, she didn't comment.

The pre-practice talk was generic, full of reasons why they were going to play better at Chester Heights and how much Coach Josephson and Coach Axelson had learned by getting everyone into the Camden game. In soccer, everyone on the team had to play at least five minutes. Because the basketball games were only twenty-four minutes and because a two- or three-minute stretch might change the momentum of a game, coaches didn't have to play all twelve players. It was "recommended" by the league, but not required.

After everyone had stretched and shot free throws— the team had gotten to the foul line a grand total of four times on Tuesday, so Andi wondered why that was a priority—they were divided up to scrimmage.

"Five who started will start tomorrow," Coach Josephson said. "Second five will be the same, too." She paused for moment and then added, "We'll let the two TV stars sub in when we get a chance."

Andi and Lisa looked at one another.

"I guess the good news is, she's not holding a grudge," Lisa said sarcastically as they walked to the sideline to watch.

"Must be in one of her books," Andi said. "Hold all grudges even if it hurts your team."

She stood with her arms folded while play started, fantasizing about what she might say to Michael Barkann the next time he showed up with a camera.

"Any better today?" Jeff asked Andi as the girls were coming off the court.

"Only if you think getting into the scrimmage for about four minutes out of thirty is better," she answered.

If there had been any doubt about going forward with his idea, Andi's answer cemented his decision to push ahead.

Practice was pretty routine, although Jeff wasn't thrilled that he was still splitting time with Arlow at the point. He was a little bit confused: He and Arlow were about the same playing the second guard spot—Arlow shot the ball about as well as Jeff—but there was no doubt the team functioned better when Jeff was at the point.

Jeff was a much better ball handler. Arlow was all

right hand; Jeff could dribble as effectively with his left hand as his right, thanks to his father forcing him to learn to dribble left-handed when he was younger. He was also far more willing to pass the ball than Arlow.

Arlow was what was best described as a "shoot-first" point guard. Jeff could shoot when the opportunity was there but felt no need to look for his shot unless he was wide-open or no one else flashed open when he got in the lane.

Near the end of practice, Coach C split the teams up, told the managers to put three minutes on the clock, and said: "Okay, I've got six gift certificates for milkshakes from McDonald's. Winners get them."

For Jeff, that was a pretty good incentive. Going head-to-head with Arlow playing point on the other team was even better.

Jeff's team won easily, in part because Jeff consistently found open teammates and Arlow didn't, but also because Jeff's team had Tavon Washington on it. Washington was the quickest player on the team and he and Jeff were an excellent combination. When Washington pitched the ball from the low post for an open three with thirty seconds left and Jeff drained it for a 15–4 lead, Coach C blew his whistle.

"Okay, guys, I think we have a winner here. Coach B will bring the certificates to the locker room. Let's gather round."

He talked about logistics for the game the next day: It would start at four, meaning he wanted everyone there at three thirty. He suggested they consider hanging around for the varsity game, in part to support the older guys, in part to learn by watching. Jeff hadn't given that much thought. He was supposed to go with his dad to a high school football playoff game the next night. The weather was going to be cold. Maybe, he thought, he should stick around and support the varsity team . . .

Coach C asked him and Arlow to bring their teammates in for a cheer. Arlow jumped the gun—again—putting a hand up and saying, "On three: Beat the Heights!"—before Jeff could get to where he stood.

Jeff didn't bother with the cheer. He'd had enough of Arlow for one afternoon. And he had something a lot more important to do than stick his arm in the air for a cheer.

Everyone started in the direction of the locker room. Jeff lingered.

"You coming?" Danny Diskin asked.

"In a minute," Jeff answered.

Danny gave him a "what's going on?" look, shrugged, and walked off.

Coach C and Coach B were talking. Jeff walked over and stood a few feet away so as not to look as if he were eavesdropping.

"You need something, Jeff?" Coach C said. He smiled. "I promise you'll get your gift certificate."

"It's not that," Jeff said. "But can we talk?"

Coach C nodded. "Sure. Come to the office. I have to give Coach B the certificates, then I've got a couple minutes."

The three of them walked to the end of the court opposite the locker rooms. There were three offices— all of them tiny—for the basketball coaches: one for varsity boys, one for varsity girls, and one that the four sixth-grade coaches all shared. It had two desks squeezed into it. Andi had told Jeff that Coach Josephson didn't use the coach's office often, instead using the larger office off the locker rooms that was for the school's gym teachers.

Coach C reached into his desk drawer and counted out six certificates. He handed one to Jeff and the other five to Coach B.

After he closed the door, Coach C pointed at the chair opposite his desk and said, "What's on your mind?"

Jeff sat and took a deep breath. "Coach, I need your help with something."

Before he could continue, Coach C put up a hand. "Jeff, if this is about you sharing time at the point with Arlow, I have my reasons."

Jeff shook his head. "No, Coach, it's not that at all. I would never question your coaching."

That wasn't completely true, but he did trust Coach C. That's why he was here.

"It's about Andi Carillo . . . and Coach Josephson."

Coach C frowned. "What in the world would that have to do with me?" he asked—a very reasonable question.

"Nothing, nothing at all," Jeff said. "Which is why I need your help."

14

JEFF WALKED COACH C THROUGH WHAT HAD BEEN HAPPENING between Andi and Coach Josephson, not skipping any details, even though he figured Coach C had some notion of what was going on.

He finished by saying, "Coach, you know Andi. She's never looked for attention. She just wanted to play soccer. It was *my* idea to get my dad involved back in September, not hers. If Coach Johnston had put her on the team in the first place, there never would have been a story."

Coach C leaned back in his chair. "Does Andi know you're here?" he asked. "I mean, did she know you were going to come and talk to me?"

Jeff shook his head vehemently. "Absolutely not. If I'd told her, she would have told me not to do it."

The coach smiled. "I think you're right," he said. "You're a good friend." He leaned forward. "But I'm honestly not sure there's anything I can do. I don't know Amy well, but I think I know her well enough to know she probably won't be thrilled if someone else tells her how to coach her team. To be honest, I wouldn't be thrilled if someone told me how to coach *my* team."

"I understand, Coach," Jeff said. "But maybe you could just explain to her that you coached Andi in soccer, you saw what she went through, and she's *not* a publicity hound. That's not telling her how to coach her team, that's just pointing out that you know one of her players pretty well and you think she might be misjudging her."

Coach C laughed. "And you think she'll take *that* well?"

He had a point. "I'm sure you could put it in such a way, you know, grown-up to grown-up, that she'd understand."

Coach C leaned back again and was silent for a moment.

"Let me think about it," he said finally. "I'd like to help. Andi's a good kid, and from what I've heard from Joan Axelson, she's one of the better players on that team—which is no surprise. But if I'm going to do it,

I have to figure a way to do it that won't offend Amy. Because, to be honest, it's none of my damn business."

Jeff was a little surprised to hear Coach C curse. In practice and in games—in soccer and now basketball—he'd never heard him use profanity. It made him think this was a serious thing to him.

"Coach, I wouldn't ask, except I think Andi's out of answers. The TV thing today apparently made it much worse. Andi's not in the doghouse, she's been kicked *out* of the doghouse."

Coach C smiled. "You've got a way with words for an eleven-year-old," he said. "Like I said, let me think about it over the weekend, once we get through tomorrow's game." He looked at his watch. "Speaking of which, you need to get home to do homework and I need to get home because it's my night to cook."

Jeff knew Coach C had three kids of his own and that his wife was also a teacher.

A text popped up on his phone. His mom was waiting outside. He'd used up his normal locker room time to shower and change talking to the coach.

He stood up and shook Coach C's hand because he thought it was the right thing to do.

He thanked him again, walked out the door, and texted his mom back. *Five minutes*, he typed.

He'd shower when he got home.

Jeff was right about one thing: Andi would have been furious had she known that Jeff had talked to Coach C. She was very big on solving her own problems. She hadn't been thrilled when she needed adult intervention during soccer season. She had no choice then but to talk to her parents about what was going on. That didn't mean she wanted them to get involved as anything other than advisors.

It was her dad who picked her up after practice. Her lawyer parents often brought work home with them. That gave them flexibility when it came to sharing pickup and drop-off duties for Andi.

Before they'd gone to college, her brothers often gave her rides. Now it was just her parents, and she knew she was fortunate one of them was almost always available to get her where she needed to go.

"So, what's the report from the department of war?" her dad said as she jumped into the front seat after tossing her backpack in the back.

Even though her dad hadn't been home that morning, she knew her mom would have filled him in on the Barkann interview and the summons to the gym office—aka the war department.

Perhaps because they were lawyers who had to listen to clients no matter how long-winded, her parents had always been good listeners. Her dad let her tell the whole story—including the crack Coach Josephson had made to her and Lisa at the start of that day's scrimmage.

"I think we need to stop for some ice cream," he said.

He knew few things cheered his daughter up more than a good ice cream cone. He soon pulled into a place called Sprinkles, which was a few blocks from their house. She ordered her usual—a vanilla cone with chocolate sprinkles—and they sat down in the one booth. Her dad, as usual, ordered a sugar-free cup of cookies-and-cream.

"So," she said, after a few passes at the cone. "Any thoughts?"

She knew her dad had them but, as usual, was making certain she was ready to hear them.

"I think you should wait and see what happens in the game tomorrow," he said. "What did you play Tuesday, about six minutes?"

"Almost," she answered.

"And Lisa, too, right?" he added, as she nodded while biting into the cone.

"If the playing time is the same or close to the same tomorrow, I think you send her a note over the weekend, asking if you can see her at lunch on Monday."

"What if she says no?" Andi asked.

"She won't. She's still a teacher. If a student wants to see her, she's obligated to do it."

Andi knew he was right. That, however, would be the easy part.

"Okay, so what do I say when I get there?" she asked.

"I'd leave that up to you," he said. "You're a smart kid. But I'd put my cards on the table. Let her know how you feel. Don't raise your voice or get angry, just tell her *why* you think you've been treated unfairly."

Andi had wanted to do that in the meeting yesterday. The Carillos were not regular churchgoers, but she knew what a "Come to Jesus" meeting was. You didn't have to be a practicing Catholic or any kind of Catholic to understand it.

She knew her dad was right—especially since that had been her gut feeling, not to mention her overwhelming desire, when sitting in the coach's office the day before.

They finished their ice cream.

"Don't tell your mother," he said as they stood. "She'll kill me if you tell her we had ice cream before dinner."

She laughed. "Your secret is safe with me."

"Good," he said, handing her a napkin. "Do me a favor and wipe the evidence off your face so we can keep the secret safe."

At lunch the next day, Jeff said nothing to Andi about his talk with Coach C and she said nothing to him about her talk with her dad.

In Andi's case, she wasn't trying to keep anything secret; she just didn't think there was any need to talk to anyone about her conversation with her father. Jeff had reason to keep quiet: Unless Coach C decided to talk to Coach Josephson, there was no reason for Andi to know what he'd done. He didn't need any lectures about her not needing a knight in shining armor. He already knew that. He just thought maybe she needed a friend.

Both had games to worry about that afternoon anyway.

The girls would be leaving school early for the bus trip down I-95 to Chester Heights Middle School.

"We have to be on the bus by two thirty," Andi said. "It's only something like sixteen miles from here, but with Friday traffic, they're leaving an hour to get there."

"So, how much do you think you'll play today?" Jeff asked.

Andi shrugged. "Based on practice yesterday, it won't be much different than Tuesday."

"Doesn't she want to *win*?" Jeff said.

"Not sure," Andi said. "I'm really not sure what she

wants. If her only goal was to win, Lisa and I would be starting. Remember, at the start of soccer, Coach Johnston kept us nailed to the bench even though the team was better when we played."

That had certainly been the case. The difference now was that they both had known why they were on the bench during soccer: Andi because she was a girl; Jeff because he had played a role in forcing the coach to allow her to be on the team. This was a mystery.

"Well, my mystery's different," he said, finally. "Coach C has to know I'm a better point guard than Arlow, but he keeps splitting time between us there. The other day when I talked to him, he just said he had his reasons and wouldn't say anything more about it."

"So you went and asked him about it?" Andi said, a little surprised. That sort of aggressive behavior wasn't like Jeff.

"Well, no, not really," Jeff said, turning a little bit red. "It just sort of came up."

"Came up?" she said. "How did it just come up?"

All of a sudden Jeff was intensely interested in the piece of cold apple pie he'd put on his plate for dessert. Andi sensed something was up.

"I think he noticed I was getting a little, you know, frustrated," he finally said. "So, after practice, he just told me I shouldn't, you know, worry about it, that he had his reasons."

He was lying. Andi knew it. Jeff never stumbled over words and he never used the phrase "you know" to break up sentences. She'd noticed that about him early on and figured it was because his father had to go on TV and speak in perfect sentences and he'd picked up the skill along the way. Now, he was stumbling as he spoke, picking at his apple pie instead of wolfing it the way he normally wolfed dessert—and turning red.

She was about to challenge him when the five-minute bell rang. She'd find out later what this was about.

"Good luck today," he said standing—clearly feeling saved by the bell.

"Yeah, you too," she said. "Let's talk tonight."

"Um, yeah," he said. "Absolutely."

The only thing missing, Andi thought, was another "you know."

It was a good thing they had left an hour to get to Chester Heights. It wasn't just the traffic. Somehow, the bus driver got confused and drove to Chester Heights High School instead of the middle school. It was 3:35 p.m. by the time they got off the bus.

Coach Josephson sent Coach Axelson to see if Chester Heights would push the start time back a few minutes, leaving her alone with the team for a moment.

"This team isn't nearly as good as Camden," she said. "For one thing, they've only got two black girls." She glanced at Maria and Eleanor and added, "Like us. So, that should even things up a bit. Their black players are both guards, so they'll probably be quick. Watch out for that."

Andi was about to say something, but Lisa Carmichael beat her to it.

"I think we have to watch out for a coach who, sight unseen, says the black kids on the other team must be quick."

Eleanor was just as angry: "Coach, do you think they'll both be eating fried chicken tonight?"

Coach Josephson stood frozen in the middle of the room, staring at Eleanor and Lisa. Coach Axelson walked into the locker room and, not knowing what had happened, said, "They'll give us an extra five minutes, Coach."

Coach Josephson didn't respond.

She pointed a finger at the two girls who had spoken up. "Apologize, right now," she said. "What I said wasn't racist and I won't have you imply that it was."

Maria spoke up. "Respectfully, Coach, I disagree. You made *two* racist comments—not one. First, that they weren't as good as Camden because they only had two African American players. Second, that the two they have would have to be quick."

Coach Josephson stared around the room. Everyone was staring back at her.

"Okay then, Medley, if you feel that way, you don't need to get dressed. Anyone else agree with her?

Without pause, three hands went up: Eleanor's, Lisa's, and Andi's. Andi knew she could dodge all of this because she hadn't said anything. But there was no way she was going to let those messed-up comments slide.

Coach Josephson looked around, waiting to see if any other hands would go up. One more did: Debbie Lee.

"Okay, fine," Coach Josephson said. "The five of you stay in your street clothes. We'll deal with this after the game's over. I am *not* a racist and won't be called one. The seven of you who want to play basketball, get dressed and warm up. We'll play with seven. That'll be plenty."

She turned and walked out.

15

FOR THE SECOND STRAIGHT GAME, COACH CRIST STARTED
Jeff and Ron Arlow at the two guard spots. This time,
though, he told them that he wanted Arlow handling
the ball at the start of the game.

Jeff was baffled. He still hadn't figured out Coach
C's reasons for having them share time at the position.
He was even more baffled when he was told Arlow
would run the offense to start the game.

He was a little slow leaving the locker room for
warm-ups. As he reached the door, Coach Benyak was
standing there. "Don't worry about it," he said. "Coach
knows what he's doing."

Jeff assumed he was talking about Arlow starting at
the point and wanted to ask what in the world he was
thinking, but said nothing.

Coach C didn't look like a genius in the first quarter.

Chester Heights was every bit as good as Camden—especially when it came to shooting the ball. Their offense was pretty basic: The point guard, who was no taller than Jeff, would work off a high-ball screen at the top of the key and get into the lane, and whenever a defender closed on him, he would pitch the ball to the perimeter to an open shooter. If, by some chance, that shooter *wasn't* open, he would quickly figure out who was open and get him the ball. It seemed as if everyone in a Chester Heights uniform could make a three.

In fact, during the first six minutes, Chester Heights attempted exactly *one* two-point shot—an open layup set up by their center, rebounding a rare miss from outside and putting the ball back in the basket just as Mike Roth arrived in time to foul.

The other eight shots taken by the visitors were all from outside the three-point line, and they made five of them. As the result, the score at the end of the first quarter was 18–8, Chester Heights.

Jeff had started reading *Sports Illustrated* online at the age of eight. His father had told him that *he* had started reading the magazine at eight and that the highlight of his week was coming home from school on Thursday afternoon and finding the magazine waiting for him.

Now the print magazine, which had been weekly for years, was only published twelve times a year. But there were online stories all the time. Jeff had read one recently on the evolution of the three-point shot, which had first come into existence on a permanent basis in high school and college basketball in 1986. The college line had recently been moved back to twenty-two feet, one and three-quarter inches, because it had become too easy a shot for too many players. But the high school line remained at nineteen feet, nine inches.

Watching Chester Heights's sixth graders shoot the ball, Jeff was convinced it was time to move the high school line back. Maybe the middle school line, too.

Coach C subbed liberally at the start of the second quarter and Jeff found himself on the bench along with Arlow, who had turned the ball over three times in the first quarter. For once, Arlow had nothing to say. Midway through the quarter, Coach C walked over and pointed at the two of them: "Michaels, Arlow, get back in. Michaels, you take the point."

By then, the score was 25–10.

On Merion's first possession after he and Arlow had gotten back in the game, Jeff got a screen from Eric Billings, who then rolled to the basket when his man came up to deny Jeff an open shot. Jeff found him wide-open for an easy layup.

As he backpedaled downcourt, Jeff heard Coach C yelling to get Arlow's attention. "Ron!" he yelled. "Do you see how it's done? That's how it's done!"

If Arlow heard the coach, he didn't act like it. Instead, he went for a steal on a pass to the wing, whiffed completely, and then scrambled back just in time to foul the open shooter as he drained yet another three.

Jeff looked at the bench to see how Coach C would react to that. There was no way to tell because Coach C had turned his back on the play and walked to the far end of the bench, hands on hips. Jeff wondered if he was still convinced that he knew what he was doing.

Not surprisingly, things were going even worse for the girls at that moment.

Andi and the other four players not in uniform sat on the end of the bench in their sweats. When the team came off the court to huddle with their coaches before the game started, the five of them stood to join the huddle.

Coach Josephson was having no part of it. "If you're not playing, you don't need to hear what's being said here," she said. "Consider yourselves lucky I'm even letting you sit on the bench."

The five of them walked back and retook their seats at the end of the bench.

"What are we going to do?" Lisa said. "This is completely out of hand."

"We could call Michael Barkann," Maria said.

"No!" Andi said quickly. "We're not doing that. All that does is prove her right: When the going gets tough, I run to the media."

"But you *didn't* run to the media on Tuesday," Eleanor Dove said. "The media came to you."

"And I'll bet they'll hear about this one way or the other," Lisa added. "Someone will drop a dime."

"Drop a dime?" the others said, looking at her quizzically.

Lisa laughed, which earned her a sharp look from the two players in uniform who weren't starting. The five starters were walking onto the court for the start of the game.

Lisa ignored the glares. "It's a phrase my dad always used about letting people know things that are going on. It's back from when there were pay phones and a call cost a dime. If you wanted to tell someone something, you'd drop a dime."

"How old is your father, a hundred?" Debbie Lee said.

Debbie was, without question, the quietest girl on the team. Andi had been surprised when she'd raised her hand to turn the benched four into the benched five prior to the game.

Everyone cracked up, causing the two coaches to glare angrily at them. They quieted down as the game started.

Not surprisingly, it was a rout from the beginning. Chester Heights was a well-coached team. Every time they had the ball on offense, they ran a play that almost always created an open shot. The Merion players looked baffled. Their center, who wasn't that tall, played near the top of the key with her back to the basket and kept finding teammates for open layups or open threes.

"They call it the Princeton offense," Maria whispered to Andi. "Every play goes through the center. She's not their tallest girl, but she's definitely their best passer."

At the other end, Chester Heights pressed from the start. Andi was certain their coach had noticed only seven players warming up before the game and had decided to exploit Merion's lack of depth. She had no reason to care why five Merion players weren't playing.

Every time Merion inbounded after a Chester Heights score, whoever caught the inbounds pass was double-teamed instantly. Sitting on the bench, Andi could see the panic in the faces of her teammates. "We never spent a second in practice working against a zone press," she said quietly to the others in the benched five.

It showed. Once, Jamie Bronson tried to dribble through a double-team and got stripped, leading to an easy layup. The next time the ball came inbounds to

Jenny Mearns, who tried to throw a quick pass back to Bronson. The ball was deflected and went right to another Chester Heights player for yet another layup.

The score was 10–0 and the game still wasn't four minutes old.

Coach Josephson quickly called time-out. For once, she was speechless.

Coach Axelson stepped into the middle of the huddle with a clipboard. Even from where she was sitting, Andi could tell that she was calmly trying to show the players how to deal with the zone press.

"You can't hold onto the ball," she said. "As soon as you catch it, the double-team is going to come." She pointed at Bronson. "Jamie, as soon as that first pass comes inbounds, I want you breaking to the basket. Remember, when they double, someone's always open."

The time-out and Axelson's coaching seemed to calm things down a little. Sure enough, on the next inbounds play, Mearns threw the ball downcourt as soon as she caught it to a streaking Bronson for a layup. At least, Andi thought, that broke the shutout.

But Chester Heights was simply too good for Merion. Occasionally, someone broke open against the press, but even when Merion did manage to score, Chester Heights had an answer. By Andi's count, ten different players scored in the first half. It was 32–10 at half-time.

"Thirty-two points in twelve minutes?" Coach Josephson said when they got to the locker room. "You call that playing defense? I'm embarrassed for you."

Andi almost laughed. If anyone should be embarrassed, it should be the coach, who clearly had no clue how to attack a zone press. Maybe she could go out and buy a book on it over the weekend.

"We could beat this team if we didn't have a group that quit on us because their feelings got hurt," the coach added.

Andi didn't think Merion would be winning if she and her teammates had all been playing, but there was no doubt the game would be more competitive. There was no doubt she and Maria would have a much better chance of breaking the press than anyone else in a Merion uniform. She felt a little bit guilty. Apparently, she wasn't the only one.

"Coach, I think we'd all be willing to play in the second half," Maria said. "If our teammates want us to play."

"No," Coach Josephson said. "You quit on these girls and . . ."

"And those girls should be the ones who decide," Coach Axelson said, interrupting.

Andi was shocked. So too was Coach Josephson, who stared at her assistant as if she'd seen a ghost.

Given the brief opening, Coach Axelson turned

to Bronson. "Jamie, you're the captain, what do you think?"

Andi was certain Bronson would stick with Coach Josephson. To her surprise, she turned to the other players. "I think we give them another chance," she said. "What do the rest of you think?"

For a moment, nobody moved or said anything. Then Randi Eisen, one of the team neutrals, said, "I think we need all the help we can get."

Others nodded in agreement. But then, Jenny Mearns looked at Bronson and said: "They're the reason we're so far behind. I say, let 'em sit."

Bronson nodded. "Let's vote on it," she said. "All in favor of letting them play, raise your hands. Three hands went up right away: Eisen, Brooke Jensen, and Ronnie Bonilla—who, along with Debbie Lee, were the neutrals on the team. With Lee one of the benched five, that was going to leave them one vote short.

Except to Andi's surprise—again—a fourth hand went up: Bronson's. The other three players, who hadn't raised their hands, stared at their leader in surprise for a few seconds. Then, all of them raised their hands—Mearns last.

Bronson turned to Coach Josephson.

"Coach, it's unanimous. We'd all like to have our whole team on the court for the second half."

For a moment, Josephson said nothing: standing

with her hands on hips, staring, first at Bronson, then at Coach Axelson.

"Okay then, if that's the will of the team, I'll go along with it." She stood up straight and pointed a finger in the direction of those who hadn't played the first half: "This isn't over, though. Your pregame behavior was unacceptable."

Someone was knocking on the door. "Two minutes, Coach," a voice said. "We need your team out here."

"Let's go, girls," Coach Axelson said, and headed for the door.

Andi found herself next to Bronson as they all went up the steps from the locker room to the floor.

"Thanks, Jamie," she said.

"Don't think I did it because I like any of you," Bronson said.

"Never crossed my mind," Andi answered.

16

THE TWO MERION COACHES DIDN'T MAKE IT OUT OF THE locker room until the buzzer sounded to clear the court for the start of the second half.

As the players walked to the bench, the coaches were a step behind.

"Okay," Coach Josephson said as she stepped into the circle. "Let's go with the five freshest players to start: Dove, Medley, Carmichael, Lee, and Carillo. Dove, you play away from the basket to give Lee some room inside."

Normally, Eleanor and Debbie wouldn't play together, but the decision to start the five who hadn't played in the first half would mean Eleanor needed to move away from the low post on offense. Andi was pretty sure she could handle it. She was probably the team's third best ball handler behind Maria and Andi.

As they came out of the huddle Andi noticed that Coach Axelson was smiling. She wondered if it had been her idea to start the previously benched five.

Merion was a different team right from the start of the half. For one thing, Maria Medley completely blew up Chester Heights's press. She was so quick that double-teaming her was a waste of time. She either raced past the double-team before it could get set up or she waited for two players to reach her and instantly found someone open.

Merion opened the half on a 9–2 run, all four baskets coming after Maria broke the press leading to layups. On the fourth one, she went past the entire Chester Heights defense, banked in a layup, and was fouled as the shot went in.

Chester Heights called time. When the game resumed, they weren't pressing anymore. Their coach clearly didn't want to mess with Maria. Andi giggled to herself, thinking about one of her favorite musicals, *The Sound of Music*. One of the songs in it has a famous line that asks, "How do you solve a problem like Maria?"

The answer, when it came to basketball, was pretty clear: Don't press her.

Coach Josephson didn't sub anyone during the third quarter. When it was over the score was 38–26, Chester Heights, Merion having outscored Chester Heights

16–6. The lead was still substantial, but the game was no longer hopelessly out of reach.

Except it was.

"Starters, back in," Coach Josephson said during the break between quarters. She looked at Andi's group. "Good job, girls. Take a break, I know you need it."

They didn't need it. They were all flying on adrenaline. They felt as if Chester Heights was on its heels, even though the easy baskets had stopped when the home team had stopped pressing.

Andi saw Coach Axelson start to say something, then stop. The starters went back in.

Chester Heights's coach clearly knew what she was doing. As soon as she saw Maria and Andi sitting on the bench, she ordered her team to begin pressing again. Ninety seconds into the final quarter, the lead was up to 44–26—a quick 6–0 run. After the last Chester Heights basket—on a clean steal from Jenny Mearns—Coach Axelson jumped off the bench and called time without so much as a glance at Coach Josephson.

She then turned to Coach Josephson and whispered something in her ear. Coach Josephson shook her head. More whispering. Finally, a nod—barely—from Coach Josephson.

"Medley, Carillo, Dove, Carmichael, Eisen—you're back in.

Eisen hadn't played at all in the second half. Clearly Coach Josephson wasn't going to go all the way back to the five who had started the half. Lee was the only player who had started the second half who didn't go back in. Given their performance, it was hard for the starters to argue.

As Andi and the others reported to the scorer's table to check-in, Andi noticed the Chester Heights coach, arms folded, smiling in her direction. Then, she turned to her point guard and said, "Drop the press, Ashley."

This, Andi thought, was a coach who knew what she was doing.

Andi's group played well for the next four minutes but couldn't get the margin into single digits. It was 51–37 when Chester Heights's coach called time-out in order to get the players on the end of her bench into the game for the final thirty-four seconds. Josephson responded by pulling all five of her players. Only Bronson, among the starters, didn't go back in the game.

She was standing as Andi and the others came to the bench. So was Coach Axelson. Coach Josephson was very busy giving meaningless instructions to those going in the game.

"You guys did well," Bronson said.

"You did," Coach Axelson added. "I hope you understand how much we need you."

The game was over a few seconds later; the final score was 53–39.

In the handshake line, the Chester Heights point guard, who was also their best player, introduced herself to Andi and Maria.

"I don't know why you guys and that tall girl"—she nodded at Eleanor—"didn't play the first half, but I'm really glad you didn't," she said. "Tell your coach if she plays you guys all the time, you'll win a lot of games."

That, Andi thought, would be easier said than done.

At that same moment, the Merion boys were trying to pull off a miraculous comeback against the Chester Heights boys.

Once Jeff took over at the point, the team functioned better at both ends of the court. The only time he wasn't running the team was when Coach C gave him brief respites in the third and fourth quarters. Jeff didn't feel tired, but Coach C believed in playing everybody and having his best five fresh for the final minutes.

By the end of the third quarter, Merion had closed what had been a fifteen-point gap to six, trailing 43–37. They got the lead down to three when Arlow took a crisp pass from Jeff, made a nice ball-fake as if to throw it inside to Matthew, and drained a three to make it 51–48 with just under two minutes remaining.

There was no shot clock, so Chester Heights began throwing the ball around, not even looking at the basket. With just over a minute to go, Coach C ordered his players to foul. "Anybody but the point guard!" he yelled, just as Jeff was grabbing the point guard.

"My fault," Coach C said.

Jeff shook his head. It had been his fault. He should have known better. The kid, who his teammates called Billy, hadn't missed a free throw all afternoon.

He kept that record intact, making two shots.

Coach C called time-out with fifty-eight seconds left.

"Plenty of time," he said. "No need to force a three here. Just take the first good shot available." He looked at Jeff: "Unless they back off you completely, which I don't think they will, get the ball in the lane and make something happen."

Jeff nodded, and seeing Billy playing up on him to deny a three-point shot, he drove past him. The center came to stop him, and Jeff slipped the ball to Washington, whose layup made it 53–50. Forty-three seconds to go.

The ball came quickly inbounds to Billy and he brought it to the frontcourt.

"Don't foul him!" Coach C yelled.

Jeff and Arlow double-teamed him and forced him to give up the ball. As soon as the other Chester Heights guard caught the pass, Danny Diskin fouled him.

It was the right move. The non-Billy guard missed the front end of the one-and-one. Merion only had one time-out left and Coach C didn't want to use it. This time, Billy played off of Jeff to keep him from driving the lane. Jeff waited to make sure he had space and then squared up for a three. It dropped cleanly through the basket with twenty-one seconds left.

Chester Heights called time.

"Get the ball out of the point guard's hands," Coach C said. "And then *foul* right away."

Jeff was stunned. "Coach, the game's tied," he said, wondering if somehow Coach C thought they were still behind.

"I know that, Michaels," Coach C said. "I don't want the game ending with that little point guard hitting a shot to beat us at the buzzer. Let's put them on the line and see if someone other than the point guard can make a free throw. Even if they make both, we'll have the ball last with a chance to win or tie.

"When we get the ball," he added, "do not call time unless you are double-teamed someplace and have no choice. Got it?"

They all nodded. This was some gamble, Jeff thought. If a college coach did this and it didn't work, the internet would be full of people second-guessing the coach. This, though, was sixth-grade basketball. The only second guesses would come from parents, only a few of whom were in the stands.

Billy walked the ball upcourt, clearly intending to run the clock down and start a play. Jeff and Arlow jumped to double-team as soon as he crossed halfcourt, and he quickly swung a pass to his left. As soon as the pass was caught, Diskin raced up to the receiver and fouled him.

The kid looked stunned. So did Billy. There were ten seconds left.

The shooter went to the line. It was one-and-one, meaning he had to make the first to shoot the second. Coolly, he swished the first. *Uh-oh*, Jeff thought, *this might backfire*. Then the kid made the second.

There was no time to worry about the gamble not working. Danny inbounded to Jeff and he raced up court. No way was Billy going to give him any space at all. Jeff gave a quick fake as if he were going to go up to shoot and then drove past Billy.

He could see the clock over the basket was at 0:03. He saw two players coming to stop him. Danny was on his left—open; Arlow was on his right—also open. Arlow was the better shooter, but somewhere in the recesses of his brain, Jeff remembered Danny bragging once about making fifteen in a row from that exact spot in the corner.

He glanced right, then flicked a pass to Danny, who

was in his shooting motion almost as soon as he caught the ball. Jeff was knocked down as he released the ball and he heard the buzzer go off. He looked up from the floor just in time to see the ball swish cleanly through the basket.

For a split second, he wondered if Danny had gotten the shot off in time, but out of the corner of his eye, he saw one of the officials with his arms up in the air in the touchdown signal, meaning the three-point shot was good.

If it had been an NBA game or a college game, the officials would have had to go to replay to make sure Danny had released the shot before the buzzer. But this was sixth-grade basketball and there were no replays. As soon as the official on the perimeter indicated that the shot counted, it counted. The game was over. Merion had somehow rallied to win, 56–55. When Danny's shot went through the basket, it was the first time in the game that Merion had the lead.

But that was enough.

The entire Merion team—with two exceptions— swarmed Diskin while Jeff was pulling himself to his feet. Before he could join the celebration, he felt someone grab him by the arm. The only other Merion player who hadn't made it to the pileup in the corner was Arlow, who had been on the far side of the court when Diskin's shot went in.

"I was wide open, why didn't you get me the ball!" Arlow yelled in his ear.

Jeff was caught off guard. They'd won the game. How could Arlow be upset?

Except he was. "Danny was open, too, standing on his favorite spot," he answered.

"I'm a better shooter than he is and you know it!" Arlow was now pointing a finger—hard—into Jeff's chest.

Jeff angrily swiped his hand away. "He made the shot, Arlow," he said. "We won. Get over yourself."

Coach Benyak stepped in between them. Why he was there and not in the middle of the ongoing celebration, Jeff wasn't sure, but he was happy to see him.

"Fellas, fellas, cool it," he said, pushing them apart. "We just had an amazing win. Let's enjoy it."

Jeff and Arlow glared at one another, with Coach B holding them apart.

"Great pass, Michaels," Coach B added. "Now, how about we enjoy this?"

He gave them each one more look and walked away.

"This isn't over, Michaels," Arlow said as he turned to walk away.

Jeff sighed. It was never over with Arlow.

17

THE BUS RIDE BACK FROM CHESTER HEIGHTS WAS ALMOST completely silent.

The only person who seemed interested in any sort of conversation was Coach Axelson, who walked up and down the aisle while they waited for the driver to get going, speaking softly to everyone, trying to encourage all twelve players.

Coach Josephson sat in the front row, on the right side of the bus, staring into her phone. That was the pose adopted, or so it seemed to Andi, by almost everyone on the bus.

Andi had texted her parents to tell them the final score and what time the bus was expected back at school. Five minutes into the ride, she saw a text from Jeff: *We won!* it said. *Came from 15 down to steal it. Danny hit the winner at the buzzer. You?*

Andi smiled wearily and texted back. *Lost, badly. More to it than score.* She paused for a moment and then added: *Want to get a pizza for lunch at Andy's tomorrow?*

They had talked in the past about how much they both like Andy's Pizza at the King of Prussia Mall. It wasn't too far from where they each lived and she hoped the parents might split the driving.

His answer came back so fast she had to smile. *Sure! Let me check with my parents about driving.*

I'll do the same. Talk tonight.

The bus was now in traffic and Andi was starting to get a headache. Jeff sent her a thumbs-up emoji in response, and she put the phone down and closed her eyes.

Coach Josephson's words in the postgame locker room kept bouncing around her brain: "This isn't over."

That certainly didn't mean, "Hey, girls, we've still got twelve conference games to play, so don't worry about the first two nonconference games." Clearly, it meant something like, "I let you five play the second half to keep from getting humiliated, but I'm still angry about what happened."

Andi was angry, too. She was pretty convinced her coach was a secret racist who had just revealed her secret.

She remembered watching a basketball game with her father in which the announcers kept talking about how *cerebral* JJ Redick—then playing for the Sixers—was. She had finally asked her father what *cerebral* meant. "They're saying he's smart," her father had answered. "It's code. They're trying to tell you the white guy is smart."

Their coach wasn't even using code. She was straight-up saying stupid things, making racist assumptions about people because of the color of their skin.

She was jolted out of her thoughts when Eleanor suddenly sat down in the empty seat next to her. Andi had been so deep in thought she hadn't even seen her coming down the aisle.

"So what do you think she's going to do?" Eleanor asked. She was speaking just loudly enough for Andi to hear over the engine and the traffic surrounding them on the highway.

Andi thought for a moment. "She won't suspend us, she can't afford to," she finally answered. "Look at what happened in the first half."

"Yeah, but if it had been her call, we wouldn't have played the second half."

"It was still her call," Andi said. "She didn't have to let it get to a team vote."

"Or maybe she miscalculated. Thought the vote would go against us."

Andi hadn't thought about that, but it made sense. She had certainly been surprised when Bronson had voted with them; she imagined the coach had been, too.

"She's in a tough spot. On the one hand, she'd probably like to throw us all off the team. On the other hand, she probably doesn't want to go zero and fourteen."

"That's why Bronson voted with us," Eleanor said, nodding in assent. "She didn't want to lose the game by fifty."

"I think we get a stern lecture on loyalty and have to run a bunch of suicides," Andi said.

"I can live with that," Eleanor said. "I probably went too far. I should have brought it up to her in private. I almost forced her into a corner."

Andi had been amazed before at how mature Eleanor was. This was another example.

"I don't think you did anything wrong, but you're pretty sensible for an eleven-year-old," she said with a smile.

"Almost twelve," Eleanor said. "My birthday party is the first Saturday in January. You coming?"

"Am I invited?"

"Absolutely," Eleanor said. "Bring your friend Jeff. I like him."

"Yeah," Andi said. "He's a good guy."

Eleanor laughed. "And cute, too."

Andi looked at her in the darkened bus to see if she was joking. Eleanor was at least seven or eight inches taller than Jeff.

"You're like a foot taller than he is," she said.

"Not that much," Eleanor said. "And when you're my height these days, most boys are going to be shorter than you."

Andi didn't have an answer for that one. So she leaned back, closed her eyes and thought about Andy's Pizza.

Jeff read Andi's text suggesting they get pizza together the next day three times before starting to respond. Then he hesitated. He didn't want to appear too eager. So he waited an entire minute before texting his answer.

He was still in the locker room, dressed and ready to go, but waiting for his mom to come pick him up. She was ten minutes away. His dad was working the Flyers game. The Stanley Cup–champion Blues were in town, so his dad had a rare hockey assignment.

Danny, carrying the game ball Coach C had presented him with, stopped and sat down on a stool next to Jeff—who was sitting in front of his locker.

"Let me guess," he said. "You're texting with Andi."

"How'd you know?" Jeff said, surprised.

"Because you've got a goofy grin on your face. You don't get that look when you're texting your parents."

Jeff had to tell someone. "She asked me if I wanted to go to the mall tomorrow to get pizza for lunch."

Danny's smile was so wide it took up about three lockers of space.

"Oh-ho, so the romance builds."

"It's not a romance," Jeff said, fully aware of the fact that his face had flushed.

Danny shook his head. "Does she know she's settling for the passer on the winning shot when she could have the shooter? You know, the guy who actually *made* the shot?"

"Should have passed it to Arlow," Jeff said. "I can see you're going to be impossible to live with."

"As opposed to Arlow, right?" Danny said, and they both laughed. Arlow had been the first guy out of the locker room, not even bothering to shower. After he'd left, Jeff had filled Danny in on what had happened after his shot had gone in.

"Yeah, well, I can deal with Arlow," Jeff answered. "I don't have to be nice to him."

"You better be nice to me," Danny said. "If only because I'm your Arlow-protector. He has no desire to get into it with me—or, for that matter, be around me."

"Why not?" Jeff said.

"Oh, I think we both know the answer to that question."

"I think you're right," Jeff said.

Danny's phone pinged. "My mom's outside."

Jeff's phone pinged even before Danny stood up. "Mine too," he said with a laugh.

They walked out together.

As they turned the corner and saw their parents' cars waiting for them on the circle behind the school, Danny said, "Have fun tomorrow, lover boy."

"Shut up!" Jeff said, punching him lightly on the arm.

He was glad it was dark. That way, Danny couldn't see that he was red-faced . . . again.

Amy Josephson was the first one off the bus when it pulled up to the back door at Merion. She didn't say good night to anybody or wish her players a good weekend. She bolted down the steps and began walking rapidly to her car.

She heard a voice behind her. "Amy, hang on a second."

It was Joan Axelson—who was about the last person she wanted to talk to at that moment. But she stopped, turned, and said, "What is it, Joan?" in as cold a voice as she could conjure.

Joan walked up quickly beside her.

"Let's go get a drink," she said.

"Can't it wait till Monday?" Amy said.

"I don't think so," Joan asked. "Come on, there's a place not far from here that'll be quiet."

"At six o'clock on a Friday night, a bar that'll be quiet?"

"Trust me," Joan said. "It's an Italian restaurant with a small, quiet bar."

The truth was, Amy could use a drink. And, as usual, she had no plans for Friday night.

"Okay, give me the address and I'll meet you there."

Joan gave her the address. "It'll take you about five minutes," she said.

Amy was skeptical about the whole thing but nodded. "I don't have that much time," she said, knowing that Joan probably knew she was lying.

"No problem," Joan said.

Joan wasn't lying about the drive—four minutes—or the place. The main room was large and filled with families out for Friday-night dinner. But the bar, tucked up front, was nearly empty and a booth in the corner was unoccupied.

They sat down and Joan asked Amy what she wanted. "White wine," she said.

Joan got the attention of the bartender, who smiled when she saw her.

"Can we have two glasses of Sonoma-Cutrer here, Mary Jane?" she asked.

Their drinks arrived quickly.

"To better times," Joan said, picking up her glass.

Amy clinked her glass but said nothing. She looked at Joan and said, "You're up."

Joan took a long sip, put her glass down, and nodded her head.

"What is it they say in sports talk radio? I have a question and a comment."

"Fire away."

"First, the question. What exactly is your problem with Andrea Carillo? You've been on her since tryouts started; you buried her on the end of the bench in our first game when she is—at worst—our third-best player. And you've gone out of your way to pick on her whenever you've gotten the chance."

"I buried Lisa Carmichael in game one, too, didn't I?"

"Yeah, you did, but I suspect her crime was being friends with Andi."

"The two black girls are friends with her, too, aren't they? And now their Asian teammate seems to be joining them."

Joan picked up her wine and took another long sip before answering.

"Okay, before you answer the Carillo question, what is it with you and your comments about people of color?"

"You too with the political correctness?" Amy answered. "Come on, they *are* different from us."

"We're *all* different from one another, Amy," Joan said, getting exasperated. "And we're all pretty much the same. Biggest problem we have in this country right now is all the labeling going on. Doing it on a sixth-grade basketball team is flat-out horrible."

Amy shrugged. "You can quit if you want to. Blacks are different from us. Hispanics—did I say that correctly for you?—are different, too. And Jews. You want me to go on?"

"No, please, please don't. But before I get out of here, what's your issue with Carillo? Being Italian American?"

Amy laughed. "Not at all," she said. "For one thing, I just agreed with Hal Johnston. Girls shouldn't be playing with boys. I learned that from my father growing up."

"When was that?" Joan said. "The nineteenth century?"

She stood up and tossed a twenty-dollar bill on the table. She had to get out of there. She had a lot of thinking to do before Monday.

18

WORKING OUT HOW TO GET TO AND FROM THE KING OF Prussia Mall turned out to be easier than Jeff had thought it would be. Jeff's mom was available to pick Andi up and drop the two kids at the mall and Andi's dad said he'd be able to pick them up a few hours later.

Jeff thought about suggesting a movie after lunch but decided not to push his luck. They agreed to eat and then spend some time walking around the mall. The drop-off would be at eleven thirty, the pickup at two. Jeff was fine with that. He suspected there was a lot to talk about.

They walked straight to Andy's—Jeff had suggested arriving at eleven thirty to avoid the Saturday lunch rush—but found it already crowded. They ordered a small six-slice pizza.

"You can take home what we don't finish," Andi suggested.

Jeff suspected leftovers wouldn't be an issue. He had been eating so much lately his parents were convinced he was in a growth spurt. He certainly hoped so.

They found a table in as quiet a place as possible and Jeff started to eat, in part because he was starving, in part because he knew Andi had a lot to tell him. Michael Roth, whose older brother—an eighth grader—was dating Lisa Carmichael, had texted him the night before to say that Lisa had told his brother that all hell was breaking loose on the girls' team.

"This is really good," Andi said after a couple of tentative bites.

"You haven't been here before?"

"I have, with my brothers, but not in a while. I'd forgotten."

Jeff reminded himself to slow down and not wolf his food. Even so, he was reaching for a second slice before Andi was halfway through her first.

As he picked up the second slice, he finally said, "So, what's up?"

Andi nodded, put her pizza down, and took a sip of the Coke she had ordered to drink.

"It's a long story," she said. "Let me start from the beginning."

She began with Coach Josephson's locker room reference to Chester Heights "only" having two black players, Eleanor's objection to the term, and Coach Josephson refusing to apologize or back down, which led to the five players not suiting up for the first half. She finished with her surprise when Jamie Bronson voted in favor of letting them play the second half, her mixed emotions about playing, and the fact that it was clear there was going to be more trouble next week.

"What do you think she'll do?" Jeff asked after Andi said she expected trouble from her coach on Monday.

Andi picked up a second slice. Jeff was about to pick up number three. It occurred to him that Andi might want a third slice. That would be disappointing.

"She's not the type to let something like this go," Andi said. "On the other hand, Eleanor, Maria, Lisa, and I are four of her best five players."

"Who's the fifth?" he asked, then realized it was irrelevant.

"Bronson," Andi answered. "If she kicks us all off the team, they won't win a game," she continued. "She won't want that, not to mention having to explain to people why she did it."

"Yeah, 'I made a racist comment and they objected' probably isn't the best reason for kicking people off the team."

She laughed. "My guess is she'd claim we over-reacted to an innocent comment, but you're right."

"And if we called Michael Barkann . . ."

She pointed a finger at him. "Don't even go there," she said.

"Only if she kicks you off," Jeff added, and Andi sat back in her chair for a moment.

While she took a few more bites, Jeff, having finished slice number three and not willing to start number four as if he were entitled to it, changed the subject—slightly.

"What's the assistant coach—Coach Axelson, right?—what's she like?"

"Very different, I think," Andi said. "The world—our world anyway—would be a very different place if she was in charge."

"So why don't the four of you—five if Lee will stick with you—go and talk to her? She's probably as frustrated as you are. She might be willing to help."

"But how can she help?"

"Not sure. I think you need to find out if she'd be willing, first, then figure out a plan."

She pointed at the last slice. "You eat that," she said.

"You sure? I've already had three."

"And you look like you could eat three more," she said, laughing. "I'm fine. Go for it."

Yet another reason, he thought as he grabbed the last slice, that he liked this girl so much.

They sat and talked some more when the last slice of pizza was gone. Jeff was sorely tempted to order a single slice but remembered what his mother always told his father about waiting twenty minutes at the end of a meal for his brain to get the message to his stomach that it was full.

They did go back for refills on soda but lost their table while they were waiting at the counter. By now, the entire dining area was packed.

"Let's walk for a while," Andi said.

They walked and talked, stopping in a sporting goods store—and buying nothing—although Jeff gawked at a $170 pair of sneakers. They stopped to see what was at the movies, even though there was no time to go see one even if they wanted to do so.

"You see *Toy Story 4*?" she asked.

Jeff was surprised to see that it was still playing because it had been out for a year. He was tempted to say no, but he'd seen it and, truth be told, had really liked it.

"I went with my mom," he said finally.

"Come on," she said, smiling. "If you saw the first three, you had to go to see the new one."

"So you went?" he said.

"Yeah, I did. I thought it was great. I liked the ending."

Jeff gave in. "Yeah, it was pretty cool. I got a little choked up."

They walked on, finally finding an empty bench. It was one thirty.

"We need to start back to the pickup point pretty soon," she said. "We're at the far end of the mall."

"Takes ten minutes tops," he said—in no rush to end the excursion. Date? No. It wasn't a date, he reminded himself.

They returned to the subject of Monday and Coach Axelson.

"If we're going to talk to her, we need to do it away from school," Andi said. "Anybody sees us—and I mean anybody—we're in big trouble. And if it's someone on the team . . . forget it."

"Text her," Jeff said. "See if she has an idea."

Andi shook her head. "No. Not until I talk to the others to see what they think."

Jeff thought that made sense. "Then you need to get the others to sit with us at lunch Monday. That won't look suspicious. You've done it before."

She nodded. "True. The problem is if Coach Josephson does something before then."

That would be a problem. "I don't think it'll happen before practice," he said.

"I hope you're right," she said.

Jeff hoped he was right, too.

Unfortunately, something did happen before practice on Monday. But the news didn't come from Coach Josephson.

It came from Coach Axelson.

Andi was the first to arrive at the lunch table and she instantly handed Jeff her cell phone—lunch period being the only one when students were allowed to look at their phones.

"Just saw this when I turned the phone on," she said.

Jeff took the phone and saw an e-mail that was addressed to the whole team.

> *Ladies, I'm writing to let you know that I submitted my resignation as your assistant basketball coach this morning. It's been an honor and a privilege to work with all of you these past few weeks, but I believe it is best for all involved if I focus going forward on my teaching responsibilities. I have no doubt that whoever replaces me will do an outstanding*

job working with you. I hope this will not be
the end of our relationships. I have enjoyed
every second working with all of YOU . . .

Jeff read it twice before handing it back to Andi. Eleanor, Maria, and Lisa were a few steps behind Andi, all carrying trays and stunned looks.

"What do you think happened?" Jeff asked.

Maria shrugged. "I think she just couldn't deal with Josephson anymore."

"I think putting *YOU* in all caps says it all," Lisa added.

Jeff thought that was accurate. "So, what are you going to do?" he asked. "This pretty much wipes out the plan to go to her for help, doesn't it?"

"Yes and no," Andi said. "I still think we should go and see her, if only to find out why she quit. She owes us that much, I think."

"She may not see it that way," Eleanor said.

"I think she will," Maria said. "She's a pretty reasonable person."

"Okay, let's say we go to her and she says—surprise—she just couldn't deal with Josephson anymore," Lisa said. "Then what?"

"We could go to Mr. Block and tell him he needs to make Coach Axelson the coach and get rid of Coach Josephson," Maria said.

Andi was shaking her head. "I think the last thing he's going to want to do is get involved with another sixth-grade coach," she said. "I know he didn't enjoy what happened with Coach Johnston during soccer season."

For a moment, Jeff wondered if it was time to involve his father and NBC Sports–Philly again. He was pretty sure that Andi would hate that idea.

"I think you go see Coach Axelson," he said. "After you talk to her, *then* you decide what to do next. But I think you better do it right away, because if you don't, there might be a new assistant coach at practice today and that'll be that."

Andi looked at the other girls. "What do you think?" she asked.

"I think we better get going," Eleanor said. "We've got twenty minutes before fifth period starts."

They decided to look first in the faculty staff room, which was off-limits to students but the likely place a teacher would be during the lunch period.

It was at the far end of the hall from the cafeteria. When they got to the door, they all stopped as if not sure what to do next. The double doors didn't have a window, so there was no way to see if Coach Axelson was inside. They all looked at each other.

"Go ahead, Andi, see if she's in there," Maria said.

"Me?" Andi said. "Why me?"

"This was your idea," Lisa said.

"Oh, yeah," Andi said, kicking herself for having the idea. "I forgot."

She took a deep breath, pushed the door on the right open, and peeked her head inside. The place was packed, teachers eating their lunch and talking to one another. Andi's eyes scanned the room while several teachers were clearly giving her curious looks.

She spotted Coach Axelson sitting at a table with the other earth science and geology teachers. She guessed this only because her earth science teacher—Ms. Marx—was sitting directly across from her. She was about to call out when she heard a voice say, "Carillo, what are you doing here?"

She knew without looking who it was: Coach Josephson.

She'd come too far to back out now. She stepped into the room and, without looking to her left, which was where she'd heard Coach Josephson's voice, waved at Coach Axelson's table.

"Coach Axelson," she said. "Have you got a minute? Several of us would like to talk to you."

She added the second sentence so Coach Axelson—and Coach Josephson—would know she wasn't the lone ranger in this.

"She's not Coach Axelson anymore," Coach Joseph-son said.

Andi still hadn't looked in her direction, rudeness she knew she'd almost certainly pay a price for at practice that day—*if* she was allowed to practice.

Coach Axelson stood up. "It's okay, Amy, I've got this," she said. "Andi, I'll meet you outside."

If Coach Josephson objected, Andi didn't hang around long enough to find out. She bolted for the door.

"Well?" the other three said in unison as soon as she walked back into the hallway.

"She's coming," Andi said. She was breathing heavily, as if she'd been running. No doubt from nerves.

It took a full minute for Coach Axelson to make it into the hallway. Several other teachers came out first, each pausing for a moment to look at the four girls as if they each had two heads.

Finally, Coach Axelson came through the door just as Andi was about to be convinced that Coach Josephson would show up first.

She looked at the four girls and nodded her head. "I figured it would be you four," she said. "Let's go up to my classroom."

19

THEY WALKED UP THE TWO FLIGHTS OF STAIRS AND DOWN the hall to Coach Axelson's classroom in silence.

When they walked inside, she took what was normally a student seat and turned it around so she could face the four of them, each sitting at a desk facing the whiteboard.

"So, before you ask your question and, in the interest of time"—she glanced at her watch—"let me answer it. You are all smart kids. You could see that Coach Josephson and I had some real differences in terms of the way we thought the team should be coached. I sat down with her on Friday after we got back to school to see if we could come to a meeting of the minds so we could continue to work together." She paused. "It didn't work out. She's the coach. It's her team. I honestly think you'll be better off with an assistant Coach

Josephson might be more willing to listen to—during practice and in games."

When she finished, they all started talking at once. Coach Axelson put up a hand. "You gotta go one at a time or I can't hear you." She looked at Andi. "You were the one who had the guts to come into the faculty room, Andi, so you go first."

The other three girls seemed to think that was a good idea.

"Okay," Andi said. "Let me start by saying this: I think what I'm about to say goes for all four of us." She looked at the others to see if anyone objected, then continued.

"Coach, we're two games into a fourteen-game season and we're emotionally exhausted. You know why, you've been there through it all. We don't want to quit the team: We all love basketball and we love playing together."

"Maybe the four of you," Coach Axelson interjected. "Not so much with some of the other girls."

"They don't much want to play with us, either," Maria said.

"Fair point," Coach Axelson said. She looked at Andi to continue.

"Coach Josephson said herself on the first tryout day that she'd never coached before. I'm not sure why she wanted to become a coach now, but I think I know enough about sports to know you don't learn to coach by reading a book."

"Also a fair point," Coach Axelson said.

"But it isn't just that," Andi said. "If she made X and O mistakes, that wouldn't be that big a deal. But she's been biased against me for some reason since day one and biased against Lisa for being my friend. Plus, she's a racist. We heard that on Friday."

Coach Axelson put up a hand. "She said some things I have a real problem with," she admitted. "I think, like all of us, she's a product of her environment. I don't know exactly where she grew up, but my guess is that it wasn't the most tolerant of communities."

"Does that make it okay?" Eleanor asked.

"No, it doesn't," Coach Axelson answered. "All I'm saying is, I don't think she's evil. Just . . . misguided."

"Misguided or not, she shouldn't be coaching us," Andi said. "*You* should be."

The five-minute bell rang.

Coach Axelson stood up. "I hear you," she said. "But I can't pull a coup d'etat here. She *is* a colleague and it would definitely divide a lot of the faculty."

Andi wasn't exactly sure what a *coup d'etat* was. She wasn't alone.

"What's a coup d'etat?" Lisa asked.

"It's when you overthrow someone who's in power," Maria said.

"Right," Coach Axelson said. "A tyrannical leader, not a sixth-grade basketball coach."

"But she *is* a tyrant," Andi said. "And we're the ones who are suffering because of it."

Kids were starting to come into the classroom. The girls had to get to their own fifth-period classes.

"Let me give it some more thought," Coach Axelson said. "No promises. But I do understand why you're all so frustrated."

The four of them began heading upstream against the tide of kids coming into the room.

"What do you think?" Eleanor said when they reached the hallway.

The late bell was ringing.

"I think if we don't get moving, we're all going to be late and in trouble," Maria said.

As usual, she was right. They all started running.

After the girls left the lunch table, Jeff pulled out his phone. He knew that Coach Crist would not be in the faculty room because he never ate lunch there. Instead, he and a couple of the other teachers walked two blocks to a diner that had very good food. Jeff had eaten there with his parents on weekends a couple of times, so he knew it was good.

They had run into Coach C and his family there

once, and he'd later told Jeff it was where he ate lunch every school day. "Menu's big enough you can eat something different every day," he said. "But most of the time, I'm happy with a burger, fries, and a milkshake."

Jeff wasn't about to interrupt Coach C's lunch with a phone call—even if he thought he'd pick up. Instead, he sent a text. *Coach, need to talk to you ASAP about problem I brought up to you Friday. It's gotten worse.*

He was pleasantly surprised when he received an almost instant answer. *Understand. Heard what happened at Chester Heights Friday. Still not sure I can do anything. We have late practice today. Come to my classroom after last period.*

Jeff knew that might already be too late, but he didn't have a lot of options. He sent back a thumbs-up emoji and then headed to his fifth-period class, which was math. He hardly heard a word anyone said the rest of the afternoon and was lucky he didn't get called on because he would have been clueless, since he hadn't been paying any attention.

As soon as eighth-period earth science—a class where he wouldn't have been listening much on any day—finally ended, he set out to find Mr. Crist's history class, which was one floor up.

The last couple of kids were on their way out of the classroom when he arrived. Coach C was standing at the whiteboard talking to two kids about a homework assignment. Jeff stood back and waited for them to finish.

Coach C saw him and signaled him to pull up a seat next to his desk.

"So, I hear Joan quit this morning," he said.

Jeff nodded.

"Do you think it was because of what happened on Friday?"

"You know about that?"

"Everyone knows about it. I haven't talked to Amy or Joan directly, but I heard from one of the other geology teachers that the two of them had it out Friday night."

Jeff didn't know that. Neither did Andi and her teammates. But that would explain a lot.

"Do you know what 'had it out,' means, exactly?'

Coach C shook his head.

"All I know is Joan was upset about what had happened in the locker room before the game Friday and tried to have a talk with Amy about it and it didn't go well."

That made sense to Jeff.

"Coach, if Coach Axelson is gone, the girls who didn't play the first half Friday have no chance to be treated fairly."

"Especially Andi Carillo, right?" Coach C said with a smile.

Jeff flushed a little. "Look, she's my friend, you know that. But really, in this case I'm talking about all of them. Isn't there something you can do?"

Coach C shrugged. "Like what?" he said.

"Talk to Coach Josephson? I mean, didn't it help when you talked to Coach Johnston during soccer season?"

"Maybe a little," Coach C said. "But that was different. I was his assistant coach and we were friends. If Amy Josephson isn't going to listen to her assistant, why would she listen to me?"

Sadly, he had a point. "What about the girls' varsity coaches?" Jeff said. "Hasn't Ms. Hanks been coaching the varsity for about a hundred years?"

Mary Ann Hanks was also a gym teacher and Jeff had heard the seventh- and eighth-grade girls loved playing for her. In fact, he'd heard it from Andi at one point when she was lamenting having to play for Coach Josephson. "If I make it to next year, it'll be nice playing for a coach who knows what she's doing," she had said.

Coach C smiled. "It's not a bad idea, but Mary Ann is Amy's close friend. In fact, I think she was the one who encouraged Amy to give coaching a whirl."

"She's her close friend?"

"So I'm told."

"Then who better to talk to her? She might be the one person Coach Josephson will listen to."

Coach C thought about that one for a minute. "Well," he finally said. "It might be worth a shot. In fact, it may be the only shot."

When Andi walked into practice that day, she found Coach Josephson standing at the jump circle with Bonnie Tuller, who taught sixth-grade English. Andi was in her class and liked her. But she wondered exactly what she knew about basketball.

Coach Josephson got right to the point after whistling everyone to the circle.

"I know you all received Coach Axelson's e-mail today saying she is stepping down as my assistant coach," she said. "Frankly, I was disappointed by Joan's decision—mostly for her sake because I don't think quitting is ever a good thing." She turned to Ms. Tuller and, with a rare smile, said, "Fortunately, Bonnie Tuller has volunteered to step in for her. Like me, she hasn't coached before—except in the backyard with her kids, which to me is excellent preparation to coach at this level. Coach, would you like to say a few words?"

Coach Tuller stepped forward and looked around. "I know none of you wanted to start the season oh and two," she said. "How about we wipe the slate clean starting today? We're playing Haverford tomorrow and conference play starts soon after that . . ."

Eleanor put her hand up and said, "Um, Coach, Haverford's a conference game."

"Don't interrupt, Dove," Coach Josephson said.

"No, it's okay, Amy," Coach Tuller said. "My mistake. I'm learning as I go here. Thanks, Eleanor."

Learning as she goes, Andi thought. Just what the team needed. Coach Tuller was clearly a nice person, but she didn't seem likely to stand up to Coach Josephson the way Coach Axelson had at least tried to do.

"Okay," Coach Josephson said. "Like Coach Tuller said, we start conference play tomorrow. Let's get stretched and do some drills, then we'll scrimmage."

Everyone looked at Coach Tuller. It had always been Coach Axelson who had led stretching and drill work. She clearly had no idea about that.

It took Coach Josephson a second or two to figure that out. She looked at Jamie Bronson. "Tell you what, Jamie, you lead the stretching today. Give Coach Tuller a chance to see what it's about."

The good news, Andi thought, was that she was so preoccupied convincing everyone that Bonnie Tuller was the next Pat Summitt that she'd forgotten her promise (threat?) not to forget what had happened on Friday.

The bad news? Everything else.

20

ONCE DRILLS WERE OVER, EVERYONE WAITED TO SEE HOW
the players would be divided up to scrimmage.

"I'm told they have a very tall team," Coach Josephson said. "So, Lee, you join the starters and, Mearns,
you be the sixth player for the starters."

Bronson had a hand up. "You talking first-half
starters from Friday, Coach, or second-half starters?"
she asked.

Coach Josephson looked at her as if she'd asked
if the next day's game was going to be played on the
moon.

"First half, of course," she said through gritted
teeth. "Rest of you are second team. Carillo, you're the
sixth player."

In other words, Andi was the twelfth player. Clearly,

Coach Axelson quitting hadn't given Coach Josephson any reason to rethink what she had been doing.

Five minutes into the scrimmage, the so-called second team—even without Andi—had outscored the first team 14–2.

"Dove, switch with Bonilla," Coach Josephson said. "Debbie, take a break. Carillo, get in."

Putting Eleanor with the first team made things more even, but the starters still didn't have anyone who could guard Maria or Andi. The good news was Eleanor was able to score enough to make things a little more balanced.

Finally, Coach Josephson told everyone to shoot free throws. There were no instructions about keeping count to see who would run suicides. Maybe, Andi thought, the coach realized that running players into the ground the day before the conference opener was a bad idea.

She thought wrong.

When free throws were over, Coach Josephson whistled them to the circle. It was 4:07 p.m.—a little early to end practice. The boys were just starting to come out of their locker room.

"As you all know, we had five players who took the first half off on Friday," she said. "So they should be well rested right now." She began pointing: "Carillo, Dove, Carmichael, Medley, Lee. You can each run three suicides."

Jamie Bronson had her hand up. "Coach, we lost that game as a team on Friday. I think we should all run."

Who, Andi wondered, had been spiking Bronson's apple juice? This was the second time she had stood up for the Doghouse Five—which is what Maria had started calling them after Friday's game.

"Well, Bronson, when they make you the coach of this team, you can make decisions like that," Coach Josephson said. "Until then, I make those decisions. Come on, girls, line up."

Before the Doghouse Five could move, Coach Tuller spoke up. It was the first time she'd spoken since her little introductory speech.

"Coach, I think Jamie is making a good point and she *is* the team captain," she said. "I think we need some team bonding right now. You're the boss, of course, but maybe everyone should run. I'd be willing to run with them."

Coach Josephson looked at Coach Tuller for a second as if she had lost her mind. Coach Tuller was the mother of three, but she was slender and appeared to be in good shape.

"Okay, fine, Bonnie. You go ahead and run with them then. Everyone line up."

As luck would have it, Andi was right next to Coach Tuller. With her long legs, Eleanor was always the fastest runner on the team. Lisa Carmichael was next.

After that came Andi, Maria, and Bronson—who was surprisingly fast for someone with her blocky build.

Andi couldn't keep up with Coach Tuller. She almost caught her on the third suicide, but not quite. Only Eleanor and Lisa finished ahead of her on all three.

"Nice going, Coach," Andi said breathlessly when she crossed the baseline at the end of the third run.

Coach Tuller smiled. "I need to do these more often," she said—also out of breath.

"I don't," Andi said.

Coach Tuller laughed. "You need more playing time," she said—and walked away.

"Hit the showers," Coach Josephson said, forgetting to bring the team in for a post-practice cheer. "Bonnie, stay here with me for a minute."

She walked toward the gym door. The boys were taking the court. Andi had no chance to talk to Jeff.

"What do you think?" Eleanor asked as they walked slowly toward the locker room.

It was Maria who answered. "I think we might have another new assistant coach by tomorrow."

They all laughed. But it really wasn't that funny.

Mary Ann Hanks was out for her post-school, preprac- tice run when the text hit her phone. It was a relatively warm day for December, but too cold to sit outside and read a text, so she finished her run and walked into her office to read the text before she took a shower. Her team practiced at five fifteen that day. Gym time had become a lot tighter since the sixth-grade teams had been formed this year, but she really didn't mind.

Her kids were both in college, so getting home early wasn't as important as it had once been. If the kids were still home, she might have been forced to give up coaching, but her husband didn't get home until after seven most nights, so even when the team had six-fifteen practice they got home at about the same time.

She walked in the back door of the gym, paused for a moment to catch her breath, and pulled her phone from the pocket inside her sweats. The text was from Jason Crist.

Can we talk for a few mins today after your practice?
She quickly texted back. *I'm not done until 6:15.*

I know. I'll shower, grade some tests and wait till you're done.

She shrugged. She and Jason had both been at the school for a long time and she liked him. But she couldn't imagine why he wanted to talk to her. *OK. Why don't you come to my office?*

The response was a thumbs-up emoji. She put the phone on her desk and went to take a shower.

During practice, she completely forgot about the exchange. Her team was 2–0 but opened conference play the next day, and she knew the games would get a lot more serious now. Merion Middle had won the conference title four times in her ten years as coach and had twice won the unofficial city championship.

At the end of a tough practice, she reminded her players to be in the locker room tomorrow by four forty-five and ready to warm up as soon as the sixth-grade game ended at about five. Their game would start at five thirty. Evelyn James, the team captain, brought Coach Hanks's team in for a cheer—"Let's go one and oh!"—referencing the start of conference play, and they all headed to the locker room.

Mary Ann walked in the other direction to her office and was surprised to see Jason Crist sitting in the chair opposite her desk. She'd completely forgotten their meeting.

"Door was open . . . ," he said.

"No worries," she answered. She gestured at the small refrigerator she kept on the floor in a corner of the office. "You want something to drink?"

He shook his head. "The answer's yes, but I'd like something a lot stronger than what you've got in that refrigerator." She laughed, leaned down, and pulled out two bottles of water. She tossed one to Jason and said, "For the road."

He opened it and took a sip. She sat behind the desk, stretched her back, which always ached a little at the end of practice, and said, "So, what's up?"

He put the water on her desk and leaned forward. "Look, Mary Ann, I probably shouldn't be here because the only team in this school that's any of my business right now is the boys' sixth-grade team."

"But . . . ," Mary Ann said.

"But there's a real problem with the sixth-grade girls' team and . . ."

Mary Ann put up a hand. "I know all about what's going on with the sixth-grade team," she said. "But you're right. How is it your concern?"

Amy Josephson had been in her office early that morning to tell her what had happened Friday before the game, during the game, and after the game—specifically her conversation with Joan Axelson. Mary Ann had been the one who had encouraged Amy to coach the new sixth-grade girls team.

That morning, she had wondered, even just hearing Amy's side of the story, if she'd made a mistake.

"Technically," Jason answered, "it's not my concern. But one of the kids on my team came to me today because he thinks what's happening to the girls—specifically the five girls who didn't play the first half on Friday—is wrong. My instinct is to agree with him—and them."

"Let me guess," Mary Ann said. "Jeff Michaels."

"Yeah, how'd you know?"

She shrugged. "He was in the middle of the whole soccer problem, wasn't he? Is he threatening to go to his father again—create more bad publicity for the school?"

Jason sat back, silent for a moment.

"Why so hostile, Mary Ann? No, he didn't say anything about going to his dad. He's friends with Andi Carillo, sure. And the others. I had him and Carillo in soccer, so he came to me. Was that wrong?"

Mary Ann sighed and put up a hand. "Sorry," she said. "You're right. You see, I knew Joan Axelson was a lot more qualified to be the head coach than Amy, but I gave it to Amy for two reasons. First, because she's older and has been at the school longer."

Jason shrugged. "I get that—sort of. But what was the second reason?"

Mary Ann had been sworn to secrecy, but that had been a couple of months ago. "Because she's going through a bad divorce. She needed a distraction and I knew she wouldn't do well working for someone younger than she is."

Jason seemed stunned. "Well, she hasn't done very well as the boss, either," he said.

Mary Ann knew he was right but wasn't sure there

was much to be done at this point. "Even if that's the case, what can I do? Her assistant, the one who had some experience, has quit. Her new assistant is less experienced than she is—by two games. And . . . even if I did something drastic, like make a change, something like that would divide the faculty. You have any ideas?"

Jason shook his head. "No, I'm not sure I do," he said. "Only thing I think I know for sure right now is I really *do* need a drink."

"So do I," Mary Ann said. "So do I."

It was the boys' turn to travel the next day. The good news was the trip to Haverford didn't require any time on the interstate. It was a few miles up Route 1 and then a few turns to get to the school.

The same five players who had started the game at Chester Heights started at Haverford. "Rotation will be the same," Coach Crist said. He smiled. "Worked out okay on Friday, so no need to change anything."

He neglected to mention that the team had played its best basketball with Jeff at the point. As they headed for the court to warm up, Coach C told Jeff to stay behind for a second. Jeff saw Ron Arlow glancing over his shoulder as he walked to the door, clearly wondering why Jeff had been told to wait and talk to the coach.

"Two things," Coach C said when they were alone. "First, I talked to Mary Ann Hanks last night."

"And?" Jeff said, quickly getting excited.

"And she's aware there's a problem. She just doesn't know what she can do about it."

"But she's going to at least *try* to do something?"

Coach C shook his head. "I didn't say that," he said. "I think she's going to give it some thought. For now, that's the best I can do."

Jeff's heart sank a little. He was pleased Coach C had talked to Coach Hanks, but—for the moment—it didn't look like it would lead anywhere.

Coach C was talking again. He snapped back to the present. "I owe you an explanation on why I'm splitting time between you and Arlow at the point," he said. "Look, you're a better point guard than he is; I know that. But I'm afraid if I don't give him time at the point, he'll sulk and his buddies might sulk, too, and, fact is, we need him—and them. Believe me, I want you on the point as much as possible. Just don't get upset when I play him there."

More disappointment. Jeff understood: Arlow was talented and temperamental. Any coach would have to baby him some of the time.

"I get it, Coach," he said finally. He got it, but he didn't like it.

"Good. Now get out there and warm up before Arlow thinks I'm making you the team's only captain."

Jeff laughed at that one—although it sounded like a good idea.

21

JEFF COULD HAVE PLAYED THE POINT FOR ALL TWENTY-FOUR
minutes and Arlow could have made every shot he took
from the shooting guard spot, and it wouldn't have
made much difference.

Haverford had eleven players who, Jeff figured,
were roughly as talented as Merion's eleven players.
But the Squirrels—the nickname they took in honor
of nearby Haverford College—had one player Merion
couldn't match: Michael Jordan.

Jeff's father had once done a story on a basketball
player at Penn named Michael Jordan. He had pointed
out in the piece that the "real" Michael Jordan had
been a high school freshman when Penn's Michael Jordan was born, so there was no connection. But he had
also found quite a few athletes named Michael Jordan

who had been named in honor of the former Chicago Bulls superstar.

This, apparently, was one of them. And, if he wasn't actually related to the Hall of Famer, he played as if he had Jordan's genes.

He wasn't that tall—Jeff guessed about five-nine—but he was at least a step quicker than everyone else on the floor and he could jump over anyone to get a shot off. Jeff knew his team was in deep trouble midway through the first quarter when Jordan stripped him, went in all alone, and dunked with one hand. For someone five-nine to dunk was remarkable. For *any* sixth-grader to dunk one-handed was whatever came after remarkable. Jeff had now seen dunks happen twice in three games. The kid at Camden had used two hands. Jordan used one and appeared to have room to spare.

Jordan didn't really guard anyone. He just roamed the floor, looking for steals. If he didn't get one, he raced to the basket when a shot went up and—almost inevitably—grabbed the rebound.

"It's like there's two of him out there," Jeff heard Coach Benyak say to Coach Crist at the end of the first quarter. By then the score was Haverford 19, Merion 7. Or, more accurately, it was Jordan 15, his teammates 4, and Merion 7. On the two baskets Jordan hadn't scored, he'd driven into the lane, drawn a double-team, and passed to a teammate for an easy layup.

"Look," Coach C said in the huddle. "I know you've never played against anyone as good as this kid. I get it. But let's stay calm and play zone and see if we can keep him from getting inside all the time."

They had practiced a two-three zone defense at times in practice but hadn't used it in the first two games. Coach C was a disciple of Duke University coach Mike Krzyzewski, who only played zone in extreme emergencies. This was clearly very extreme.

The first time Jordan brought the ball up in the second quarter and saw the zone, he began smiling. "Zone!" he called out to his teammates.

Apparently, they'd seen this before. They all shuffled around and the kid playing center came to the top of the key and set a screen for Jordan. He dribbled behind it and smoothly shot—and swished—a three. Jeff found himself looking over at Coach C as if to say, "Now what?"

They stayed in the zone and Jordan, apparently bored, passed more often to his teammates. It was 35–15 at halftime. The only way Merion was going to have a chance was if the Haverford coach agreed to let them play seven guys against his five. Even that might not have helped.

Jeff hadn't noticed how packed the gym had become once the game started. It probably seated about five hundred, and every corner was full. Apparently, the word was out that the sixth-grade team had a star in the making.

Jordan didn't play at all in the fourth quarter. The score was 53–22 after three quarters, and the Haverford coach decided to have mercy on his opponent. Jeff had a feeling that was going to be the case for a lot of Haverford's games. With Jordan sitting on the end of the bench with a towel over his head, Merion managed to play the fourth quarter to a 10–10 standoff. Without Jordan, the teams were—as Jeff had suspected— evenly matched.

The final score was 63–32. Even with Jordan not playing the last six minutes, Haverford had scored sixty-three points, which was amazing in a twenty-four-minute game at any level.

Ted Washington, Tavon's brother who kept stats for the team, told Jeff later that Jordan's three-quarter totals were thirty-six points, fourteen rebounds, eight assists, and eight steals. It had felt more like 20 steals to Jeff.

When they got back to the locker room, Coach C just shook his head as they all sat down on stools.

"Fellas, you've got nothing to feel bad about," he said. "I have a feeling someday you'll tell people you played against the Michael Jordan of the twenty-first century. His biggest problem is going to be all the attention he's going to start getting very soon.

"So we're going to pretend today never happened. The good news is, we don't play them again until the last game of the season, so let's try to get on an eleven-game winning streak between now and then. We've got Ardmore at home on Friday. Unless Jordan transfers there between now and then"—he got a laugh with that line—"it's an eminently winnable game. So, let's shower fast and get back to school. I know you've all got homework to do."

Jeff moaned to himself. He had plenty of homework to do. Getting visions of Michael Jordan out of his mind while he was studying would not be easy.

The Haverford girls' team wasn't nearly as good as its boys' team. There was no female equivalent of Michael Jordan or anyone close to that. They *were* tall, but not very athletic. Debbie Lee was as tall as any of them and more talented.

Of course, Coach Josephson insisted on the same five starters, so the score stayed close for a quarter— 11–10, Merion. But when she put Andi and Lisa Car-michael into the game to start the second quarter to join Eleanor, Maria, and Jamie, the game became a runaway quickly.

Haverford didn't have any guards who could handle the ball against the quickness of Maria and Andi, and with Lisa joining Eleanor inside, Merion dominated, in spite of Haverford's height. In the first four minutes of the second quarter, Merion outscored Haverford 13–0, pushing the lead to 24–10. The Haverford coach called time and Coach Josephson took all five players on the court out—insisting that Dove and Medley need a rest.

"We're fine, Coach," Maria said when Coach Josephson explained this in the huddle.

"I'll decide that," Coach Josephson answered, giving Maria a sharp look.

The last two minutes were even and Merion led 28–14 at the break.

In the locker room, Andi, sitting nearest to the corner where the coaches went to talk while the players rested, overheard Coach Tuller saying, "Amy, we've got to go with the kids who started the second quarter. They've earned it."

"Bonnie, you've been to one practice and been part of the first half of one game and now you're the expert on who should play?" Coach Josephson answered.

Andi didn't hear the answer. The two coaches had apparently walked out of earshot.

Maybe the group that had started the second quarter had earned the right to start the third, but Coach Josephson went with the five who had started the game. Fortunately, Eleanor and Maria were part of that group, and the third quarter ended with Eleanor catching a lob pass from Maria for a layup that made the score 40–23.

Everyone played in the fourth quarter. Andi hit two open threes and was fouled while making the second one. As she walked to the free-throw line, she saw Brooke Jensen and Jamie Bronson reporting to the scorer's table. Bronson came in for her pal Jenny Mearns. Jensen, however, stayed at the table, indicating to the official that she was coming in for the shooter—Andi.

Andi wasn't that surprised. There was only 2:14 left in the game and the lead was now a very comfortable 53–31. Jensen was part of the second five that Coach Josephson had played while leaving Andi and Lisa Carmichael on the bench, but in reality, she was probably the twelfth-best player on a twelve-girl team. Getting her some playing time in the last couple minutes of a blowout made sense.

Andi made the free throw, exchanged a hand-slap with Jensen, and received congratulations from her teammates as she came out. She had played about fourteen minutes—a season high—and had scored fifteen points. She had taken four three-point shots and made them all. A pretty good day.

As she walked to the end of the bench and sat down next to Maria and Eleanor, she realized she was smiling—probably for the first time all season. She put her head in a towel to wipe the perspiration from her face and became aware that someone was standing in front of her. She pulled the towel away and looked up to see Coach Josephson standing there.

"You played well today, Carillo," she said. "But you need to learn to pass more often."

Andi was about to say something like, "Coach, why pass when I have a wide-open shot?" but opted for, "Thanks, Coach, I'll work on it."

"You're a much better person than I am," Maria said as the coach walked away. "I'd have told her to stick it."

"Which would have accomplished what?" Eleanor said.

Maria grinned. "I don't know. But I would have enjoyed it."

The final score was 56–39, after Haverford was able to score a few easy baskets in the final couple of minutes.

It was nice to win. Andi was still convinced they could have at least split the first two games if Coach Josephson had kept her best players on the floor for the most minutes instead of playing her silly mind games. They were 1–0 in the conference. Andi reminded herself they had started 0–2 in soccer and had tied their first conference game. Based on that, they were ahead of schedule.

A winning locker room is always louder than a losing locker room. Even Coach Josephson seemed upbeat.

"Now you see how we can play when we play as a team," she said. "Everyone contributed today—everyone. That was a great win. We have the late practice tomorrow, early on Thursday. Friday, the bus will leave for Ardmore at two thirty. I hear they won their conference opener today, too, so that will be a big game."

She was actually smiling. Andi was trying to remember if she'd ever seen her smile before. After they did their cheer—"Beat the Antlers!"—Maria walked past Andi on her way to the shower.

"Great win?" she said softly. "Did she watch that team play? You, Eleanor, and I could have beaten that team three-on-five."

Andi laughed. Then she thought about it for a second. Maria might have been right.

She remembered a quote she had once read from the football coach of a struggling team: "You never throw a win back. Every one of them is worth having."

This team, she suspected, was in no position to throw a win back.

Jeff was climbing wearily onto the bus, visions of Michael Jordan's dunk still very clear in his mind's eye, when he saw that Andi had texted him. He'd been thinking of texting her once on the bus but was almost afraid to ask what had happened. What if Michael Jordan had a twin sister?

He smiled when he saw the text.

We won! Haverford was so bad even Coach J couldn't screw us up. U?

He sat down and began typing a response. Danny Diskin sat down across from him.

"Let me guess," he said. "Andi."

Jeff smiled. "Yeah," he admitted.

"They won," Danny said, causing Jeff to look up sharply from his phone.

"How'd you know?" he asked.

Danny grinned. "I have a source inside the team."

"Who?" Danny asked.

"Not telling."

Then it hit Jeff. "Eleanor," he said with what was undoubtedly a smug smile. "I see you talking to her every chance you get."

Danny shrugged. "Just means I've got good taste."

"Did her text mention how bad Haverford was?"

"Matter of fact it did. She said even their coach couldn't screw this one up."

Jeff burst out laughing. "That's what Andi said!"

Then Jeff went back to responding to Andi. *Congrats. A win is a win, right? We got crushed. They had a kid named Michael Jordan—seriously—who might be the next MJ.*

She sent back a smiley face.

Jeff was trying to think of a response when Danny looked up again.

"Hey, lover boy, Eleanor says you should ask Andi to go to the movies with us on Saturday."

Danny had started calling Jeff lover boy during soccer season when it had become clear that he had a crush on Andi.

Jeff didn't think that was a great idea. Fortunately, he had a built-in excuse. "St. Joseph's is playing North Carolina in the Palestra Saturday. I'm going with my dad."

"Okay." Danny nodded. "Maybe we'll do it sometime later in winter recess."

"Yeah, sounds good," Jeff said.

It *did* sound good. Whether he could actually make it happen was an entirely different story.

22

AMY JOSEPHSON WAS ENJOYING HER SECOND CUP OF coffee the next morning when there was a light tap on her office door.

"Come," she said, and looked up to see her friend Mary Ann Hanks walking through the door, Philadelphia Flyers coffee mug in hand. Mary Ann was a dyed-in-the-wool Flyers fan, no doubt influenced, at least in part, by the fact that her husband had played college hockey.

"Hey," she said, looking up. "Nice win yesterday."

Hanks's varsity had beaten Haverford's varsity in a tight game, which Amy hadn't seen since she'd been on the bus back to school with her own team. On Tuesdays, the sixth graders left right after their game. On Fridays, with the weekend coming up, they stayed to watch the older kids play when the game was at home. It wasn't a rule, but it was expected.

"Thanks. You too," Mary Ann said, sitting down. "I remember my first win. It's a nice feeling, isn't it?"

"You remember back that far?" Amy said, teasing her friend. Then she added, "Yeah, it felt good, especially after those first two losses."

"How's it going with Bonnie as your assistant?" Mary Ann asked.

Amy shrugged. "Okay, I guess. Honestly, Joan knew a lot more about basketball than she does, but . . ."

"But she tried to tell you some things that you didn't want to hear."

That brought Amy up short. She considered Mary Ann a friend, maybe her closest friend on the faculty. All of a sudden, it was clear that this wasn't a social call.

She drained her coffee, stood up, and poured another mug—hers said KANSAS, in honor of her alma mater—and held the pot out to Mary Ann to see if she needed more. Mary Ann leaned forward while Amy emptied what was left into her mug. She remembered that she couldn't stand hockey.

"For the record, I didn't fire her," Amy said, sitting back down. "She quit."

"I know," Mary Ann said. "I talked to her. Why don't you tell me what happened in the locker room at Chester Heights?"

Mary Ann Hanks was the senior person in the athletic department. She had been at the school longer than any of the other coaches—two men and two women—who taught gym. Technically, she had no authority over anyone. But most people deferred to her when there were decisions to be made—like on the subject of gym time. She had been the one who had made the schedule to alternate boys' and girls' practice times each day.

Now she was sitting calmly, sipping her coffee, but clearly challenging Amy on some level. They had worked together for five years, but never before as coaching colleagues.

"I said something that offended the two black girls," she said finally. "They didn't like the fact that I pointed out—accurately—that Chester Heights didn't have as many black players as Camden had and that . . ."

"They wouldn't be as athletic," Mary Ann said.

"Well . . . yeah. Because it's true."

"Amy, that's a ridiculous stereotype."

"There's a reason why things become stereotypes," Amy said. "It's usually because they're true."

"If you were an eleven- or twelve-year-old African American kid, can you see why that stereotype might be offensive?"

Amy thought for a moment. "So I'm supposed to

cater to the fragile emotions of sixth graders—even if they *should* know that wasn't my intent?"

"That's *exactly* what you're supposed to do," Mary Ann said. "You're coaching sixth graders, remember?"

"Don't kids need to hear the truth about things as they get older?"

"What truth are you telling them? That white people like you expect them to be better athletes because they're black? If you want to tell them a truth, point out to them that, even today, being African American means you are going to be subjected to silly stereotypes."

Amy was just about done with this conversation. She hadn't done anything wrong and she hadn't meant to offend anyone. Before she could cut things off, Mary Ann was speaking again.

"Okay, I hope I've made my point. Now, one other thing. What have you got against the Carillo kid? I hear you've been all over her since practice started."

At least that one was easy. "She's a prima donna," Amy said. "That Michaels kid got her on TV during soccer and she still thinks she's some kind of star."

Mary Ann shook her head. "Hal Johnston got her on TV with his knuckle-dragging views on boys playing with girls. And she *was* a star because of what she did on the field. So, what's your *real* problem with her?"

Amy had several answers to that question, but none she wanted to share. "Did she come to you and complain?" she asked.

Mary Ann shook her head. "As a matter of fact, no. It was Jason Crist. He apparently heard it from some of his players."

"What would his players know about what's going on inside my team?"

Mary Ann smiled. "Amy, you don't think sixth-grade girls and sixth-grade boys talk to one another? Especially when they all play basketball?"

Amy really didn't want to hear any more. In the back of her mind was the thought that she'd just kick the kid off her team and be done with it. Then again, she'd probably run back to the media.

"I'm trying my best to be fair to her," she said. "It isn't my fault she's a whiner."

"Who says she's a whiner?"

"Well, she must have complained to someone for it to get to Jason Crist."

"Amy, your team plays right before my team plays every game, remember? I've seen how you use her— and don't use her. Regardless of what Jason's told me, it's clear-cut to anyone watching that your four best players are Dove, Medley, Carmichael, and Carillo— not necessarily in that order."

"I'm not sure that's true."

Mary Ann stood up. "Let me tell you something, they're the only four from your group I guarantee will play for me next year."

"Fine," Amy said. "Play 'em all you want. Until then, I'll play 'em all I want."

Mercifully, that ended the conversation. After Mary Ann left, Amy sat down in her chair and took her last sip of coffee. It was cold.

Andi probably should not have been surprised when Danny Diskin joined their lunch group on Wednesday. She knew that he and Eleanor had been texting after the game the day before because Eleanor had shown her a funny text from him about playing against a Michael Jordan who might be better than the real Michael Jordan.

She'd giggled reading it, then said, "You like him, don't you?"

Eleanor shrugged and said, "What's not to like?"

So when Danny got to their table and said, "Room for one more?" it was Eleanor who moved her seat closer to Andi in order to make space for Danny to pull up a chair.

Much of the lunch conversation centered on Jeff and Danny explaining what they had seen the day before at Haverford.

"So," Maria said. "He's how tall and he dunked?"

The two boys looked at one another. "About my height," Danny said. "Like five-nine, I'd say."

Jeff nodded. "Maybe five-eight, no more than five-ten. There was a kid from Camden who was maybe five-seven who dunked. But he couldn't play like this guy. Spud Webb won the NBA dunk contest at five-seven," he added. "And Nate Robinson won it at five-nine."

Jeff was a dunk-contest junkie, which he knew made him one of the last people alive who actually still cared about it.

"They were grown—no joke intended—men," Andi said. "This kid is how old? Eleven, maybe twelve?"

Danny nodded. "It was pretty amazing. If he had played us one-on-five, Haverford still might have won."

"Almost makes you wish we wouldn't be up at their place playing when they come back here to play in February," Eleanor said.

"Maybe we can make you a video," Danny said, sounding just a tiny bit jealous.

"Maybe you can," Eleanor said, picking up on the tone and clearly enjoying it.

Jeff decided to change the subject.

"So, what's the deal with the new assistant coach?" he asked the girls.

Maria shrugged. "She's fine. She's a nice person. But I don't think she knows much about basketball."

Andi nodded. "Yeah, we're two for two now. Maybe Coach Josephson can loan her one of her coaching books."

"Don't bet on it," Eleanor said. "I don't think she wants her to know enough that she might challenge her decisions."

"You mean the way Coach Axelson did, right?" Danny said.

They all nodded. "She knew basketball and she was a nice person," Andi said. "Which meant that it was impossible for her to work with Coach Josephson."

"Why do you think she's so . . . difficult?" Danny said, after searching for a word.

"She's not difficult," Eleanor said. "She's awful. She's clearly got a racist streak and she's got some kind of problem with Andi that I don't understand."

"Well, we get a break from her after Friday," Andi said. "Maybe she'll come back after the holidays filled with holiday spirit."

"Yeah, I'll bet," Jeff said. "Bah humbug for all."

Everyone laughed. The five-minute bell rang. "Speaking of bah humbug . . . ," Andi said as they all stood to clear their trays and head to class.

Holiday break was on Coach Josephson's mind at practice that afternoon.

"We've got two more practices this week, then we go to Ardmore, and then we don't see each other for two weeks," she said. Then, to Andi's surprise, she smiled. "I'm sure you are all looking forward to not seeing me for fourteen straight days."

She paused a moment, just in case she caught someone nodding their head—or so Andi suspected because she was looking right at her.

"If we can win Friday at Ardmore, we're two-and-oh in the conference going into break. We don't want to lose the momentum from yesterday. If you guys can get gym time if only to shoot a little bit during break, that would be great. We aren't allowed to hold official practice at all while school's out."

Andi's family made an annual post-Christmas trip to Williamsburg. Her brothers would both be home and would make the trip. She wasn't worried about gym time.

Practice was no different than it had been all year. The starters remained the same and so did the second team. Andi and Lisa were subbed in as the scrimmage moved along. Andi knew she had been the team's best player in the Haverford game. She'd seen the final stats as kept by Tina Murphy, who was the team's manager. They may not have been 100 percent accurate, but they were probably pretty close.

She'd scored fifteen points—making five of six shots,

including all four of her threes—and had four assists, four rebounds, and four steals, all in a little more than half the game.

And yet she was still playing behind girls she could beat in a game of one-on-one using just her left hand. She was seriously getting tired of it.

Two days to break, she told herself. *Not the time to start something with the coach.*

When practice ended, Coach Josephson told them she was happy with what she was seeing from the team. Andi had several thoughts on that comment but kept them to herself. She was turning to head for the locker room when she heard the coach's voice.

"Carillo, before you shower, come to my office for a minute, please," she said.

Two words crossed Andi's mind as she followed her coach across the court: Bah! Humbug!

23

COACH JOSEPHSON POINTED AT THE CHAIR OPPOSITE HER desk after Andi followed her into the small office. She reached into a refrigerator, pulled out a bottle of water, and asked Andi if she wanted one. Andi nodded and said, "Yes, thank you."

They sat down opposite one another. Coach Josephson took a long sip from her water bottle and said, "So, Miss Carillo, I understand you and I have a problem."

Andi wasn't going to be drawn in by a general statement that might lead her down a path where she didn't want to go. In fact, she was fairly certain she didn't want to go down any path right now.

"Problem, Coach?" she asked.

"I'm told you aren't happy with your playing time," the coach said.

That one was easy to handle.

"Coach, I think I'm like anyone else on this team—or any team. I want to play. I think I can contribute more if I play more."

Coach Josephson took another swig of water. "In other words you think you *should* play more."

Andi shrugged. "Sure I do. I think Lisa should play more, too."

"So, you think at eleven you know more about basketball than I do."

For the first time a hint of hostility crept into her voice. It was a trap question.

"I didn't say that."

"In saying you think that you and Lisa should play more and, by extension, others should play less, aren't you saying you know more basketball than I do?"

"Coach, would you want a player on your team who *didn't* want to play more, contribute more?"

Andi liked that answer. She thought it would—should—put the coach on the defensive. She was wrong.

"I want players on my team who don't question my authority," she said—real anger now in her voice. "I want players on my team who don't run to the media when they don't get exactly what they want. I want players on my team who don't go whining to the entire school when they aren't getting what they want."

She was on the edge of her chair now, glaring at Andi with nothing less than pure dislike in her eyes.

"Coach, I haven't gone to the media. That camera crew showed up for the first game just to do an update on me after what happened in soccer season . . ."

"Uh-huh. And how did you end up talking to them during soccer season? By whining that Hal Johnston wasn't being fair to you and then whining you weren't playing enough even after he was gracious enough to put you on the team."

Andi had been taking a sip of water at that moment. When Coach Josephson used the word *gracious*, she actually spit up a little water.

"Coach, he was *ordered* by the principal to put me on the team," she said. "It was hardly an act of grace."

"Uh-huh. So, this time when you make the team, but you aren't playing enough—in your opinion—you went running to your old pal Coach Crist for help."

"I did not!"

Andi was shouting. Not a good idea, and she knew it right away. "Sorry," she said. "But that's just not true. I haven't even talked to my parents about my playing time."

"If you didn't go to Coach Crist, then who did?" she said. "I don't think he talked to Mary Ann Hanks about you being treated unfairly without someone bringing it up to him. Do you?"

Suddenly, Andi knew exactly who had talked to Coach Crist.

"I can tell you for a fact it wasn't me," Andi said. "I've barely spoken to Coach Crist since the end of soccer season. I've hardly even seen him except going on and off the floor at practice."

"History says you run to the grown-ups when you don't get your way."

Andi sighed. "I asked for help *once* when I was being unfairly denied the chance to play soccer."

"Playing field hockey with the rest of the girls would have been beneath you?"

"No. I've never played field hockey. I've played soccer. And I'm good at it. I proved that."

"And you think you've proved you deserve more playing time on my basketball team, right?"

Andi paused a split second and then said, "Yes, I do. And I don't think I'm the only one who feels that way."

Coach Josephson stood up.

"I'll see you at practice tomorrow."

She turned her back on Andi to reach into the refrigerator again. Andi turned and walked out.

"Jeffrey Daniel Michaels!"

Jeff froze at the sound of Andi's voice cutting through the din of pre-first period in the locker area of the second-floor hallway the next morning. There were exactly two people in the world who called him by his full name—his mother and his father. And they only did so when he was in trouble.

He wasn't exactly sure how Andi knew his middle name, but based on her use of it and her tone, he was fairly certain he was in trouble. She was walking down the hallway in his direction, her long strides covering the ground between her and where he stood in front of his locker with almost frightening quickness.

He suspected the smart thing to do was run. But that would only delay the inevitable—whatever it was.

"Good morning," he said, giving her a bright-as-the-sun smile as she pulled to a stop in front of him.

"Good morning, nothing," she said. "You went to Coach Crist about my problems with Coach Josephson."

Something in Jeff's gut told him denial would be futile.

"That's not exactly true," he said. "I mentioned to him that the entire girls' team was having trouble with Coach Josephson. He would have known anyway when Coach Axelson quit."

It occurred to him when he brought that up that perhaps he could have claimed he'd done nothing, and it was probably Coach Axelson quitting that had tipped Coach Crist off that something was up. But he'd never been very good at lying. This moment was another example.

"Uh-huh," she said, arms folded across her chest. "And where do you think he thought your information came from? Did you *not* single me out as one of the players who was unhappy?"

"I might have, yeah."

"And did you really think it wouldn't come back on me sooner or later if he said anything to anyone?"

"Did he go to Coach Josephson? I told him not to do that—honest."

She almost smiled. "No, he didn't go to Coach Josephson, he went to Coach Hanks and then *she* went to Coach Josephson."

Now, it was Jeff's turn to smile. "That was probably pretty smart of him, huh? Wouldn't Josephson sort of have to listen to Hanks?"

"She listened all right. She listened just enough to call me into her office yesterday and chew me out for being a whiner."

"I'm sorry," he said. "You don't deserve that."

It really was unfair. Andi was anything but a whiner. It had been *his* idea back in the fall to take her story public to force the school to give her a fair chance to play soccer. She had told him *not* to do anything about the current situation and he hadn't listened. Now, he'd gotten her in trouble.

"You're right, I don't deserve that," she said. Her voice was a lot softer now. A number of people had been staring at them when she first stalked up to his locker. "But I know you were trying to help. You made a mistake. It happens."

"I really am sorry. How can I make it up to you?"

"Have Coach Josephson kidnapped by Santa's elves? Or think up something a lot smarter than your first idea."

The five-minute bell rang.

"Saved by the bell," she said. "The good news is, you have all of break to come up with a brilliant idea."

"What do you think will happen tomorrow?"

Andi shrugged. "I don't know. We'll find out when we get there."

They got to Ardmore at three fifteen on Friday. Thirty minutes later, when they came back to the locker room after pregame warm-ups, Andi found out.

She certainly wasn't surprised when the names of the same five starters were on the whiteboard. "We'll sub pretty much as we've subbed previously," Coach Josephson said. "I think we found something close to the right combination on Tuesday."

The thought crossed Andi's mind that *any* combination would have worked on Tuesday.

They did their pregame cheer and headed in the direction of the court, which was up a short flight of stairs from the locker room.

"Carillo, hang back a minute," Coach Josephson said. She looked at Coach Tuller, who was standing next to her. "Bonnie, go on up and keep an eye on warm-ups, okay?"

Coach Tuller nodded and followed Eleanor, the last player out the door, out of the locker room.

"I've given some thought to the conversation we had yesterday," she said. "I agree with you on one thing: a competitor *should* want to play. But my problem with you isn't wanting to play. If you had a problem with playing time, you should have come to *me*. I'm the coach. Not Joan Axelson, not Jason Crist, not Mary Ann Hanks, and certainly not the media."

"Coach, I never went to—"

Coach Josephson interrupted. "Maybe we can start off on square one after the holidays. For the moment, it's clear you questioned my authority to others and that's unacceptable."

"Coach, I didn't question your authority to anyone—"

She cut her off again. "You're a basketball fan, right? Do you think Bob Knight would tolerate this sort of thing from one of his players?"

Oh, God, Andi thought, *she must have read another*

book. She'd just compared herself to Bob Knight, one of *the* greatest basketball coaches of all time.

"So, I'm going to do what Bob Knight would do in this situation. I'm not throwing you off the team because he never did anything that might hurt the rest of the team to punish one player. You won't play today, but after the Christmas break, you'll get one last chance."

"You think my not playing today won't hurt the team?" Andi asked.

"You have an answer for everything, don't you?" the coach said.

Andi didn't have an answer for that one. Which was probably a good thing.

The last day before winter break was the boys' turn to lose again, and the girls' turn to get embarrassed.

Coach Josephson never told the other players that Andi wouldn't be playing, but it was apparent to all of them by Andi's body language when she finally joined warm-ups that something had happened in the locker room and it wasn't good.

It was Eleanor who asked first, as she was rebounding a layup for Andi.

"Not playing today" was all Andi said. She could see her friend's shoulders sag. Andi had told everyone

about the Wednesday meeting, and they had all figured there would be some sort of reprisal, but when
nothing seemed different during Thursday's practice,
they had all hoped the Josephson temper-tantrum bul-
let had been dodged.

Wishful thinking.

With Andi riding the end of the bench, Merion never
made a game of it. As usual, the starters put them in
a hole almost right away, the team trailing 13–7 after
one quarter. Coach Josephson changed things up a little in the second quarter, adding Lisa to the second
five, but it didn't help much. It was 25–15 at halftime.
Early in the third quarter, Maria picked up her third
foul diving for a loose ball and had to come out.

"What kind of dumb play was that?" Coach Josephson said as Maria came to the bench.

Maria gave her a sharp look. "Dumb? I was going for
a loose ball. We need all the help we can get out there,
especially without our best shooter in the game."

Coach Josephson put her hands on her hips. "So now
you want to coach the team, too? Tell you what, go sit
with your friend and watch. We'll be fine without you."

Maria glared for a second, then walked down and
sat next to Andi.

"Don't feel bad," Andi whispered. "We weren't going
to win with you in foul trouble anyway."

"I didn't even foul the kid," Maria said.

She was right about that. Two players going for a loose ball, each with a hand on it. The ref should have no-called it but hadn't.

With Maria out, whether because of foul trouble or coach's ego, the game got out of hand quickly. Every time Eleanor touched the ball, she was double-teamed, and every time she pitched to an open teammate, the open teammate missed. It was often the kind of shot Andi made with consistency.

The final score was 51–32.

"We've got a lot of work to do after the Christmas break," Coach Josephson said to the team. "And some of you need to do a lot of thinking about whether you want to be part of this team. There's an old saying, 'You're either for us or against us.' Some of you girls need to figure out which one you are."

"You read that in a book, Coach?"

Andi turned at the sound of the voice. It was Jamie Bronson.

The silence that followed was more shock than anything else.

Coach Josephson stared at her team captain for a split second. "Like I said, for us or against us," she said. "You *all* need to think about that."

Then she turned and walked out.

They were 1–3. Happy holidays. Or, bah humbug, depending on your point of view.

24

"THE PROBLEM IS, WE'VE GOT SOME GOOD PLAYERS, BUT no great ones. And Coach Crist still keeps insisting on playing Arlow at the point."

It was the first Monday of winter recess—two days before Christmas and, not surprisingly, the mall was packed with shoppers.

Jeff and Andi were sitting in the food court, sharing another Andy's pizza. The idea of getting together had been hers. She still had some shopping to do, liked the idea of company—especially knowing how crowded it was going to be—and loved the idea of sharing another really good pizza.

Plus, she had plenty she wanted to talk to Jeff about, although she made it clear that if he repeated a word to *anyone*, she would never speak to him again.

"So, nothing dramatic then," he said when she finished her threat.

She smiled. It was hard to get angry at him, harder to *stay* angry. His sense of humor was—what was the word her mother used?—disarming.

She had finished buying presents for her brothers and still had to figure out what to do about her parents when they decided to take their pizza break.

"So, tell me why you have *no* shopping to do?" she asked as they dug into their first slices.

"Because we have a family tradition of getting our Christmas tree and doing our holiday shopping on the Saturday after Thanksgiving," he said. "It's not crowded because so many people shop the day before on Black Friday, and my dad doesn't have to work because he's got an Eagles game the next day."

"So how do you buy presents for each other if everyone's there?"

"I go with Dad to get presents for Mom. Then he and Mom switch off and she and I get some things for Dad while he gets something for me. Not that hard. We probably spend more time worrying about what to get the cats than the humans."

"They complain a lot, do they?"

Once Jeff had explained the magic of the Michaels's holiday shopping, Andi asked about the boys' loss on Friday to Ardmore. Both basketball teams were now

1–3. The difference was that the girls had a conference win.

That was when he had launched into his speech about Ardmore having a kid the Merion players couldn't guard. "He wasn't as talented as the Jordan kid at Haverford, but he must have been six-four and he had really good hands. They just kept throwing the ball toward the rim and he'd catch it and score. The only way we could stop him was to foul."

"So, you need a star and you haven't got one," she said.

"We also need me playing the point the entire game," he said. "It's not that I'm great or anything, but at least I pass the ball. I checked over the weekend with Gary, who keeps our stats, and do you know how many assists Arlow has in four games?"

She figured she needed to guess low. "Eight," she said.

"Four," he answered. "You'd have to get more than one a game by accident."

"Especially if you're spending half your time at the point."

"Exactly," he said. "I asked Gary if Coach C knew that stat and he said he must because he asks for all the stats to be e-mailed to him after every game."

"That's just weird," she said. "You know he wants to win and you know he's not a guy to hold grudges—unlike my coach."

"I know," he said. "So, speaking of grudge holders."

She sighed and told him in detail about Friday. He had texted her Friday night after Danny Diskin had told him that Eleanor had reported that Andi hadn't played at all at Ardmore. She hadn't written back until Saturday, which concerned him because he wondered if she blamed him for the benching, but then suggested meeting at the mall on Monday for shopping and pizza. That had been a relief.

Other than making him swear a blood oath he wouldn't repeat anything she told him, Andi had apparently forgiven him for going to Coach Crist.

She sighed now and walked him through the events of Friday, from the pregame locker room to Bronson's book crack in the postgame locker room.

Jeff was surprised to hear the Bronson part of the story.

"Does she have potential to maybe be a decent person?" he asked.

Andi shrugged. "Not sure. Before the season I would have said no way. Just a bully, a female Arlow. Now, though . . . I kind of wonder."

Jeff thought about that for a minute, tearing apart a second slice of pizza in the process.

"I'm guessing if you just show up for practice on the first day of school, this isn't going to get any better," he said, after taking a long sip of water to wash the pizza down. "In fact, it may get worse."

"Worse?" Andi said. "How can it get worse?"

"I don't know," Jeff said. "She could try to throw you off the team. Say that you're disruptive and she's doing it for the good of the team."

"I would think the other players would object to that."

"Exactly," Jeff said. "So why not beat her to that punch? Why not see if you can get up a petition to have her removed as coach before she either keeps you on the bench or tries to toss you? You know Eleanor, Maria, and Lisa will sign it, right?"

"I think Debbie Lee probably would, too," Andi said, playing along but still not certain about any of this.

"But the key would be getting Jamie Bronson and her three disciples—what are their names?"

"Alayne, Jenny, and Hope," Andi said.

"You get Bronson and those three and you've got at least nine votes. My guess is those three in the middle will swing with whomever has the most support."

Andi thought about it for a minute.

"That's pretty risky, isn't it? Even if I get the signatures and we take 'em to Mr. Block, he's not going to want to fire a coach because the players are complaining about her. Not unless we can prove abuse of some kind."

"She's never threatened to hit anyone or anything like that, has she?"

"No. She's not even that much of a yeller. It comes down, really, to picking on me and, to a lesser extent, Lisa."

"And the crack about African Americans in the locker room at Chester Heights."

"Yeah, though she hasn't said or done anything like it since then. On the other hand, she's never apologized, either."

"And she doesn't pick on Maria and Eleanor?"

"They're two of her best players. She may be dumb, but she ain't stupid."

"In that case, you probably have to wait for her to make her next move. But keep this in mind as a possible plan B."

"You think she'll make the next move?" Andi asked.

Jeff grinned. "What are the chances you come back from the holidays and she opens practice by saying, 'Andi, I messed up. I'm putting you in the starting lineup on Friday'?"

"Zero," she said.

He pointed at the last slice of pizza. "Want it?" he asked.

"All yours," she said.

While Andi's family headed for Williamsburg, Jeff's family stayed home. The holidays were a busy time for

Tom Michaels: all the Big Five schools had games, as did the Sixers and the Flyers. There were high school basketball tournaments going on and—most important, of course—the Eagles had two games left and needed to win one to clinch a wild-card berth, two to win the division.

Jeff's mom, a Montessori schoolteacher, was more than happy to have some time to chill and prepare her classroom for the post-holiday restart of school.

Coach Crist had told his players to take it easy during the break and play hoops with friends only if they felt like it, but be ready to work hard when they came back to school on the Tuesday after New Year's. Their first game back would be on Friday.

"Gives us three full days of practice to get back in the swing of things," he'd said. "We go to Main Line on Friday and we better be ready. We can't keep losing conference games." He smiled. "Of course, if the sixth-grade version of LeBron James shows up, I'll understand. Short of that, we need to start winning."

Jeff and Andi had texted a couple of times during the break. Andi sent Jeff a photo of her standing with her two brothers and a man and a woman dressed in eighteenth-century colonial-period dress. Jeff noticed that her brothers were considerably taller than Andi. He wondered how tall she would be.

He sent her a photo of him standing on the

fifty-yard-line at the Linc prior to the Eagles game with the Cowboys. Michael Barkann was also in the photo and Jeff noted, *He says he's here to help when needed.*

Andi texted back right away. *Did you say something to him?*

Not a single word. Don't want to be in Andi-purgatory for life. He brought it up. I suspect he was joking. But . . .

But nothing.

Stay calm. Let's not panic until it's time to panic.

It first occurred to Andi that it was time to panic during the first practice of the New Year. It had snowed in Philadelphia the night before school started and the opening on Tuesday was two hours late. The short-ened day left everyone feeling feisty and in a good mood when the girls hit the floor for the three-fifteen practice.

Coach Josephson welcomed them back briefly and told them the next three days would be critical to get ready for the game Friday at home against Main Line.

"They're one-and-one in conference just like we are," she said. "A game we need to win."

They went through their usual routines: stretching, drill work, free-throw shooting. The notion of counting free throws and making people run had mercifully become a thing of the past. Andi wondered if it was because she was the player least likely to have to run.

Coach Josephson divided them into two teams to scrimmage—nothing new. Same starting five, same second five, Lisa and Andi as the sixth man for each team.

About five minutes in, Coach Josephson called a foul on Eleanor—the coaches always reffed the scrimmages—which caused Eleanor to look at her as if she were seeing double.

"Carmichael, go for Mearns," the coach said after the whistle.

Andi started to walk onto the court to take Ronnie Bonilla's spot at guard, which had been normal procedure. Bonilla started to walk to the sideline.

"Hang on," Coach Josephson said. "What are you doing, Carillo? Did I tell you to sub in?"

"No, Coach, but I thought . . ."

"Don't think, Carillo. Not your strength. When I want you to sub, I'll let you know. Bonilla, get back in there. Let's play."

They played on without Andi. And played. And played. She never saw the court for the rest of the practice.

When practice ended and they headed to the locker room, Coach Tuller stopped her as she was leaving.

"Andi, don't get too down," she said. "Coach is just trying to make you understand about the chain of authority. In class, if you don't like a grade, you go to the teacher, not around the teacher to the principal. This is no different."

"Are you the good cop?" Andi asked.

Coach Tuller smiled. "I'm just trying to be the conciliator. The team needs you. I want to see you back playing as soon as possible."

"How soon do you think that'll be, Coach?" Andi asked.

The smile faded. "I don't know," she said. "I wish I did. I guess Coach Josephson would say that's up to you."

Andi knew the words that came out of her mouth next were a mistake, but she couldn't help herself. "Like hell it is," she said, turning and walking away.

It was time, she thought, to give some serious thought to Jeff's plan B. This had gone far enough. In fact, it had gone too far.

25

WHEN ANDI DIDN'T GET TO SCRIMMAGE FOR EVEN ONE second on Wednesday or Thursday, she began writing the petition she planned to present to her teammates after Friday's game—assuming she didn't play again, which seemed likely.

She started and stopped and started again a number of times. She first addressed the petition to Mr. Block, the school principal who had stepped in to get her on the soccer team—after Jeff's dad and a columnist named Ray Didinger had brought the situation to the public's attention.

Mr. Block's first response, Andi remembered, had been to allow Coach Johnston to cut her from the team.

She then looked up the name of the chairwoman

of the Merion Middle School Board of Directors, a group of parents who were supposed to settle disputes within the school that the principal or teachers could not resolve. Her name was Ann Cowett and her e-mail address was listed in the school's online directory.

Andi even thought for a moment that she should direct the petition to Coach Josephson's former and current assistants. Both had witnessed Coach Josephson's behavior, Coach Axelson to the point where she had quit her coaching job. Maybe they, as teachers, were the ones to take the issue to Mr. Block or Ms. Cowett and her fellow parents on the board. Or perhaps she should address it to Coach Hanks, who she knew had been made aware of the problem by Coach Crist.

She asked Jeff what he thought. He briefly campaigned for her to go back to NBC Sports–Philly. Bad publicity for the school had worked during soccer season; why not go that route again now? Andi thought about it but rejected it because she knew it would confirm what Coach Josephson had been accusing her of—whether it was true or not. Eleanor, Maria, and Lisa were all of different minds about who the petition should be addressed to, but all agreed the earliest to even think about making a move was after practice the following Monday.

"It could be she's going to make her point this week and then move on," Eleanor said. "I'm not saying that's right, I'm saying it might be what she's doing."

Lisa nodded. "But if you still aren't practicing on Monday with a game on Tuesday, it's time to do something. This has already gone too far. Friday's a done deal. We can't let it go further than that."

Friday, as Lisa had predicted, was a done deal. There was little doubt that Merion could have used Andi's shooting and ball handling—but especially her shooting—against Main Line. Their coach had apparently looked at the statistics from Merion's last prebreak game, against Ardmore, and noticed that Merion had shot one out of fourteen from beyond the three-point line. Whether she noted that a player who had shot four out of four the previous game didn't play, no one knew.

Main Line opened the game in a two-three zone, basically daring Merion to shoot the ball from outside. Every time Maria tried to attack the lane, a second defender came to meet her. She could kick the ball to a shooter—but it didn't do much good if the shooters were firing blanks.

Getting the ball to Eleanor was almost impossible because Merion had someone dropping down to double-team her constantly. When she did get the ball, she had absolutely no space to work with—a player behind, a player in front, and occasionally a third player leaning in to swipe at the ball.

She and Maria did their best to keep the game close. Lisa didn't get into the game to add a third scorer until there were three minutes left in the first half. By then, Main Line led 24–12. Lisa's presence opened things up a little—she made two threes—but it was still 30–20 at the half. There was no doubt in Andi's mind that if she and Lisa had both played the entire half, Merion would be leading. With two outside shooters in the game, Main Line would almost certainly have been forced to abandon its zone, and that would open up the lane for Maria's drives and for Eleanor to score from the low post.

But Andi stayed nailed to the bench in the second half and Lisa didn't get back in until under four minutes were left and the margin had grown to 49–30. Merion simply couldn't score with only two real scorers in the game. The final was 55–36.

"That's a loss to a team we could have beaten," Eleanor said as they walked off after the postgame handshakes. "I'm sick of this."

"Start writing," Maria said. "And write fast."

The boys had gone to Main Line and picked up their first conference win.

That was good news. In even better news, Jeff had played a key role in the victory. The only bad news was that the team had probably played its best with Ron Arlow at the point.

No day was perfect.

Coach C had started the two guards—Arlow at point guard and Jeff at shooting guard—and, once again, Jeff was left to wonder what he was thinking. Maybe he knew that Main Line's point guard was lightning-quick, but just five-three. That meant Arlow benefited greatly from high-ball screens set by Merion's big guys—notably Eric Billings and Tavon Washington. He made four threes in the first quarter, and Merion led 18–12 after the first six minutes.

Main Line switched to a zone defense and the game turned into one of those back-and-forth battles that are tense and fun at the same time. The little Main Line point guard, whose named turned out to be Reilly Atkinson, played on the wing in the one-two-two zone Main Line switched to, and he used his quickness on several occasions to dart into passing lanes for steals that led to layups.

Coach Crist switched Jeff to the point, which was no picnic with a five-ten forward playing at the top of the zone. Main Line led 43–41 after three quarters. It turned out Merion's best offense was to get a shot up against the zone and then watch Danny Diskin and Tavon Washington take advantage of the seams in the zone to grab offensive rebounds.

Merion had the lead, 51–49 with the clock under a minute, when Jeff, unable to see clearly around his giant tormentor, tried to shot-fake and then pass to Diskin on the wing. For about the fifth time in the game, Atkinson darted into the passing lane, stole the ball, and took off toward the basket, with Jeff in pursuit. Just to be sure he turned a mistake into a really bad mistake, Jeff fouled him as he laid the ball in with nineteen seconds left.

As the shot went in and the whistle blew, Jeff heard three voices all saying the same thing: "Michaels, what the hell were you thinking?" The voices he could hear clearly were Arlow and Coach C. The third voice was inside his head.

What the hell was I thinking?

Atkinson calmly swished the free throw to make it 52–51, Main Line. Coach C called his last time out.

He didn't say another word to Jeff about the play. Instead he said simply: "Clear-four," an end-of-the-clock play they'd worked on in practice. The point guard would get the ball to the top of the key, while the other four players went to the baseline. "Michaels, you've got the point," he said. "If they don't double-team, keep going to the basket. If they do, you know what to do. Forget the clock here. Just get a shot up as soon as one is available. Everyone crash the boards on a miss."

Jeff nodded. He'd run the play successfully in practice. This, of course, was different.

They lingered to put their hands into the huddle—all twelve of them—actually, eleven, because Arlow was already walking onto the court, clearly upset that Coach C was putting the ball in Jeff's hands.

"We're out of time-outs," Coach C said. "If they press, you gotta get it inbounds."

They did press, and it took Jeff several seconds to get the ball across midcourt. The clock was at eight seconds by the time he got near the top of the key. The big forward was waiting for him, guarding him man-to-man. Jeff had a quickness advantage. He gave a head-fake as if to shoot and instead went to the basket. The one-four alignment had spread the defense out. Jeff saw the help coming as he got into the lane and went up as if to shoot. It was Tavon Washington's man who had come to help with Jeff. Tavon curled to the basket, hand up, and Jeff spotted him.

Tavon caught the pass with three seconds left and banked the shot in as the clock hit one second. At this level, the clock didn't stop on a made basket and, Jeff realized later, Main Line had no time-outs left either.

The clock went to zero, the buzzer sounded, and everyone in red had their arms in the air. Merion had won, 53–52. The bench swarmed Tavon and Jeff.

Jeff still had a big smile on his face when Arlow walked up to him. "Good play," he said, putting out his fist for a bump, which Jeff returned. "Of course, if I'd had the chance, I'd have done the same thing."

"Really?" Jeff asked.

Arlow smiled. "Yeah, you're probably right," he said. "I'd have taken the shot. And made it."

26

IT HAD NOW BECOME A SEMI-REGULAR THING FOR ANDI and Jeff to meet on Saturdays. That pleased Jeff, even though there were no signs from Andi—at least none he could detect—that their meetings were anything more than two friends getting together to hang out.

This Saturday, though, was different. First of all, the weather was unexpectedly warm for January, so they decided to meet up at a neighborhood park for some one-on-one, rather than go to the mall. On the court and off, Andi was all business, and Jeff understood. Her playing time in practice and in games had been so limited that she had a lot of pent-up energy and plenty of frustration to match. She took it out on him, sinking some ridiculous threes, rebounding aggressively, and generally wiping the beat-up concrete court with him.

Jeff couldn't have been happier.

Afterward, while they cooled down on a bench, Andi asked for his input on the petition she'd been talking about.

"You can't make it too hostile," he said.

Andi was sitting next to him, a yellow legal pad on her lap. Jeff figured she'd gotten it from one of her lawyer parents.

"I know that," she said. "But I'm not concerned about tone right now. I'm concerned about content. What points do I bring up, so it doesn't come across as someone whining about playing time or the group blaming the coach for us not playing better?"

Jeff nodded. "I get it. Here's the thing: Whatever you write, you have to get the whole team to sign it. It can't just be you, Eleanor, Maria, and Lisa. It can't even just be the neutrals. It has to be all twelve of you. Even if it's eight against four, the coach can say that six of you are just whining about playing time and that Eleanor and Maria overreacted to an innocent comment."

Andi knew Jeff was right. It wasn't that unusual for teams that were losing to have players complaining about playing time or even how the offense was being run. Having two starters—Eleanor and Maria—sign the document would help, but there was little doubt Coach Josephson would say they were holding a grudge because of what had happened at Chester Heights.

An idea flashed through her head. "What if we got eight players *and* Coach Axelson? I'll bet she'd agree with everything I'm going to write—especially since it's all true."

Jeff was shaking his head. "Look, Coach C didn't really want to get involved because he didn't like the idea of one coach questioning another coach or, for that matter, one teacher questioning another teacher. There's no way any teacher, especially a relatively new one, is going to sign a document calling for the overthrow of another teacher."

"She won't go for a coup d'etat, huh?" Andi said, deciding to flex her vocabulary muscles for a moment.

"A coo-day-what?" he said.

"It means to overthrow a government in French," she said. "Forget it. Anyway, you're right."

"About Coach Axelson?" he said.

She nodded. "Yeah. About that. And about needing all twelve names on the petition, letter, document—whatever we end up calling it. I need Jamie Bronson. If I get her, I'll get everyone."

"What are the chances she'll go along with you?" he asked.

She sighed, while he chewed on a protein bar. "Before the first game, I'd have said somewhere between zero and ten percent," she said. "Now, I'd say fifty-fifty. One thing is clear: She doesn't like losing any more than I do."

"So, you write it, e-mail it to her, and ask what she thinks?"

"Are you crazy?" she said, finally opening the extra bar Jeff had brought for her. "First of all, this doesn't go anywhere until my parents have seen it, you've seen it, and Eleanor, Maria, and Lisa have seen it. Then, after everyone's had their say and *only* then, I will set up a meeting with Jamie."

"How do you propose to do that? You can't just sit down with her at lunch and you can't talk to her before or after practice on Monday because you'll be seen in either place by people with big mouths or, worse, by the coaches."

"I know that," Andi said. "I need to meet her some-place where it's just the two of us. First, though, I have to get this thing written and edited and in exactly the shape we want it in whenever it's delivered."

"So, we aren't going to shoot some HORSE or some-thing?" Jeff said, taking a swig from his water bottle and throwing his wrapper in the trash after.

She was typing a message into her phone. "I just asked my dad to pick us up here in thirty minutes," she said. "You seem a little off your game today, so I'll let you go first."

* * *

Andi spent most of Saturday afternoon writing. Not wanting to wait until Monday, she decided to take a chance and e-mail what she'd written to Jeff, Eleanor, Maria, and Lisa. If it fell into the wrong hands, so be it. This was pretty much a make-or-break endeavor anyway.

Everyone wrote back with an idea or two after reading what she'd written. She wrote down all the suggestions and then sat down to write a second draft, including some of the input she'd gotten. The one thing they all seemed to agree on was that it needed to be as unhostile and unthreatening as was possible when trying to pull off a coup d'etat.

After talking to her friends, she took the petition draft to her parents, explaining it was only a second draft.

"You sure you want to do this?" her mom said. "You—and the others—could get thrown off the team."

Andi shrugged. "Mom, I haven't played a minute in a game or practice since before winter recess, so—big deal. And I'm not submitting this unless the whole team signs it. She can't throw *everyone* off the team."

"But she'll know you're the ringleader," her dad said. "She might just come after you."

"Fine," Andi said—meaning it. She was ready for a fight.

By dinnertime, she had finished a final draft. The petition, which was what it had to be, was addressed to Mr. Block. But all three women who had coached the girls' basketball team were copied: Coach Josephson, to make it clear that the girls were being transparent about the issues they had with her; Coach Axelson, because they wanted to be sure Mr. Block would talk to her; and Coach Tuller, who they thought would be a neutral party. After Andi initially rewrote, she went back to make the petition as brief as possible. Her parents had always told her that overkill on any document was a mistake.

Dear Mr. Block:

We are writing today to ask for help with a very delicate situation. We understand that Coach Josephson has worked very hard to try to make our sixth-grade girls' basketball team successful. We certainly do not want anyone to think we blame our current 1–4 record on her. We are all responsible.

But there is a strong feeling among all twelve of us that Ms. Josephson lacks the experience—as she explained to us on the first day of tryouts—and perhaps the temperament to coach our team. We realize coaching a group of competitive 11- and 12-year-old girls can't be easy, but all of us—whether starters who have played often or nonstarters who have played little—feel that she is having a difficult time with the job. We don't claim to be mind readers, but she does not appear to be enjoying what she's doing and, as a result, neither are we—and that's NOT because of our record.

We believe the decision by Coach Axelson to leave the team is a reflection of this. Coach Axelson played college basketball, and we believe her decision to leave stemmed from her feeling that Coach Josephson wasn't flexible enough to grow with the job—just as we are all trying to grow as players.

We respectfully ask that you discuss with Coach Josephson the possibility of stepping down and perhaps allowing Coach Axelson to coach us the rest of the season. We want to make it clear we are grateful to Coach Josephson for the time and energy she has put into the job. We are just hoping to make things better for everyone involved—players and coaches.

We would welcome the opportunity to discuss this further with you. Thank you in advance for your attention and concern.

Yours Truly,

There was ample space at the bottom of the printed-out page for—Andi hoped—twelve signatures.

She had incorporated a number of suggestions into what she had initially written. On her father's recommendation, she had cut a sentence saying that the players were not in any way questioning Coach Josephson's character. "You bring it up, you're basically saying that character is an issue," he said. "You don't want to do that."

At her mother's suggestion, she had added the sentence about welcoming the opportunity for further discussion, because that was a clear next step if Mr. Block decided to take the matter to the next level. Eleanor had come up with the idea to add the word *delicate* to the opening sentence. Jeff's contribution had been adding the word *respectfully*, and Maria had suggested being specific about making things better for everyone by adding *players and coaches* to the end of that sentence.

Once she had incorporated the suggestions into the final version, Andi came to the step that would be far more difficult: figuring a way to sit down with Jamie Bronson and then convince her to put her name on the petition.

The school's website didn't have e-mail addresses for students—just for their parents—but the players had been given a sheet after the final cuts that included e-mail addresses. That was an important step for Andi: She could write directly to Jamie without having to go through her parents.

She sent the e-mail on Sunday morning. It was brief, but carefully crafted: *Hey Jamie—I'm hoping you and I can get together and talk at some point in the not-too-distant future. You may have Sunday plans with your family, but I can free up any time if you find a few minutes. We can discuss where to meet if you think you can do it. Please let me know . . . Best Regards . . . Andi.*

She had thought about suggesting a place to meet—the mall, perhaps—but, at Jeff's suggestion, left that out. He pointed out that might come off as presumptuous.

Andi sent the e-mail at ten thirty. By noon, she was convinced she wasn't going to hear back and would have to try to talk to Bronson face-to-face in school the next day, which would be awkward under any circumstances. Maybe, she thought, this had been a vanity exercise, a chance to vent along with her friends. Clearly, it wasn't going anywhere.

Then, at twelve fifteen, a note popped into her in-box: *Hi Andi—Sorry for the delay. Was at church with my parents. Mandatory, every Sunday. Glad to get together this afternoon. I'm free up until five o'clock. Got any ideas where to meet? . . . Jamie . . . PS—Bringing anyone with you or is it just you and me?*

Jamie included her phone number so Andi could just text her back. Andi was tempted to wait a few minutes if only not to seem overeager. But what the heck, she figured. Jamie had to know she'd been waiting for a response.

How about the King of Prussia Mall? Good food court there. Shouldn't be too busy Sunday afternoon . . . Oh, it'll just be me.

This time the answer popped right back: *Know it well. I can get my mom to drop me. Does 3 work?*

That was smack in the middle of the Eagles–Lions playoff game. Andi didn't care. *Perfect. Meet you at the food court.*

The response was a thumbs-up emoji.

Andi sighed. "Okay," she said to herself. "Here we go."

27

BOTH OF ANDI'S PARENTS WERE HOME, AND HER MOTHER volunteered to take her to the mall so her father could watch the finish of the Eagles and the Lions. Her dad wasn't that big a sports fan—except when it came to the Eagles. Her mom, on the other hand, loved baseball and the Phillies.

Eleanor, Maria, and Lisa all made noises about going along to show support, but Andi quieted them down by telling them Jamie had specifically asked if she'd be bringing anyone. Jeff didn't bother bringing it up; he knew he'd be shut down quickly if he did. Knights in shining armor need not apply.

The Eagles were trailing 17–14 when Andi's mom dropped her off near the food court entrance just before three. The place was almost empty. Most of the city was at home living—and dying—with the Eagles, who were playing the wild-card round in Detroit.

It felt unexpectedly odd to Andi to walk into the food court and not see Jeff. Instead, Jamie was already there, sitting at an empty table, looking at her phone.

"Hungry?" Andi asked as she walked up, trying to keep things casual for as long as she possibly could.

"No, not really," Jamie said. "Ate lunch not too long ago. Wouldn't mind a milkshake, though."

They quickly agreed on McDonald's. There was literally no one in line; a first, Andi thought, in her life. She ordered vanilla, Jamie chocolate.

Andi steered them to a table on the edge of the food court where no one was around. The quieter the better, she figured.

"So," Jamie said. "What's up, Carillo?"

No small talk, just cutting to the chase. Fair enough.

Andi had worn her backpack into the mall. Now she put it down next to her and pulled the petition from it. There was no sense saying anything. It was pretty self-explanatory.

"I'd like to know what you think of this," she asked, handing it to Jamie.

Jamie put her milkshake aside, wiped her hands on a napkin, and started to read. Almost right away, she looked up at Andi and said, "Seriously?" Andi's heart sank. Jamie kept reading, getting to the end without further comment.

"I know it seems crazy and it may seem like this is just me whining about playing time, but . . ."

Jamie put up a hand. "Let me read it again," she said.

They both lapsed into silence as Jamie read one more time. She finished, took the top off her milkshake—as Andi had already done—and took a sip, careful not to spill. McDonald's shakes were too thick to drink through a straw.

"Okay," she said finally, then paused. She looked her teammate in the eye. "Andi, this *is* crazy." It was the first time she had ever called Andi by her first name. "I mean, even with all that went on, you never tried to get Mr. Johnston removed as soccer coach."

"This is different . . ."

Jamie put up a hand again. "You got me down here because you want to know what I think. Let me tell you."

Andi, the daughter of two lawyers, had a habit of anticipating people's answers and interrupting.

"Like I said, it's crazy. I don't see how Block could possibly do anything other than maybe call Coach Josephson in and ask her what the heck is going on. She'll say it's just a handful of players who think they should be playing more and that'll be the end of it."

Andi waited to make sure she wasn't interrupting. "Unless all twelve of us sign it."

Jamie nodded slowly. "Unless all twelve of us sign it. That's why I'm here. You need me, don't you? If I sign it, my three friends will sign it. That will make eight—I assume Eleanor, Maria, and Lisa are on board with this already, right?"

Andi nodded.

"And Debbie would be inclined to side with you. So, if I signed and Jenny, Alayne, and Hope followed me, that would leave Randi, Brooke, and Ronnie. They'd probably go along with the majority—either way, I'm guessing."

She was guessing, Andi was certain, correctly.

"So, I'm sort of the swing vote, right? I go along and you can almost certainly get all twelve names on this thing."

She wasn't smiling as if to say, "Gotcha." Her tone wasn't smug or sarcastic. It sounded thoughtful.

"I know it's a tough call," Andi said, not wanting to come across as putting pressure on her.

"It *is* a tough call," Jamie said. She leaned back in her chair. "You're basically asking the principal to fire someone who volunteered to do this and is getting paid practically nothing for giving up her afternoons five days a week."

"Every coach in the school does the same thing,"

Andi said. "Like you said, she volunteered. No one forced her to do this."

Jamie said nothing in response. Andi was tempted to fill the void but remembered something she'd read about waiting when people were quiet to give them a chance to think.

"Did you know she's going through a divorce?" Jamie finally asked.

Andi didn't know. She wondered how Jamie knew—but realized it didn't matter much.

"No, I didn't," she said quietly. "I'm sorry. That might explain why she's in a bad mood so much of the time."

"Or not. She could be happy to be rid of her husband. It also might explain why she's coaching," Jamie said. "I know her daughter's in college. She might be pretty lonely right now."

Andi's stomach was turning over. She didn't want to bring more unhappiness into a life that might already be unhappy. Then again, did that make it right for her to make an entire team—or most of an entire team—miserable? This time she didn't say anything for a full minute. Jamie waited patiently.

"Let me put it to you this way," Andi finally said. "Regardless of her personal circumstances, from what you've seen so far, should she be coaching this team?"

There was another long silence—broken suddenly by a loud cheer coming from a nearby TV set. Several people were standing around it. Clearly, the Eagles had just scored. If Jamie cared, she didn't show it.

"Repeat your question," Jamie said.

Andi did.

This time, the answer came right away. "No," Jamie Bronson said. "She shouldn't be coaching. I think I knew that when she made the crack in the locker room at Chester Heights. I don't even think she meant it maliciously, it was just . . ."

"Stupid?" Andi said.

Jamie shook her head. "No, not stupid. Ignorant."

She took another sip of her milkshake. "I'll talk to the other three and get back to you by lunchtime tomorrow."

She was as good as her word—better, in fact.

Just as Andi and Jeff were sitting down at lunch, Jamie walked over and handed Andi a large envelope. "I think everything you need is in there," she said, without so much as glancing at Jeff. "Let me know what you decide to do with it."

Andi and Jeff sat down and Andi pushed her tray aside and opened the envelope. She looked at it, smiled, and handed it to Jeff, just as Eleanor, Maria, Lisa, and Danny—now a regular at the table—arrived.

Below the "Yours Truly" were four signatures: *Jamie*

Bronson, Hope Allison, Jenny Mearns, and *Alayne Jolie*. Next to Bronson's name were parentheses with the words *Team Captain* inside.

"Wow," Jeff said. He could think of nothing to say beyond that, so he handed the document back to Andi before he got pasta sauce on it.

As the others sat down, Andi passed it around.

"Who'd have thunk it?" Lisa said, intentionally misspeaking.

"Not me," Maria said. "I know there were a couple of clues she wasn't happy, but you must have done a great job yesterday, Andi."

Andi thought perhaps she should stand and take a bow. Then again, the fact that Bronson had been willing to meet with her was a pretty clear indication that she was willing to listen.

"Turns out there's more to her than meets the eye," she said. "She's pretty thoughtful."

"So, what's next?" Danny asked.

Andi looked around the room to see if they were attracting any attention.

"First, the four of us need to sign it," she said. "Then, when I get to the locker room before practice, I have to grab the other four, show this to them and get them to sign it."

"What if the coaches see you?" Jeff asked.

"They don't come into the locker room before practice,"

Eleanor answered. "But there won't be that much time." She looked at Andi. "You need to get a copy for each one so they can read it at once rather than pass it around."

Andi nodded. "Problem is, the only place to make a copy of anything is the school office. I can't just walk in and say I need to make copies of a petition to remove our sixth-grade basketball coach."

"Yeah, but I can go in there to say I'm making copies of a poster for tryouts for the sixth-grade spring play, which I'm codirecting," Danny said. Danny was taking an elective theater class, and he and a girl named Valery Levy had been named codirectors of an April production of *Twelfth Night*.

"You sure?" Andi asked.

"Give it to me right now," he said. He glanced at his phone. "I'll be back in ten minutes."

He was back in a few minutes. "I made ten copies to make it look more real," he said, passing them to Andi.

"What happens when there are no posters up around the school?" Eleanor asked.

"I'll burn that bridge when I get to it," Danny said with a wide smile.

Andi thanked him and put the copies of the petition into the envelope she'd been handed by Jamie. Her mind was going a million miles an hour. She was confident she'd get the remaining four signatures. The question was: Then what?

Burn that bridge when I get to it, she thought.

The five-minute bell rang. They all stood up and looked at each other.

"We need to talk more once we have the other four signatures," Maria said.

"Let's get the signatures, then worry about that," Lisa said.

"A-men to that," Andi said. "A-men."

As soon as last period was over, Andi bolted from her earth science class and headed straight to the locker room. Since the girls were on the road the next day—at Malvern—they had the early practice. She walked into the locker room and found it empty.

She began changing into her practice gear while waiting for others to start arriving. Eleanor and Maria showed up first. "No one yet, huh?" Maria said, stating the obvious.

A minute later, several players came piling in, including Debbie Lee, Brooke Jensen, and Randi Eisen. Andi handed them the document as they headed in the direction of their lockers. "Do me a favor and read this before you change," she said. "As you can see, eight of us have already signed it. If you want to sign, too, I have the original."

They looked at her a little bit funny but took what

they were handed and sat down on stools in front of their lockers to read.

Naturally, Ronnie Bonilla—one of the four whose signatures Andi still needed—was the last to arrive. Andi had the feeling that everyone was looking at her as she handed the document to her and said, "Ronnie, please read this as quickly as you can."

It was 3:10 p.m.

Debbie and Randi signed almost as soon as they walked in the door. A moment later, Ronnie did, too. They now had eleven signatures. It was 3:12. Brooke Jensen was sitting on her stool, still looking at the document. Finally, as the others were walking out the door, she walked over to Andi, still holding it.

"I can't sign something like this without talking to my parents first," she said. "I'm not saying I disagree with anything you've written, but to challenge authority this way . . . I'm just not sure."

"You know everyone else has signed this," she said.

Brooke nodded. "I know," she said. "I get it. I'll let you know tonight."

Andi understood her position and respected it. She knew she probably wouldn't have gone ahead with the whole thing if her parents had disapproved. It was also entirely possible that when Brooke explained the situation to her parents, they'd tell her it was okay to sign. But for the moment, she was stuck on eleven signatures.

She needed twelve.

"I understand, Brooke," she said.

Jensen seemed frozen in front of her.

"We better get going," Andi said, standing up. "Or there's going to be an authority figure very upset with us."

Brooke's face broke into a wide smile and the two of them sprinted through the door to the court.

Andi stopped while leaving the court after practice to update Jeff. He agreed she needed all twelve signatures. "Eleven is good," he said. "But twelve means they have to pay attention."

Practice had been the same that day as the week before—Andi spectating throughout the scrimmage period. At one point, Coach Tuller walked over to her during a water break and said, "Stay ready, Carillo."

"Why?" Andi answered.

Coach Tuller didn't respond. Clearly, she'd just been mouthing a sideline cliché—maybe she was reading books now, too?—and hadn't expected a sharp-tongued response.

The boys' practice was routine, except for the fact that Ron Arlow was absent. Coach C told the team that Arlow had left school early, feeling sick. Coach C was waiting to hear back on whether he'd be in school the next day and available for the Malvern game.

Jeff wasn't sure how to feel. Arlow was one of the team's better players, but he certainly wouldn't mind playing the point for an entire game and wouldn't miss his presence in the locker room. Coach C seemed to read his mind. While everyone was shooting free throws, he waved him over to where he and Coach B were standing at midcourt.

"So, I'm guessing you aren't going to be broken-hearted if Ron can't go tomorrow," he said with a smile.

Jeff shrugged as if to say it was no big deal one way or the other. "Coach, he's one of our better players . . ."

"But he can be a pain in the butt, and this way I'll have to play you at the point most of the game."

Jeff nodded. "True."

"Which one?" Coach B asked—also smiling.

"Both," Jeff answered.

"I appreciate your honesty," Coach C said. He blew his whistle to get everyone back onto the court.

Jeff really liked Coach C. He just wished he'd be a little less mysterious about Ron Arlow.

28

ANDI WAS FINISHING HER HOMEWORK, HER CELL PHONE sitting next to her on her desk, when it buzzed with an incoming text.

Eleanor, Maria, and Lisa had all texted earlier wondering if she had heard anything from Brooke, to whom she'd given her number after practice. Jeff had texted twice. She had told all of them she would let them know if and when she heard something.

She reached for the phone, figuring it was probably Jeff again even though she'd told him to try to be patient.

The text wasn't from Jeff.

Can you meet me at your locker ten mins before first period in the morning? I will sign then.

Andi almost jumped out of her chair. She had to get

her fingers under control just to reply: *You bet. See you then. Thanks!*

She then sent a group text to Eleanor, Maria, Lisa, and Jeff: *She says she's signing!*

The answers came back quickly, all celebratory. But Eleanor's included an additional two words: *What next?*

That was a good question. She would have the document with all twelve signatures in hand before first period. She had several options: sit down with everyone at lunch and decide what to do next, wait and see how the game the next day went and then make a decision, or just walk into Mr. Block's office at lunchtime and hand it to his assistant in an envelope clearly marked for Mr. Block's eyes only. Then again, they had cc'd the coaches, so she owed it to them to get it into their hands, too. But when? Before the game?

She thought about asking her parents, then decided against it. The truth was she didn't want to think like a lawyer at that moment. She wanted to figure this out for herself—but she needed some help. The best voice, she decided, would be someone not on the team.

She called Jeff.

"What's your gut telling you?" he asked.

"That I should take the thing to Block's office at lunch tomorrow and ask the assistant to help us get extra copies into the coaches' mailboxes in the faculty room," she said. "There's no way to go into the pool up to our waists anymore. We're either in or we're out."

Jeff paused for a second. Andi wondered if he was figuring out her pool analogy.

"I agree," he said finally. "I mean, even if Coach Josephson sees this before the game, what's she going to do, bench you?"

Andi laughed. "She can't bench all twelve of us unless she wants to forfeit the game." She hadn't thought of that possibility, but she now realized it *could* happen. She had another thought. "If she's still the coach on Wednesday, I'm going to be off the team anyway. She'll see me as the ringleader and blame me."

"You are the ringleader."

"I know. And if someone asks me about that, I'm not going to deny it."

"What do you think Block will do?" Jeff asked.

"I have no idea," Andi said. "Honestly, I have no idea."

Andi got to her locker the next morning at eight fifteen, wanting to be sure she didn't keep Brooke waiting. By eight twenty, she was getting nervous and running out of ways to look busy. She could only take books out and put them back in the locker so many times.

Just as she was starting to think Brooke might have changed her mind, she saw her walking quickly in her direction, easy to spot even in a crowded hallway, because she was taller than just about anyone else.

Andi reached into her locker for the original copy of the petition that the other eleven players had signed. She held it at her side, not wanting to thrust it at Brooke in case she was having any second thoughts at all.

"Sorry," Brooke said. "Just got a late start and I was all the way in the back of the bus."

"No worries," Andi said. "You still okay to sign?"

Brooke nodded, reaching into her pocket for a pen. Andi handed her the document.

"I hope this didn't cause any problems at home," Andi said as Brooke's eyes worked their way down the petition to where there was room for her to sign.

"Actually, my parents asked me one question: 'Do you agree with your teammates?' I said I did, and they said, 'Then you should sign it.'"

She finished writing her name, handed the document back to Andi, and said, "Now what?"

"I'm bringing it to Mr. Block at lunchtime," Andi said. "The coaches will probably have seen it by the time we get on the bus today. So be prepared."

Brooke nodded. "I guess we all better be prepared."

She was right. They all better be prepared, Andi most of all.

The five-minute bell rang. Brooke waved and headed off. Andi reached into her locker one more time for the envelope she'd been carrying the document in, carefully put it back inside, and stuck it into her backpack. She took a deep breath, squared her shoulders, and headed for class.

Maria, Eleanor, and Lisa insisted on going with Andi to the principal's office.

"Show of unity," Eleanor insisted. "It's better if the assistant tells Block there were four of us, rather than just you."

Andi liked that idea—loved it, actually—since the thought had occurred to her that upon hearing that Andi had dropped the petition off, Mr. Block's first reaction might be, "Her? Again?"

This would lessen that possibility—at least a little. The assistant, Ms. Dumas, wasn't exactly helpful. She wasn't thrilled when they asked to use the copy machine to make the three extra copies for the coaches' mailboxes. When Andi asked for three extra envelopes, she rolled her eyes.

"We're not a Staples store, you know," she said.

Ms. Dumas was about Maria's height and, according to what Andi had heard, had worked in the school office forever. In fact, the rumor was she'd been there when the school opened in 1964. Exaggeration . . . perhaps.

"It's really important," Lisa said. "Otherwise we wouldn't ask."

Ms. Dumas looked up at Lisa—who was probably close to a foot taller than she was—and sighed. Then she reached into her drawer and produced three legal-sized envelopes. Andi put the original document into the envelope already marked for Mr. Block, and then she and Maria wrote the coaches' names on the other three, put the copies inside, and handed them back to Ms. Dumas.

"Mr. Block is at lunch," she said. "I'll give him his copy when he returns and put the others' in their mail-boxes."

She looked at the four girls, who were far taller than she was, and then at the envelopes marked for the coaches. "I'm guessing this is about basketball?"

"Yes, ma'am," Andi answered.

She nodded. "Fine then," she said, and sat back down at her desk, indicating she was finished talking to the girls.

They looked at each other, turned, and walked out. The die was cast. No turning back.

Andi didn't hear a word either teacher said in her two afternoon classes. She was waiting to be called to the principal's office or to have Coach Josephson stalk into one of the classrooms and demand to see her.

Neither happened. After sixth period, she headed

to the gym to get her basketball uniform from her locker, pulling her cell phone from her backpack as she walked there and powering it back on.

There was a text . . . from Jeff. *Anything?*

He had apparently sent it between fifth and sixth periods—against the rules—but Jeff wasn't always big on rules. Sometimes he looked at them as a suggestion.

She looked through her texts and e-mails. Nothing.

Coach Josephson was sitting in her usual seat on the bus when the girls boarded, looking at her phone. If she had seen her copy of the petition, she gave no indication of it. She didn't look up to say hello to anyone—which wasn't unusual.

Everything was the same when they arrived at Malvern. The same five would start. Coach Josephson told them she had spoken to a couple of coaches who had played Malvern and had been told they relied on their guards, who were both very good shooters.

"Medley, Eisen, you're going to have to really defend those girls," she said. "No open shots. Don't let them pick you."

Andi resisted the urge to shout out, "You don't say 'pick you' in basketball, you say 'screen you.'" It didn't matter. Telling a player not to get screened was a little like saying "Don't miss any shots." You were going to get screened. The key was to get help on a switch if need be, but they had never worked on that in practice.

Coach Josephson's scouting report turned out to be accurate. Malvern's offense was simple. The point guard brought the ball up, and the two forwards came to the top of the key and screened—on every possession. If someone switched—Jamie Bronson was actually very good at it—the guard with the ball would reverse it across the court to the other guard. On occasion, if Merion's inside defenders came up to try to stop an outside shot, the ball would be thrown inside to someone who was open. More often, one of the guards would shoot.

The game stayed close because Malvern had as much trouble guarding Merion as Merion had guarding Malvern. The Mounties had no one quick enough to stay with Maria, and she consistently got into the lane to score or set up Eleanor. It was 17–15 after one quarter, and when Lisa came into the game in place of Alayne Jolie—giving Merion another legitimate scoring threat—the Mustangs took the lead before two late three-pointers by Malvern's point guard tied the game at 31–31 at halftime.

"Good job, girls," Coach Josephson said during the break. "We'll go back with the usual five to start the third quarter." Everyone looked at one another. They had, as usual, played better with Lisa in the game in Alayne's spot.

The third quarter was much like the first, except that Malvern had switched to a zone to make it tougher for Maria to get into the lane and Merion was struggling to score. It was 43–37 after three quarters.

Lisa went back in at the start of the fourth quarter and promptly hit a three to cut the margin to 43–40. But Merion simply couldn't get a stop. After yet another three made it 49–42 with 4:01 left, Eleanor called time-out. This was unusual—to say the least. The players had been told in preseason that the coaches would call all the time-outs.

"Is something wrong?" Coach Josephson asked Eleanor as the players came to the bench. "Are you hurt?"

"No," Eleanor said. "But I'm sick—sick of losing games we should win. We need Andi in the game. We need her shooting and her defense."

"I make those decisions, Dove," Coach Josephson said.

"She's right, Coach," Coach Tuller said, surprising everyone by speaking up and disagreeing with her boss.

"I agree," Randi Eisen said. "Put her in for me. I can't guard that girl. She's too quick. Andi's much quicker than I am."

The horn to return the teams to the court was sounding. Coach Josephson looked around the huddle. Then she put her hands on her hips.

"Fine, play it that way, then," she said. "Carillo, you're in for Eisen."

She was saying something else, but Andi wasn't

listening. She was pulling off her sweats and racing to the scorer's table. She was very glad she had spent time shooting threes in warm-ups, something she had done largely to entertain herself, never figuring she would get into the game.

It was Merion's ball. Maria brought the ball up. Eleanor called for the ball in the low post and Maria got it to her. Instantly, she was double-teamed, Andi's defender leaving her alone to go and help. Eleanor pitched the ball right to Andi and, perhaps because it had been so long since Andi had touched a ball in a game, yelled, "Shoot it, Andi!"

Instinct took over. Andi caught the ball, squared her feet just behind the three-point line, and shot. She knew it was in as soon as she released it.

It was 49–45. As Andi ran downcourt, the girl who had left her to double-team Eleanor ran past her and said, "Where've you been all day?"

Andi laughed. It felt great to be playing basketball again.

29

ANDI'S PRESENCE ON THE COURT SEEMED TO GIVE THE
entire team an emotional boost. On her first defensive
possession, the ball swung to the guard who had seemingly made about a hundred threes. Andi was there,
hand in her face, having gone over a screen (a pick, in
Josephson-speak) to get there.

The guard, whose teammates called her Nicole,
looked surprised. She fumbled the ball for a split second, then tried to pass, only to have Lisa dart into the
passing lane to steal the ball cleanly and take off for a
layup that made it 49–47.

Malvern's coach called time. Coach Josephson had
little to say in the huddle. Coach Tuller stepped in and
said, "Just keep doing what you're doing, girls. They're
rattled."

She was right. Malvern, which seemingly hadn't

missed for twenty minutes, suddenly couldn't make a shot. The Mounties decided not to double-team Eleanor the next time downcourt, and she scored easily to tie the game. Then they went back to doubling her and sending Lisa's defender to help. Eleanor looked at Andi, then swung the ball to Lisa, who drained another three. By the time the run was over, Merion had scored twelve straight points to lead 54–49.

Malvern began fouling, and with Maria, Andi, and Lisa controlling the ball, Merion made seven out of eight free throws down the stretch. The final score was a stunning 61–55. In the four minutes Andi played, Merion outscored Malvern 19–6.

"Well," Maria said in the euphoric locker room, "if that was our last game, we went out in style."

In the afterglow of the comeback, Andi had completely forgotten about the petition. Maria was right, though. Their future was very clearly in doubt. But for now, the present was pretty great.

Coach Josephson's postgame speech was brief. "Good win, girls," she said. "Practice tomorrow at four fifteen."

She turned and walked out without waiting for the players to do a postgame cheer. They all looked at each other. Chances were a lot would happen between now and four fifteen tomorrow.

Bronson walked to the middle of the locker room

and put a hand in the air. "New season!" she said. They all joined in loudly.

Andi was just beginning to wonder if Ms. Dumas had passed the petition on to Mr. Block when she received an e-mail shortly after eight o'clock that night.

It was addressed to all twelve members of the sixth-grade girls' basketball team and was very direct. *Would like to see two representatives from your team in my office at the start of lunch hour tomorrow to address this issue. Arthur L. Block, Principal.*

"Not exactly infused with warmth," her father said when she showed it to her parents.

"Well, the petition doesn't make his life any easier, does it?" her mother observed.

A text popped into her phone. It was from Jamie Bronson. *Should probably be you and me, huh? If you agree, I'll send a text to all suggesting that.*

Andi was happy to see that Bronson wasn't going to back off now that Block had responded. She answered with a thumbs-up.

"Any idea what he'll do?" her mom asked.

"Hard to read tone in a one-sentence note, but I don't think he's going to be jumping up and down and saying, 'Great idea, girls!'" her dad said.

Andi wasn't sure about much, but on that subject, she had no doubts.

The verdict on having her and Jamie go to see the principal to represent the team was unanimous.

And so, at 11:35 the next morning, Andi walked into the principal's outer office. Jamie was already there. Ms. Dumas needlessly pointed her to a seat.

"I wonder if Josephson's coming," she whispered to Jamie as she sat down.

"You'd think so, wouldn't you?" Jamie said. "The petition is about her."

Ten minutes later Mr. Block's door finally opened. Amy Josephson walked out, glanced at the girls and, without so much as a nod, walked out. They looked at one another clearly thinking the same thing: not good.

Mr. Block appeared in the doorway.

"Ladies, come in," he said.

They walked inside.

"Ms. Carillo, I know," he said. Turning to Jamie he said, "You are?"

"Jamie Bronson," she said, putting out a hand. "I'm captain of the team."

Mr. Block nodded. "And you selected Ms. Carillo as your second because of her past experience complaining about coaches?"

Wow, Andi thought. *Not a good start.*

"No," Jamie answered with admirable cool. "I asked her to come with me because she's probably the smartest kid on our team."

Good answer, Andi thought—*whether it was true or not.*

Block nodded and pointed them both to chairs opposite his chair on the other side of the desk. Arthur Block *looked* like a school principal. He was about forty, with short-cropped brown hair and the kind of glasses you'd expect a principal to wear. Andi had thought him a decent guy during the soccer crisis, although his first instinct when Andi had been cut had been to say he'd given Coach Johnston his word that he could select the team without outside interference. Only after Jeff's dad and other media members had gotten involved had he buckled and put Andi on the team.

Now he sat looking at what Andi guessed was a copy of the petition. "As you saw, I've just spoken with Coach Josephson about this," he said, holding the petition up for them to see. "As you might imagine, she's not happy. She feels she's put a lot of effort into coaching you girls, and while she admits making some mistakes as a first-time coach, she's baffled by the animus in this document."

Andi was baffled by the word *animus*—in part because she wasn't 100 percent sure she knew what it meant, but also because they had worded the petition as mildly as possible to try not to be too confrontational. Clearly, they'd failed.

It was Jamie who answered.

"Mr. Block, let me say this as the person in the room who has started every game and was selected by Coach Josephson to be team captain," she said. "I signed the petition and encouraged others to sign it because the things that bothered me about the decisions Coach Josephson has made have very little to do with basketball."

She recounted the incident in the locker room at Chester Heights. She talked about the coach's hostility toward Andi from day one and how it had affected her judgment on Andi—and on Lisa Carmichael, who was clearly Andi's friend—and how that had hurt the team. She noted that Joan Axelson had been upset enough to quit as assistant coach.

"The only reason we won yesterday," she said in conclusion, "is because Coach Tuller and the other players more or less insisted that Andi play in the fourth quarter. If not for that, we'd have lost again."

Mr. Block sat back in his chair for a moment. He was looking at notes he had obviously made earlier.

"The Chester Heights incident was brought to my attention and Coach Josephson feels there was an overreaction to it. She says she misspoke and when she tried to apologize . . ."

"Tried to apologize—she's never apologized to anyone for anything!" Andi realized she was halfway out of her chair and shouting. "Sorry," she said, sitting back down.

"Andi's right," Jamie said. "There was never an apology."

Mr. Block was silent for a moment.

"Well, I'm going to be honest with you. I just now tried to convince Coach Josephson to stay on the job, to try and clear the air with all of you—whatever that might involve. She told me she has no desire to coach any of you anymore. Apparently, she had already talked to Coach Tuller before our meeting, because I have an e-mail from her saying she supports Coach Josephson and doesn't want to coach anymore, either.

"So, for the moment, you are a team without a coach."

Andi was surprised by Coach Josephson quitting—she had thought she wouldn't go down without a fight. She was even more surprised by Coach Tuller walking away. There had been clear indications that she disagreed with Coach Josephson's tactics, most notably yesterday.

"We could get Coach Axelson to come back," Andi said.

"I am willing to ask her," Mr. Block said. "My guess, though, is that most, if not all of the faculty, is going to stand behind Ms. Josephson on this. Frankly, I agree with them. As of this moment, I'm inclined to simply cancel your remaining eight games. We don't *have* to have a sixth-grade girls' basketball team. We started the sixth-grade teams for the benefit of the students. So far, they've pretty much been nothing but a headache."

Those were pretty strong words. But Mr. Block was angry about the situation, and what had happened during soccer season—even if it hadn't been her fault—was clearly part of the reason for his demeanor.

"When will you decide what to do next?" Jamie asked. "I mean, should we expect to practice today?"

Mr. Block sighed. "As of right now, no. You can't practice unsupervised. And at the moment, there's no one to supervise you."

Andi was holding out hope that Coach Axelson would come back. "Sir, you really should ask Ms. Axelson."

"I will," Mr. Block said. "But I wouldn't get my hopes up if I were you."

Andi and Jamie raced to the cafeteria as soon as they left the principal's office. There were still twenty minutes left before fifth period. They were hungry and they had to report what had happened to the rest of the team.

As soon as they picked up trays, they were besieged.

"Let us grab some food, then meet at the table where Andi usually sits and we'll fill you in," Jamie said, holding her arms up to shield herself from the questions coming all at once.

Two spots had been cleared for them at the table. The rest of the team sat or stood around it. Jeff and a number of the players from the boys' team stood on the fringes of the circle listening. Since Jamie was the captain, Andi let her do the talking.

She walked through the meeting in Mr. Block's office: Coach Josephson and Coach Tuller quitting in response to the petition, Block's anger, and his prediction that no one else would be willing to coach them. She concluded by saying, "I think Coach Axelson is our best hope."

"No, she's not," Maria said. "Lisa and I ran into her in the hallway on our way here. She said she thought the petition was way out of line."

"In fact," Lisa added, "she said there's no one on this faculty who's going to step in now. Then she said, 'You girls went too far, too fast.'"

There was silence at the table.

"So, does that mean the season's over?" Jenny Mearns asked.

"It might," Andi answered, speaking for the first time. "Mr. Block says we can't practice today without a coach."

"What about the game Friday?" Brooke Jensen asked.

"Same thing," Jamie answered. "No coach, no game."

The five-minute bell was ringing. They all started in the direction of the door and their fifth-period classes. Jeff hung back to wait for Andi.

"I'm really sorry," he said as they walked to the door.

She shrugged. "You know, the funny thing is, if I'd known she was going to listen to Tuller and let me play yesterday—play our best team—I probably wouldn't have delivered the petition. Then we'd still have a team."

Jeff shook his head. "She'd have been her old self in practice today. You said she didn't say anything about how well you played or how the game changed when you went in. You did the right thing."

"Maybe," Andi said as they reached the hallway and were about to head in opposite directions. "But we sure as heck didn't get what we wanted."

Jeff remembered something his father often told him: Just because a coach makes the right call doesn't mean you get the right result.

This was certainly proof of that.

30

WHEN THE BOYS' PRACTICE ENDED AT FOUR FIFTEEN, IT FELT
strange not to see the girls ringing the court for their
practice. One way or the other, Jeff was accustomed
to seeing a girls' team—either the sixth-grade girls
when the boys had the early practice or the varsity
girls when they went at four fifteen—waiting to take
over the court.

"I suppose I could keep you guys out here for a while
longer," Coach C joked. "But we'll let the varsity girls
get a little bit of an early start."

Ron Arlow was back at practice, looking hale and
hearty and once again, he and Jeff split time at the point
guard start. The one-game joyride was clearly over.

Jeff didn't really give that much thought during
practice. His mind was on the girls' dilemma—debacle

was more like it—and what might be done to help them or, more accurately, to save them.

Unfortunately, he had nothing—not a single idea. Unless someone on the faculty stepped forward and agreed to coach, the girls' season would be over.

There was a good deal of discussion in the locker room after practice about what was going on with the girls. Most of the boys were sympathetic. To no one's surprise, Arlow was not.

"It's your girlfriend, Carillo—again," he said, pointing a finger at Jeff. "She whined her way through soccer season and now she's whining again and somehow convinced everyone else to go along with her."

"Does the fact that everyone else signed the petition tell you something, Arlow?" Jeff said, feeling himself turn red, more with anger than embarrassment at Arlow calling Andi his girlfriend.

"Yeah, well, everyone knows she's a troublemaker. Been going on for months."

"You just don't like her because she's a better soccer player than you *and* because she wouldn't go to the dance with you," Danny Diskin said.

Arlow didn't have an answer for that one. Most of the others were hooting at him—because they knew Danny had nailed him on both fronts. Jeff high-fived Danny and headed for the shower. As soon as he felt the warm water on his back, his mind returned to the girls' plight.

Come on, Jeff, think, he thought. Nothing was coming to mind.

He'd forgotten that his father was picking him up, but he brightened when he saw his car because he remembered *why* he was picking him up. One of his dad's good friends was Fran Dunphy—the recently retired Temple basketball coach. Dunph—as everyone called him—still taught a class at Temple and would often bring in guest speakers from all walks of life to talk about their experiences. His dad was speaking to the class that night, and Dunph was buying dinner beforehand at the Capital Grille as his "payment." He had urged Tom Michaels to bring Jeff along, having known him since he first started going to Temple games as a toddler.

They parked with the valet in front of the restaurant, which was at the spot where Broad Street emptied into City Hall Square, at exactly five p.m.—the time the valets came on duty and the time of the reservation. Dunphy was waiting inside the front door.

The restaurant manager—who screamed, "Dunph!" when he spotted the old coach—led them to a corner table. Jeff had filled his dad in on what was going on with the girls' team on the drive to the restaurant. As soon as they sat down and ordered drinks, his dad began telling Dunph the story.

"Never knew sixth-grade sports could be so intense," Dunph said with a smile. He looked a lot younger than seventy, his hair graying but still flecked with brown, his eyes alive, his smile easy. "There's really no one who will step in and coach them? I mean, if the two assistant coaches understood the woman wasn't being fair to the kids, why wouldn't they want to help?"

"It's political," Jeff said. "No one wants to be seen as not supporting another faculty member."

"What about supporting the kids?" Dunph asked. "Shouldn't they be more important than a teacher's ego?"

It was a good question. An idea flashed through Jeff's head—a bad one, or at the very least an impossible one.

"Coach Dunphy?" he said.

"Come on, Jeff, I've known you since before you could walk," the coach said. "It's Dunph or Fran."

Jeff knew that, but in this context, he wanted to emphasize the word coach. "Okay, fine, sure, I mean, Dunph, why don't *you* coach them? It's just eight games and I've seen you quoted in the papers as saying you've got too much free time . . ."

"Jeff, don't be ridiculous," his dad said. "Dunph coaching sixth-grade girls? Come on."

"I'd have no problem coaching sixth-grade girls," Dunph said, stunning Jeff. "Coaching is coaching. And if the point of coaching is to help kids out—which is what it's *supposed* to be—why wouldn't I coach a group of girls who need a coach?"

"You mean you'll do it?" Jeff said.

Dunph held up a hand. "Slow down, Jeff. The easy part right now is finding time. I've got charity commitments on some weekends and I have class every Wednesday night and Friday morning, but right now, that's about it." He smiled. "It's too cold to play golf."

"So, what's the hard part?" Jeff's dad asked.

Dunph shrugged. "You think the principal would let me do it? Sounds like he's pretty much with the coach and against the girls. And, even if he did let me do it, I'm sure there would be an insurance issue and maybe a union issue since I don't work for the school."

Jeff and his dad were both nodding.

"But if we could figure that part out?" Jeff asked. "Would you do it?"

Fran Dunphy smiled as a waiter arrived carrying drinks. "Absolutely," he said. "In a heartbeat."

Five minutes later, after everyone had ordered dinner, Jeff excused himself to go outside to call Andi. Naturally, she didn't answer. He texted: *Call me ASAP! Really important.*

He paced up and down on Broad Street for about two minutes before the phone rang.

"What's so important?" she said.

He told her.

"Seriously, Fran Dunphy would coach *us*?" she practically screamed into the phone.

"Yes, but there's the insurance issue and the union issue."

"Let me talk to my parents. They're lawyers. They'll know what to do."

Jeff went back inside, just as Dunph's linguini with shrimp, his dad's stuffed lobster, and his New York strip were arriving.

He reported back on what Andi had said about talking to her parents. That sounded like a good idea to both men.

Dunphy had a big smile on his face as he dug into his dinner. "If we can pull this off," he said, "I think it could be fun. A lot of fun."

Jeff's father raised his glass. "You finished with five hundred eighty wins, right?" he said as Dunphy nodded. "Here's to five eighty-one."

The three of them clinked glasses—two of them holding white wine, one Coke. Jeff was completely fired up.

Once Andi had explained everything to her parents—and had convinced them she wasn't kidding about Fran Dunphy being willing to coach their team—it was her mother who spoke first.

"The only way this is complicated is if Block decides

he doesn't want to get into some kind of fight with his faculty," she said. "The easy part is the union. There are plenty of people who work at that school who aren't part of the teachers' union. They just have to give Coach Dunphy a contract that meets all the requirements of a non-union employee."

"What about the insurance?" Andi asked.

"Same thing," her mom said. "As long as he's a school employee, he can coach the team and they're covered."

Andi's mind was going in about a hundred directions at once. In a period of about eight hours they had gone from taking on their coach, to their coach quitting, to being told by the school principal that no one would coach them, to an apparent offer from Fran Dunphy to coach them.

Fran Dunphy.

Andi didn't follow college basketball as closely as Jeff, but she knew enough about it to know that Dunphy was known as "Mr. Big Five." He had played on very good LaSalle teams in the late 1960s, had gotten a master's degree at Villanova, and had been hugely successful coaching at Penn and Temple. The joke around town was that St. Joseph's needed to hire him in some capacity to complete the sweep.

And now he was willing to coach a sixth-grade team?

Jeff had told her he would be home at about nine after he and his dad attended Dunphy's class. She texted him and asked him to call before he went to bed. He called her back from his dad's car.

"So, did your parents have any ideas?" he asked.

"Yes," she said, and explained.

"So, the key then is Block being willing to do it—or to let Coach Dunphy do it."

"Exactly. Do you think there's any way he can come with us to meet with Block? If he's actually there, I think it'll be harder for Block to say no."

"I agree. When should we ask him to come?"

"I'll get to school early in the morning and ask for another meeting with him at lunch. If Coach Dunphy can come in then—perfect."

"Let's hope," Jeff said.

There was silence for a moment, until Andi asked, "Jeff, who came up with this idea?"

More silence. Then Jeff said, "Well . . . I did."

"Then let me tell you something, Jeffrey Daniel Michaels, if we pull this off, I'll forgive you for going to Coach Crist."

"Seriously? I'll be off the hook?"

"Close," Andi said. She had a big smile on her face. She suspected Jeff did, too.

When Andi walked into the principal's office the next morning, she was surprised to see Mr. Block standing at Ms. Dumas's desk talking to her. When he saw Andi, he frowned instantly but said in a polite tone, "Can I help you with something, Ms. Carillo?"

"Mr. Block, I know how busy you are, but do you think you could meet with us at lunch again today?"

"What's the subject?" Mr. Block asked, clearly skeptical.

"Our basketball team," Andi answered.

"I don't know that there's anything more to discuss," he said.

"Well, sir, we do and we'd be grateful if you could give us just a few more minutes," Andi said, keeping her voice as soft as possible.

Mr. Block sighed and looked at his watch for no apparent reason.

"Fine," he said, after what seemed like a long silence. "Come straight here after your fourth-period classes. I can give you about ten minutes."

Andi suspected they'd need more than that. She also suspected he had more than that.

"Thank you, sir," she said, turning to leave before he could change his mind.

Andi called Jamie to explain what was going on so she could help spread the word with the team. Then she texted Eleanor, Maria, and Lisa to fill them in. Like her, everyone had been disbelieving.

"Talk about going from bust to boom," Jamie had said.

Next, Andi texted Coach Dunphy directly—Jeff had given her his cell number—to confirm an eleven-thirty meeting in the principal's office. Just before she turned her phone off for first period, he texted back: *See you there.*

It had been decided that Jamie and Andi would again represent the team. Last night, Jeff and Andi had discussed the idea of one of her parents coming in to explain how Coach Dunphy could take over the team without breaking any school or conference rules. They had decided against it. If Block needed to talk to a lawyer, Andi's parents would be available. Meanwhile, Jeff had promised to get his dad to bring Coach Dunphy up to speed about her parents' advice.

The morning crawled by. Andi was asked several times about the team, "firing" Coach Josephson, and the season being over. She'd just answered with a smile, "It's never over till it's over."

When the fourth-period bell finally rang, she dodged the hallway traffic and ran all the way to the principal's office. She hoped Coach Dunphy would be on time. She arrived at the same moment as Jamie. Together, they walked into the school office.

Ms. Dumas was standing at her desk, mouth open. Coach Fran Dunphy, dressed in a blue pinstriped suit, was standing in front of her with a wide smile on his face.

Andi and Jamie introduced themselves.

"The leaders of the revolution," he said with a smile.

The door to Mr. Block's office opened. When the principal saw Coach Dunphy, his mouth dropped open, too.

"Mr. Block, thanks for taking some time," Coach Dunphy said, extending a hand. "I'm Fran Dunphy."

Block took the offered hand and stared. Apparently, he'd forgotten his own name.

31

ONCE MR. BLOCK RECOVERED HIS COMPOSURE, HE INVITED Andi, Jamie, and Coach Dunphy into his office. Ms. Dumas came in and asked if anyone would like anything to drink—a first in Andi's previous visits to the principal's office.

Mr. Block asked for some coffee—Andi suspected he might prefer something a lot stronger—and Coach Dunphy said a bottle of water would be nice. Ms. Dumas scurried out.

Mr. Block looked at Coach Dunphy and said, "Coach, it's an honor to meet you, I've followed your career for a long time . . ."

"Too long," Coach Dunphy said with a smile.

Mr. Block laughed uncomfortably at the joke, then continued. "That said, with all due respect, what are you doing here?"

Coach Dunphy looked at Andi and Jamie to make sure they didn't want to answer the question before responding.

"I understand you need someone to coach your sixth-grade girls' team the rest of the season," he said. "As you know, I'm retired, and my weekday afternoons are free right now. So I'm here to offer some help."

"You mean coach the team?" Mr. Block said—in a tone that made it clear that if Coach Dunphy had said he was here to buy the school he wouldn't have been any less stunned.

"Yes, exactly," Coach Dunphy said.

Mr. Block was about to answer when Ms. Dumas returned with a mug of coffee for Mr. Block and a bottle of water for Coach Dunphy. Mr. Block took a sip of the coffee, leaned back, and said, "I'm curious, how exactly did you hear about our problem?"

He was looking at Andi when he said it.

"Well, Tom Michaels and I have been friends for years," Coach Dunphy said. "Tom came to speak to my class at Temple last night, and he and his son Jeff filled me in on what was going on here. Very unfortunate situation, obviously. I'm sure you don't want the girls to lose their season, so I said I thought maybe I could help."

"If the season ends, it'll be the girls who brought it

on themselves," Mr. Block said, the ice that had been in his voice a day earlier returning.

Coach Dunphy shrugged. "I'm not here to judge that," he said. "I'm here to see if I can help a bunch of kids out."

Mr. Block took another sip of his coffee, then folded his hands on the desk. Andi sensed he was stalling.

"Well, it's very generous of you to want to help out," he said finally. "But, unfortunately, it's impossible for a nonemployee to supervise students in any capacity." He shrugged as if to say "end of story."

Coach Dunphy smiled. "I understand that. But I've talked to a couple of lawyers who tell me that I can sign a contract—you can pay me one dollar—making me an employee."

Block seemed surprised by the quick response, but rallied: "There's also the union issue. You can't possibly join our teachers' union."

"You have lots of employees on staff—your assistant out there, I'd imagine for one," Coach Dunphy said, nodding in the direction of the outer office, "who aren't in the union."

Mr. Block was silent. He sat back in his chair, leaned forward, picked up the coffee again, drank, and sat back one more time.

"I'm going to have to give this some thought," he

said. "I need to talk to the superintendent of schools and see what she says."

He stood up to end the meeting.

Coach Dunphy didn't move.

"The girls have a game tomorrow," he said. "They didn't practice yesterday. I'd like to be able to meet them and get to know them a little as players before coaching a game. I understand they practice at four fifteen. Can we try to get this done by then?"

Mr. Block shook his head. "Well, even if we get approval, even if I decide to go ahead, I don't see how it can be done by then."

"Why not?" Coach Dunphy said. "You must have a standard employee contract that just needs to be filled in with my information, dates, salary. That shouldn't take long."

Mr. Block was clearly taken aback by Coach Dunphy's aggressiveness. Andi was surprised, too. The Fran Dunphy she'd always read about was about as polite as anyone in sports. Clearly, though, he didn't have much patience for bureaucratic stalling tactics.

"Leave me your cell phone number," Mr. Block said. "I'll be in touch."

"Soon, I hope," Coach Dunphy said.

He stood up, put out his hand, and said, "Look forward to working with you."

After shaking hands with the principal, he led Andi and Jamie out of the office.

The word that Fran Dunphy had been in the principal's office volunteering to coach the sixth-grade girls' team spread through the school like wildfire. The entire cafeteria knew before lunch was over, and so did the faculty—tipped off, apparently, by Ms. Dumas.

As soon as last period was over, Jeff went to find Andi. There was a text from Coach Dunphy waiting for him when he turned on his phone: *Nothing yet.*

Andi had gotten the same text. She and Jeff were talking in front of her locker when both of their phones buzzed. A new text from Coach Dunphy.

Block just asked me to come to his office—alone. I think you and Jamie should be there.

Andi looked at Jeff. "What do you think?"

"I think he's right," Jeff said. "It's your team."

Andi texted back asking when the meeting would take place.

Five minutes. I'm right down the street at the Madison Diner.

See you there, Andi texted back, and then called Jamie to loop her in.

Getting to the principal's office was a challenge,

since it seemed as if everyone in the hallway wanted to know what was going on.

She was—unfortunately—the first to arrive.

"I believe this is a private meeting," Ms. Dumas said when she walked in. "Adults only."

Before Andi could respond, Coach Dunphy walked in with Jamie right behind him.

"I asked the girls to join us," Coach Dunphy said. "It's *their* team."

"Well, we'll see what Mr. Block has to say about this," Ms. Dumas said, just as Mr. Block—right on cue—appeared in the doorway.

"It's fine, Ms. Dumas. Come on in, everyone."

They sat in the same three seats they had occupied earlier.

Mr. Block got right to the point. "I've talked to the superintendent of schools and I've also talked to counsel and I'm told that we can do this," he said. "I'll be honest and tell you, Coach Dunphy, I'm not thrilled by this. I understand you want to do this for the girls, but I'm not a big believer in rewarding misbehavior."

"The misbehavior here was Coach Josephson's," Jamie said, surprising Andi—especially since she was thinking the exact same thing.

"We'll agree to disagree on that point, Ms. Bronson," Mr. Block said, waving a hand.

"Mr. Dunphy, I'm going to allow this—at least for

now. I know my faculty won't be happy, but for the moment I will say I made the decision for the sake of the players."

"That's the only reason for you to make it," Coach Dunphy said quietly.

"I'll need you to fill out paperwork before practice today, which I'm told is at four fifteen. Ms. Dumas will give you what you need."

He stood up. The meeting was over. He didn't extend a hand, just waved in the direction of the door—and Ms. Dumas.

Andi didn't care. They had a coach—a *real* coach.

Jeff had wondered if Coach C would have anything to say about the possibility of Fran Dunphy coaching the girls. By the time the boys gathered for their three-fifteen practice, the entire school was aware of what was going on, so there was no reason to pretend otherwise.

He didn't have to wait long for an answer.

"I know you guys have heard about what's going on with the girls' team," Coach C said when they got to center court for their prepractice talk. "I can tell you the faculty isn't going to be happy if Mr. Block allows Fran Dunphy to coach the sixth-grade girls. The support for Coach Josephson is pretty close to unanimous."

Then he smiled. "On the other hand, we're talking about a Hall of Fame coach and I'm sure he is doing this for good reasons, not bad ones. But we'll see if it happens. Right now, we've got a game at King of Prussia tomorrow and they're the only unbeaten team in the league. We beat them, we're a game out of first place. So, let's focus on that."

They practiced hard, with Jeff and Ron Arlow back to splitting time at the point. Jeff knew it was wrong, but he couldn't help but wish that Arlow had been a little bit sicker and hadn't come back to school so fast.

At 4:10 p.m., Jeff noticed members of the girls' team coming into the gym dressed in practice gear. That *had* to mean Mr. Block had decided to allow Fran Dunphy to coach the team. Sure enough, a moment later, Coach Dunphy himself walked onto the court, wearing a maroon T-shirt that said TEMPLE BASKETBALL on it. He stood at the baseline with Andi and Jamie and watched as the boys wrapped up.

Jeff *knew* Coach C had seen the girls and their new coach, but he gave no indication that he'd noticed anything unusual. A moment later, practice was over and they circled their coach again. He reminded them to be on the bus at two thirty the next day, asked Arlow and Jeff to lead a cheer—"Beat KOP!"—and sent them to the locker room.

As the girls took the court to warm up, Jeff was amused to see Coach C stopping to shake hands with Coach Dunphy. They spoke briefly, before Coach Dunphy gave Coach C a friendly pat on the back and headed to midcourt. Jeff thought for a second about running over to say hello, then decided it was a bad idea. Arlow had already made a crack in the locker room about Jeff and "his daddy" riding to Andi's rescue again. He didn't need to make a point of the fact that he knew Coach Dunphy.

Coach Dunphy had told the girls to warm up the way they normally did—which meant two layup lines. Andi could feel the adrenaline pumping through her and could tell everyone else felt the same way.

After several minutes, she heard Coach Dunphy say in a clear voice: "Everyone, here please."

He wasn't wearing a whistle. It was pretty apparent he didn't need one. Everyone raced to the center jump circle.

"Before we start, I'd like each of you to introduce yourself to me," he said. "I will try to be sure I learn everyone's name as quickly as possible. I already know some of you, but I need to know all of you. And, even though I should be able to figure it out watching you play, tell me what you think of as your position."

He looked directly at Maria Medley. "You can skip the part about your position."

Everyone laughed.

They went around the circle. Andi and Jamie went last.

Then they did some warm-up drills and returned to the circle.

"I asked Jamie and Andi to give some idea of how you guys have been lining up. On their recommendation, here are the five I want as starters—at least for now: Bronson, Carillo, Medley, Dove, and Carmichael." The second team—for now—will be Jolie, Allison, Mearns, Lee, and Eisen. Jensen and Bonilla will sub in as the day goes along."

The scrimmage was spirited. Coach Dunphy occasionally said "Stop, everyone" or "Hang on" to make corrections on things like footwork or how to set a screen. It was the first teaching the girls had received all winter.

When they were finished, he gathered them again and told them he was honored to have the chance to coach them. "I don't know a thing about King of Prussia's team," he said. "We'll all have to learn as we go tomorrow."

He looked around the circle and then added, "Jamie has suggested to me that I make Andi Carillo her co-captain. Any objections?"

Everyone shouted, "No!"

Coach Dunphy nodded. "Okay then, Jamie, Andi, get 'em in."

Jamie hadn't warned Andi about this. Now she looked at her and said, "Lead the way, captain."

Andi was beaming. She stepped into the circle and waited for Jamie, and they put their hands up together: "Let's go one and oh!" she said—her meaning clear.

They stepped in and shouted, "Let's go one and oh!"

Everyone was grinning as they headed to the locker room.

32

ANDI NOTICED THE CAMERA CREWS SETTING UP THEIR
equipment as soon as she and the rest of the Merion
sixth-grade girls' team came onto the court the next
afternoon to warm up. *Oh, no*, she thought, *I should
have known.*

Clearly, word had spread quickly in the Philadelphia media that the great Fran Dunphy was going to
coach a sixth-grade girls' basketball team. Andi should
have realized that was inevitable but hadn't given it
any thought. She'd just been so happy to have a real
coach in charge that she hadn't thought about the
ramifications.

The first of those ramifications had been evident
during school. When she passed teachers in the hallway, they all looked away. At one point, during earth
science, she'd raised her hand to answer a question

and the teacher, Ms. Marx, had looked at her and said, "Oh, Andrea, let's give the other kids who don't have the answers for everything a chance."

Pretty nasty, Andi thought. It also probably reflected the way a lot of the faculty felt. The presence of the media was only going to make things worse. She dreaded being asked to talk after the game—win or lose.

By the time the game started, the little gym was full. Andi guessed the place seated about five hundred people. The average attendance for most sixth-grade basketball games might have been fifty on a big night: family, close friends, a few kids who liked basketball. Now there were people standing in the corners of the gym because the bleachers were packed.

"Good thing no one's called the fire marshal," Eleanor whispered as they watched the King of Prussia starters get introduced.

Like Merion, King of Prussia was 2–2 in conference play. But the Merion team that had been 2–2 was very different from this Merion team. To begin with, the best five players started. What's more, the team now had a coach who knew how to make adjustments during the game. Merion bolted to an 18–8 lead at the end of the first quarter—Andi making two threes and a layup off a beautiful pass from Maria to lead the way.

With Coach Dunphy going to the bench, KOP cut the margin to 27–20 at halftime, but the starters blew the game open again in the third quarter. The final, with the bench playing the entire fourth quarter, was 54–42. It hadn't really been that close.

The building was loud throughout. More than once a cheer started that said simply: "Dunph! Dunph! Dunph!"

It was pretty clear whose side the students were on.

Once they reached the locker room, Coach Dunphy told them how proud he was of the way they'd played and that he hoped this was the start of something good—and fun. Then, he brought up the media horde that awaited them.

"I will, of course, talk to everyone and explain why I'm here," he said. "It's up to the rest of you whether you want to talk to anyone. I know there is some unrest among your teachers about this, so if you don't want to talk because it might cause trouble for you in your classes, I will explain that to all the reporters."

That sounded like a great idea to Andi. Eleanor Dove raised her hand.

"Coach, I think one of us should speak for the players," she said. "And, unless I'm wrong, I'm pretty sure Andi doesn't want it to be her."

Andi was nodding her head vigorously, agreeing with Eleanor.

"So, how about Jamie?" Eleanor said.

Jamie clearly didn't want to do it, either. "It was a long day in class today," she said.

Maria jumped to her feet. "I'll do it," she said. "I honestly don't care if the teachers are upset. We did what we had to do. That's exactly what I'll say."

Coach Dunphy looked around. "Everyone okay with Maria being the spokesperson?"

The answering shouts were unanimous.

"Thanks, Maria," Andi said after their postgame cheer.

"Hey," Maria said. "Who can get mad at me? I'm adorable."

By the time Andi showered and dressed and walked back into the gym, she could see Coach Dunphy surrounded by cameras, tape recorders, and notebooks. Maria was still in the locker room, probably primping, Andi figured, for her close-up.

She was glad to see that everyone was focused on Coach Dunphy and walked quickly to where her mom, who had come to the game, was waiting for her.

"Great playing—by all of you," her mother said before Andi cut her off.

"Let's get out of here before any of them"—she nodded in the direction of the media—"notice me."

"Camera shy?" her mom said with a big smile.

"Absolutely. Anyway, we voted to let Maria be the spokesperson for the players."

"How'd that happen?" her mother said as they walked quickly to the gym door.

"She volunteered."

"Brave girl."

Andi wasn't sure if Maria was brave or just unafraid. Maybe they were the same thing. Either way, she was relieved. Until her cell phone buzzed with a text.

I saw you and your mom duck out. I understand why you don't want media attention. But I'd like to talk to you—at least on background.

Andi groaned. Leave it to Stevie Thomas to be the one seeing her leave. When her mom asked what the groan was for, she read her the text. "Text him back and tell him you'll talk to him as long as he doesn't quote you. He did say background—that means no quotes."

"But, Mom . . ."

"He was very fair to you in the fall and he didn't write anything after that first game when he could have."

She was right. She texted him back and he asked if he could call in about an hour.

Fine, she texted back. Why was it, she thought, that nothing was ever simple?

The boys were also greeted by a media crowd when they walked into the gym at King of Prussia. When Jeff and

Andi compared notes later, it was clear it wasn't nearly as big a crowd as the one back at Merion, but it was not insubstantial.

"What is the deal with all this?" Danny said to Jeff as they warmed up.

"The Eagles' season is over," Jeff said, grimacing at the memory of their loss in Detroit. "The Flyers don't play tonight; the Sixers are out of town. And the high school games are at night. So, they're all bored and here."

He knew he was right because his father had told him he was working the newsroom that night to coordinate the high school coverage since it would be the focus of the ten o'clock news show. Or maybe not, Jeff thought, looking at the cameras.

The media—and everyone else—got to see a very good game.

KOP led 45–43 with ninety seconds to play. Coach C called time.

"Let's shorten this game a little bit," he said in the huddle. "Jeff, Ron, you guys control the ball outside for a while. We aren't playing for the last shot—not down two—but wait for my signal before you start the offense. They're not going to attack because they're ahead and their big guy has four fouls."

He looked at Jeff and Arlow. "You guys understand? Share the ball. No shot until I say so."

They both nodded.

Coach C was right; no one from KOP attacked as Jeff and Arlow played catch with each other on the perimeter. A couple of times Danny Diskin or Eric Billings came out to catch a pass when a defender moved into the passing lane.

Finally, with thirty seconds left, Coach Crist stood and yelled, "One-four, Michaels, take the point."

That meant he wanted them to run the same play that had won the Main Line game: Jeff controlling the ball up top, getting into the lane, and creating a shot for someone. Jeff's defender was up tight on him, not wanting to give him space for a three.

Jeff made a quick head-fake, put his head down, and drove the lane. Two defenders closed on him and he flipped the ball to Arlow—who was open for an instant. A defender ran at him, but it was too late. Arlow released the shot and stood posing, knowing it was going in.

Only it didn't go in. It hit the back rim. There was a wild scramble and Danny eventually tipped the ball back in the direction of midcourt. Jeff ran it down. The clock was under ten seconds. Arlow had his hand up, calling for the ball again.

Jeff made a pass-fake as if he were going to throw him the ball and then, with his defender diving left to try to deflect the pass, he pulled up just outside the three-point line and took the shot. The ball hit the bottom of the net with the clock at :02. One of the KOP kids grabbed it and tried to throw it to a teammate—who did catch it just shy of midcourt. But his heave was short and wide left as the buzzer sounded.

Final: Merion 46, KOP 45.

Everyone—except Arlow, of course—mobbed Jeff, who kept trying to point at Danny. "He deflected it back to me," he kept saying. "Mob him."

"Shut up, Michaels," Danny said, laughing. "You're the hero. Enjoy it."

Jeff decided he was right. So he enjoyed it.

Three schools: Main Line, King of Prussia, and Haverford were now tied for first place in the conference at 4–1; Merion and Ardmore were both 3–2. Jeff had wondered how Haverford had lost a game but got his answer in the handshake line: Michael Jordan had apparently rolled an ankle and hadn't played in his team's game against KOP.

The kid from KOP who gave him this news said to him, "Wish you'd been out today the way Jordan was when we played them."

"I'm no Jordan," Jeff answered, laughing.

"No kidding," the kid said. "But you're pretty good in the mortal division of this league."

After Coach C congratulated them on the win and told them that they were now a game out of first place in the conference, he told them what they already knew.

"There are a lot of media types out there," he said. "They aren't here because this was a big game in the conference. And Michaels, they aren't going to want to talk to you because you hit the game-winning shot." He smiled. "I think you all know that. All I can say is, be careful what you say. You know my colleagues on the faculty aren't happy about what's gone on with the girls' team and I'm sure they'll all be watching, listening, and reading tonight and over the weekend. Don't make Monday difficult. If it's going to be a problem, let it be the girls' problem. Our biggest concern right now should be Bryn Mawr Tech coming to our place on Tuesday. Everybody understand?"

The talk sobered them up a little after the postgame celebration. When Jeff came back into the gym, he heard someone calling his name. He looked up and saw Brian Schiff, who had worked at NBC Sports–Philly so long that the joke in the newsroom, according to his dad, was that Shifty—as everyone called him—had interviewed Ben Franklin shortly after his discovery that lightning produced electricity.

"The Eagles were off that day," Shifty would say in response. "Ben was a good talker."

Shifty was walking in his direction, hand out. "Great game, Jeff, congrats," he said. "How about talking to us for a minute?"

"But not about the game, right?" Jeff said.

Shifty smiled. "I'd rather talk about the game and your shot, you know that. But . . ."

"I know," Jeff said putting a hand up. "It's okay."

Shifty was producing; the person on camera was Kelli Johnson, who was very tall and very pretty. His dad had told Jeff she had come to Philadelphia from San Francisco recently.

"As soon as we finish with this kid, we'll get you in and out of here," Shifty said.

Jeff looked around. Another camera crew from Channel 3 was talking to Coach Crist, and several people with tape recorders stood in a circle around Danny.

The kid talking to Kelli Johnson was Arlow. They had apparently just started a moment earlier, so Jeff and Shifty stood off to the side.

Kelli Johnson was midquestion. "So, you *don't* support the girls' team decision to stand up to their coach, then?" she said.

"Not even a little bit. I played with Andi Carillo during soccer season. She was a good player, but like a lot of girls, she's a whiner—no offense. That's what this is about."

Kelli Johnson didn't ask another question, didn't

even bother to thank Arlow. She looked at Jeff and said, "Please tell me you're Tom Michaels's son."

Jeff smiled. "That's me."

Arlow shot Kelli Johnson a disgusted look as he walked away. "Oh, yeah," he said. "I'm the bad guy for telling the truth. Go ahead, Michaels, tell everyone how wonderful your girlfriend is."

He stalked away.

Jeff shrugged and said to his retreating back, "Happy to."

33

BRIAN SCHIFF FORMALLY INTRODUCED JEFF TO KELLI JOHN-
son. Jeff was tempted to ask if he could stand on a box
for the interview. In high heels, she was easily six feet
tall. She seemed to read his mind.

"Don't worry, Jeff, we'll only be on camera together
for a few seconds—if at all," she said. "I'll ask the first
question and then it'll be just you on a one-shot. We
might not even show me asking the question."

Jeff knew what a one-shot was—one person on
camera—after years of hearing his dad talk in TV
lingo.

"Thanks, Ms. Johnson," he said.

"Kelli," she said.

She was, Jeff decided, as nice as she was tall.

Not surprisingly, the first question was about his
role in Fran Dunphy becoming the coach of the girls'

team. He had decided to just tell the truth. He walked through his dad's friendship with Coach Dunphy, the class, the dinner, and his idea.

"So, you just thought of it on the spot?" Kelli Johnson said.

"It was almost like I was thinking out loud," Jeff said. "I said it almost the second I thought it. I never thought it could actually happen."

"Why do you think Coach Dunphy agreed to do this?" she asked.

Jeff was ready for that one. "He's spent his whole life trying to do two things: help his players grow as people and, of course, win games. This was a chance to help out some kids who really needed him."

She thanked him, turned back to the camera, and said, "Michael, back to you."

"So, Mr. Barkann is in the studio tonight?" Jeff asked her after Shifty had said, "Perfect. Wrap it."

"No, he's actually at your school. My interviews will be intercut with his."

"Wow. This will be a long piece, then, I guess."

She nodded. "Oh yeah. This is an amazing story."

Jeff knew she was right.

Jeff had texted Andi to congratulate her on the girls' win and to report that the boys had pulled out another close one. She called him as soon as she got home so they could exchange details.

She was excited to hear he'd hit the game-winning shot, but discouraged when he reported that Arlow had attacked her when talking to the TV reporter.

"Did the reporter say anything when he said that?" she asked.

"Not a word," he answered. "I think she just wanted to be done with him."

"Any chance they might not run it?"

"I doubt it," he said. "You know how TV is. I'll check with my dad and let you know."

Andi sighed, hung up, and remembered she'd forgotten her promise to talk to Stevie Thomas. He called soon after dinner, saying he had waited a while longer than they had planned, to give her time to eat.

It was hard not to like the guy.

After they had again agreed that Andi wouldn't be quoted on anything, he asked her to walk through what had happened, leading to the petition.

"I talked to Jamie Bronson," he said. "She said she was jealous of you when practice started because you'd become such a big star during soccer season, but realized once the season started that Coach Josephson was treating you badly and that the team needed you to play."

Andi had never had that conversation with Jamie but was grateful to hear it.

"How nervous are you about dealing with angry teachers going forward?" Stevie asked.

"Very," Andi answered honestly. "I hope their anger will pass, but who knows? It's entirely possible that the more we win, the more upset they'll become because it will prove us right."

"Dunph says it's hard to judge by one practice and one game, but he thinks you guys are good."

"We're certainly a lot better with him coaching us," Andi said. "And you know what, you can quote me on that."

She knew she was hardly going out on a limb saying it. Stevie laughed. "I can't imagine anyone disagreeing with that comment."

Soon after she hung up with Stevie, Andi got a text from Jeff: *Dad says Arlow stuff is airing. His boss said, "It's part of the story. We can't bury it."*

She watched the station's ten o'clock news show with her parents. The lead story was a preview of the Flyers game the next afternoon against the Islanders. The second story was about a buzzer-beating high school game in the vaunted Philadelphia Catholic League.

"And when we come back," anchor Dei Lynam said, "yet another remarkable story involving sixth graders at Merion Middle School."

After the break, Lynam introduced the piece by saying simply, "In the fall, we reported on the exploits of young Andi Carillo after she was initially refused a spot on the boys' soccer team at Merion Middle School. Eventually, she became a star. Now, young Ms. Carillo is part of the girls' basketball team at Merion Middle, but—at least right now—she is *not* the star of the story. Michael Barkann begins our reporting from Merion Middle School."

Lynam disappeared and a shot of Fran Dunphy standing in front of the bench and talking to Maria Medley appeared. Over it came Barkann's voice.

"You are not hallucinating, folks, that *is* the great Fran Dunphy coaching the Merion Middle School sixth-grade girls' team to a victory over King of Prussia this afternoon. Dunphy retired from Temple a year ago with five hundred and eighty victories, but now, he's back coaching under very different circumstances."

Dunphy came on camera next, talking about a casual dinner conversation with his old friend Tom Michaels and his son, Jeff, that had led to Jeff telling him the sixth-grade girls needed a coach or their season would be over.

"I've got some free time at this stage of my life," he said. "How could I say no?"

Maria was next, talking about how amazing it was to be playing for Coach Dunphy. Barkann pointed out that the reason he was there was that no one on the faculty was willing to replace Coach Josephson after the team had petitioned for her ouster.

Maria hit it out of the park.

"Trust me, we didn't take that step lightly," she said. "We tried to understand that Coach Josephson was coaching for the first time. But her ego got in the way of trying to help us become a better team. She sat Andi Carillo on the bench when she was arguably our best player. She made a racially offensive comment in front of the whole team that I think all of us were offended by. We didn't know what else to do."

"Wow," Andi's dad said. "She looks eleven, sounds eleven, but talks like she's about thirty."

Andi agreed.

Soon after, Barkann said, "Let's go now to Kelli Johnson, who is with the Merion sixth-grade boys' team at King of Prussia Middle School."

"Feels like they're covering the Eagles," Andi's mom said.

Kelli Johnson came on camera for a moment, talking about Jeff's role in Fran Dunphy's hiring to coach the girls, and then his role in winning the game for Merion. The last few seconds of the game rolled on camera, and Andi got to see Jeff grabbing Danny Diskin's tip back, making the winning shot, and being mobbed by his teammates. She felt very proud of him.

Then he was on camera talking about how he'd come up with the idea to ask Coach Dunphy to coach the girls.

When he finished, Kelli Johnson was back on camera, saying, "Dei, unfortunately, not everyone on the boys' team supports the girls." And there was Arlow, with a caption identifying him as BOYS' CO-CAPTAIN, spewing about Andi into the camera.

Andi had briefed her parents about Arlow. Even so, her dad drew back as he finished and said, "Something's wrong with that kid. Seriously wrong."

Kelli Johnson had tossed back to Barkann, who shook his head and said, "I've dealt with Andi Carillo a good bit, Kelli, and I can honestly say she is anything but a whiner."

That made Andi feel very good. Then Barkann added, "Dei, we requested interviews while we were here with former coach Amy Josephson and principal Arthur Block, and both turned us down. Back to you."

Stevie Thomas's story on the front page of Sunday's *Philadelphia Inquirer* sports section included a sentence very high up that said, "Lawrence Gutman, an eighth-grade chemistry teacher who is the chairman of the Merion Middle School branch of the teachers' union, said the union plans to seek an injunction

Monday preventing Fran Dunphy from continuing to coach on the grounds that only union members should be allowed to directly supervise students."

When Andi showed that to her parents, they looked at one another. "I've got a pretrial hearing Monday," her mother said.

Her dad nodded. "I can do it. But we should check with Tom Michaels to make sure Dunphy hasn't already got someone."

They did that—through Jeff, who called Andi back to say that Coach Dunphy would be delighted to have Tony Carillo represent him and, by extension, the entire girls' team.

"He wants to know when this will come to court and if he needs to be there," Jeff told Andi.

Her dad nodded. "Tell him to give me a call. When you seek an injunction like this, they usually get you in front of a judge right away. It'll probably be Tuesday, but it could be Monday afternoon. And yes, if he can make it, he should be there. Better he answer the judge's questions than me."

Fran Dunphy called a few minutes later. The two men talked for a while. After hanging up, Andi's dad said that technically, the school board should be fighting the injunction on the school's behalf, but he wasn't terribly confident about how enthusiastic that defense would be.

"They could even go so far as to say, 'We will abide by anything you do, your honor,' and leave it at that."

"Which," Jeannie Carillo added, "won't help our case at all."

"No, it won't," Tony Carillo said. "It will depend, ultimately, on which judge we get. If it's a pro-union judge, we're probably dead. If it's not, it will still depend on how he or she feels about sixth graders for all intents and purposes overthrowing a coach who is doing the job for almost nothing."

"Coach Dunphy's doing it for one dollar," Andi said.

"Good point," her dad said. "I'll use that."

It was lunchtime the next day that they found out who the judge was and when the hearing would be held. The judge was Jacob Levin, who, according to Andi's dad, was known as a very pro-union judge who had been supported by the local unions in Philadelphia throughout a long career on the bench. The hearing was at nine a.m. the next morning.

"Given that you guys have a game tomorrow afternoon, he's likely to rule right away," Tony Carillo told his daughter. "And, just being honest, I'm not really optimistic. The school system just filed a brief saying they had no objection to the injunction."

"In other words, they're more or less agreeing with the union," Andi said.

"No," her dad said. "They're *completely* agreeing with the union. We're going into court tomorrow as big-time underdogs."

Andi was reminded of the biggest upset in college basketball history: The University of Maryland–Baltimore County—a sixteenth seed—beating Virginia—a number-one seed—in the NCAA basketball tournament. Prior to that game, number-one seeds had a 135–0 record against number-sixteen seeds.

"Is this Virginia vs. UMBC?" she asked her dad.

He smiled. "Only if we're lucky," her dad said.

34

FRAN DUNPHY HAD ALWAYS UNDERSTOOD THAT DEALING with the media came with the job when you were a college basketball coach. But he was never one of those coaches who craved attention the way some do.

Now, as he walked up the steps to the Philadelphia courthouse on Tuesday morning and saw the camera crews rolling, he could only shake his head and think, *What in the world have I gotten myself into?*

Jeff Michaels's request, while a bit off the wall, had seemed a reasonable one. A bunch of kids needed help; he had the time and he had the experience to help. So, why not?

The answer was now right in front of him. He was in the middle of what was becoming a media maelstrom.

No good deed goes unpunished, he thought as he reached the top of the steps and several reporters—men and women he knew—asked him to stop and answer a few questions. "After we have a ruling," he said. That was what Tony Carillo had told him to say.

The lawyer was waiting for Dunphy in the lobby, just beyond the metal detectors everyone had to clear to get into the building. They had never met, but Carillo recognized him and walked over and introduced himself.

"Tom Michaels tells me we've got an uphill fight," Dunphy said.

Carillo nodded. "Yes—and no. Judge Levin has about ten grandchildren, so even though he's a pro-union guy, I think he'll take into account what ruling against us would do to twelve kids."

They walked up the stairs to the third floor, where the courtroom was located. It was 8:55 a.m., and when they walked to the door, the security guard put up a hand and said, "No seats." Then he recognized both men.

"Sorry, counselor," he said. Turning to Dunphy he said, "Good luck in there, Coach. Lot of folks pulling for you."

Dunphy shook his hand briefly, then followed Carillo inside.

The guard hadn't been kidding. The courtroom was packed. It looked like the scene from *Miracle on 34th Street* when the judge had to rule on the existence of

Santa Claus. This wasn't nearly that important. It was about sixth-grade girls' basketball.

Carillo stopped for a moment to say hello to the union's lawyer. He introduced her as Carol Burmeister. She was, Dunphy guessed, about thirty-five. Dressed in a tailored suit, her dark hair cut stylishly, she had an easy smile.

"Big fan," she said to him. "Went to Penn."

As they walked away, Carillo said softly, "Don't be fooled by her looks or her charm. She's as smart and tough as anyone in this courthouse."

"That's certainly good news," Dunphy answered.

Judge Levin came in a moment later and everyone stood. When they all took their seats, the judge said good morning to the two lawyers and then said, "Ms. Burmeister, you're up."

A bit informal, but all business.

Carol Burmeister was as good as advertised: She railed on the injustice of the girls signing a petition against their coach, who was being paid the grand total of $250 for the season and giving up her free time after school so they could *have* a team; she pointed out the dangerous precedent of letting someone "walk off the street" to supervise eleven- and twelve-year-olds, someone who had no middle-school teaching experience, adding, "with all due respect to Coach Dunphy." She pointed out that this sort of thing would undermine the union, because schools at all levels—up to high school—might hire retired coaches looking for something to do and take away full-time and part-time jobs from "legitimate teachers." She finished by saying that if the judge wished, she could very quickly produce Coach Josephson and both the women who had worked as her assistants to testify to the fact that a group of "budding adolescents" had badly overreacted to the discipline the coach had tried to bring to the team.

Levin leaned forward in his chair and pointed at Tony Carillo. "Mr. Carillo, your turn."

The good news was that Tony Carillo had anticipated Burmeister's arguments. He pointed out that there was probably nothing more cliquish than a group of, "to quote Ms. Burmeister, 'budding adolescents,' and yet all twelve girls—including the starters and the team captain, had felt the situation dire enough to sign the petition—knowing there could be serious consequences.

"It wasn't as if Coach Dunphy was waiting in the wings, Judge," he said. "The first thing that happened was that the school principal shut down the season. Since then, I'm told almost all the girls have been subjected to—at best—ice-cold treatment from other teachers in the school."

At that point, Carol Burmeister objected.

"Hearsay," she said.

"Sustained," the judge said.

Tony Carillo nodded at Burmeister, then continued.

"There's no precedent being set here, Your Honor. This is a one-time thing, eight games. Coach Dunphy has no interest in coaching these girls beyond that. He was asked by a friend to rescue these girls from losing their season. Your ruling could be restricted to this case as a one-time-only thing."

"Mr. Carillo, I don't need you to tell me what my ruling can and can't do," Levin said sternly.

"Of course not, Your Honor. Thank you." If the judge's admonition shook Tony Carillo, he didn't show it.

"The bottom line here is the union will not be hurt by Coach Dunphy coaching these girls for seven more games, but the *girls* will be hurt if their season is cancelled because the union is trying to make a point about kids speaking their minds."

"Objection."

Judge Levin looked at Burmeister. "Overruled. Counsel has the right to express an opinion . . . Mr. Carillo, would Coach Dunphy object to coming up to the witness stand so I can ask him a few questions?"

Tony looked at Dunphy. "Happy to," Dunphy said, standing up and walking to the witness stand. The judge reached down to shake his hand. "It's a pleasure to meet you, sir," he said. "I'm a Princeton grad, but I forgive you."

Everyone laughed at that.

"Sir, you aren't under oath," Levin said once Dunphy had taken a seat. "This isn't a formal hearing that way. But I'd appreciate honest answers to my questions."

"Guaranteed," Dunphy answered, looking the judge in the eye.

For the next ten minutes, Judge Levin walked Dunphy through everything that had happened since the previous Wednesday night, when he'd gone to dinner with Tom and Jeff Michaels at the Capital Grille.

"If I rule in your favor, you promise not to come back and coach at Penn again?" he said to more laughter.

"I promise that regardless, Your Honor. But you'd probably be better off with me coaching again than with Steve Donahue there."

More laughter. Dunphy wondered if the judge's jokes meant anything. The judge thanked him, and he returned to sit next to Carillo.

Judge Levin said nothing for a moment, then leaned forward again. "Both sides have made compelling cases," he said. "I understand why the union would be upset about this and see potential danger in it down the line. I also understand why Coach Dunphy would want to help a group of kids who just want to play basketball.

"I think I need to hear from the parties directly involved before I rule. Ms. Burmeister, how soon can you get Ms. Josephson in here?"

"Well, Your Honor, she's a teacher and it's a school day . . ."

"I understand that. But she must have a lunch hour and surely someone can cover for her for a class or two if need be."

Burmeister nodded her assent.

"Mr. Carillo, how about getting at least one player here?"

"Lunch is at eleven thirty, Your Honor. I'm sure I can have someone here by noon, latest," Tony Carillo said.

"Good. We'll recess until noon."

Andi saw the text as soon as she pulled her phone from her backpack while walking out of her fourth-period class. Her first thought was that the judge had already made a ruling—which probably wasn't good.

She was wrong. *Meet me in usual spot outside right now. Already signed you out. Will explain.*

When Jamie and Jeff came running down the hall

to ask if she'd heard from her father, she showed them the text.

"Better get going," Jamie said.

"Good luck—whatever it is," Jeff added.

Andi headed for the door, hearing shouts from various kids asking if there had been a ruling from the judge yet. It seemed as if the whole school knew what was going on.

As they drove to the courthouse, her dad filled her in. "I'll lead you through the story," he said. "Just tell it the way it happened."

"And what about cross-examination?" As the daughter of two lawyers and someone who'd watched courtroom dramas on TV, Andi knew the opposition lawyer would get to question her.

"Just answer honestly," her dad said.

They cleared security without much trouble; most people were headed out of the building at lunchtime, not into it. Andi walked into court and was happy to see Coach Dunphy already there. She was less happy when she saw who was sitting across the aisle from him: Coach Josephson.

"Just be polite, say hello, and sit down next to Dunph," her dad whispered, as if reading her mind.

She walked down the aisle in front of her father. Coach Josephson was glaring at her. "Hello, Coach," she said, looking her in the eye for a moment.

"It's not 'Coach' anymore," Ms. Josephson replied, turning away to talk to her lawyer.

Andi's dad patted her on the back. "You did fine."

A moment after they were seated, the judge came in and everyone stood, then sat.

He looked at the other lawyer. "I presume, Ms. Burmeister, this is Ms. Josephson?"

Burmeister stood. Apparently, you never addressed a judge while seated. "Yes, Your Honor, this is Amy Josephson."

"Thank you for coming on such short notice, Ms. Josephson," the judge said.

He turned to Andi's dad. "And who have you got with you, counselor?"

Andi's dad stood. "Your Honor, this is my daughter, Andi. She is the cocaptain of the Merion sixth-grade girls' team."

The judge nodded. "Andi, thank you for coming. Would you mind coming up here and sitting in this chair next to where I'm sitting?"

Andi understood. She walked to the chair and stood, waiting for someone to swear her in—the way she'd seen on TV.

The judge understood. "Andi, this is a hearing, not a trial, so you won't be under oath. But I would appreciate it if you'd answer the questions honestly."

"Yes, Your Honor," Andi said, and sat down.

Her dad went first. He led her through all that had happened, beginning with the first day of tryouts. As instructed, Andi answered in detail, especially when walking through the locker room incident at Chester Heights. Her dad also asked her to explain how divided the team had been at first—making the point that it had taken a lot to get them to the point where all twelve of them signed the petition.

Finally, he thanked her and sat down. The judge nodded at Ms. Burmeister, who stood and walked to stand directly in front of Andi.

She started with the soccer season, asking Andi about how she had "publicly humiliated" Coach Johnston to get on the team and then to play more. Andi's dad had told her to expect something like this and to stay calm. She did.

"I wanted to play and thought I was good enough to play," she said. "Coach Johnston told the school principal the only reason he cut me was because I was a girl. My friend Jeff Michaels told his dad what was going on and he thought it was worth a story on NBC Sports–Philadelphia."

Burmeister seemed surprised. "You're saying it wasn't your idea to take your case to the media?"

"No, ma'am, it wasn't."

"But you went along with it, right?" she said, recovering.

"Yes, ma'am. I wanted to play."

She moved forward quickly to the media turnout at the first game. Andi explained that she had known nothing about it beforehand and really didn't want any publicity during basketball season.

"Well, you've got it now, don't you?" Ms. Burmeister said, drawing a laugh from the crowd.

She went on to ask Andi if she and her "friends" hadn't overreacted or misunderstood an "innocent" comment in the Chester Heights locker room.

Andi jumped on that one. "If it was an innocent or misunderstood comment, why didn't Coach . . . Ms. Josephson, just say she was sorry or that she hadn't meant it that way?"

"Your father prepared you well, didn't he?" Burmeister said.

Talking about Andi's benching, she just said, "Wouldn't you agree that a coach, even an inexperienced one, probably knows more about who should play and who shouldn't than an eleven-year-old?

Andi couldn't believe she'd asked that question. It was like throwing a batting-practice fastball to Bryce Harper, the Phillies superstar right-fielder.

"I would agree that Fran Dunphy knows more about who should or shouldn't play than an inexperienced coach does, and he started me and started Lisa Carmichael in his first game as our coach, and we won easily."

The courtroom was murmuring loudly. Her father would tell Andi later it had been because an eleven-year-old kid was outsmarting one of the city's better lawyers.

Burmeister seemed to understand. She thanked Andi and the judge told her to step down.

"Ms. Josephson," he said. "Your turn."

35

CAROL BURMEISTER WALKED AMY JOSEPHSON THROUGH
the saga of the Merion Middle School sixth-grade girls'
basketball season, just as Amy's dad had done with
her. But the spin was entirely different.

She had Ms. Josephson explain why she had wanted
to coach and how hard she had worked all summer
and fall to be prepared. Josephson talked about trying to find the right combination of girls to play when
the games began and how sorry she was that the two
African American girls and some of their teammates
had completely misunderstood her point prior to the
Chester Heights game.

She went on to say that Andi Carillo was a talented
player, but from day one it had been apparent to her
that she thought she was above all rules because of
the notoriety she had gained during soccer season. Yes,

Hal Johnston was a friend and she had sympathized with what he'd gone through, especially after coaching Ms. Carillo for a few days. She had been stunned and hurt by the petition, and even though Mr. Block had urged her to continue coaching, she had stepped down because if the girls wanted someone who would coddle them, well, so be it.

"So, in the end, you stepped down because you thought you were doing what was best for the girls you'd worked so hard to coach, correct?" Ms. Burmeister said.

Andi almost gagged.

"I didn't think it was best for them to be coddled, but I *did* think they'd be happier if I stepped down. So I did it to try to make them happy."

Ms. Burmeister turned the podium over to Andi's dad.

"I'm going to steer clear of your treatment of my daughter," he said as he stood. "Because, obviously, I'm biased. So, let's talk about the other eleven girls on the team."

He talked about Lisa Carmichael's benching and all the suicides she'd asked eleven-year-old girls to run—asking her to explain what they were. "I understand one of your assistants ran with the girls one day," he said. "Did you ever run?"

"She's much younger than I am," Ms. Josephson said.

He then asked about Joan Axelson's resignation. As it turned out, he'd hit a nerve—the right one to hit.

"She was disloyal from the start," Ms. Josephson said. "Clearly, she wanted my job. She undermined me with the players—particularly your daughter, who she encouraged to question me every chance she got. She seemed to think that because she played college basketball, she knew more about the game than I did."

"Is it possible she was right?" Tony Carillo said in a gentle tone.

"No—I mean, well, anything is possible. But I doubt she spent the summer studying coaching books."

"So, like the players, ultimately she turned on you?"

"From the beginning. Then there was that ridiculous scene after the Chester Heights game when she tried to convince me that what I'd said in the locker room was somehow wrong."

She was rambling now. How could a twenty-three-year-old know more about *anything* than she did? How dare she question her feelings on race? "I work with black people every day," she said. "I teach them. I coached them—even if they don't listen!"

"Your black players didn't listen to you?"

"No. They were impossible. As bad as your daughter!"

"But two of your best players."

"Well, yes. They can play ball. And run. And jump. No surprise there."

She stopped suddenly, looking around. The courtroom had gone completely silent.

"Your Honor," Burmeister said, standing. "May we have a five-minute recess?"

"No need, counselor," Tony Carillo said. "No further questions."

Andi saw tears in Amy Josephson's eyes as she shakily walked back to the table where Burmeister was still standing. Andi almost felt sorry for her former coach. Almost.

Levin waited until Burmeister and Andi's dad had taken their seats and gave a deep sigh.

"Even though I knew there was a game this afternoon, I had planned to take a while to consider both sides of this issue," he said after a moment. "I'm not big on rushing to judgment. But it's clear to me now that there's no need. The motion for an injunction is denied. Coach Dunphy, Ms. Carillo, good luck today."

Andi couldn't believe it. Except she could. Ms. Josephson's meltdown on the witness stand had made Judge Levin's decision easy.

Fran Dunphy was shaking her father's hand. "You were Barney Greenwald and she was Captain Queeg," he said.

"So, you saw *The Caine Mutiny*?" her father said.

"Read it, too," Dunphy said.

"Whaaa?" Andi said.

"I'll explain in the car," her dad said. "We all need to get going."

They stopped at McDonald's on the way back to school because Andi was starving. On the way, her father explained that *The Caine Mutiny* was a famous book—and movie. In the movie, Humphrey Bogart played Captain Queeg, the incompetent and often-cruel captain of the *Caine*, leading to a mutiny. During the trial of the mutineers Queeg melted down under cross-examination much the way Ms. Josephson had melted down.

"The only thing missing today were the steel balls," her dad said.

"Steel balls?"

"He had two little steel balls he rolled in his hands whenever he got nervous. Ms. Josephson could have used them today."

It was midway through fifth period when Andi walked back into the school. She had to go to the principal's office to get a note excusing her lateness. Ms. Dumas barely looked at her as she filled it out. When she signed it and handed it to Andi, she said, "I guess you girls got your victory in court?"

Apparently, word had gotten back to school very

quickly that Coach Dunphy would still be coaching that afternoon.

"We get to have a season, yes, ma'am," Andi said. She left before Ms. Dumas could answer.

When she got to her English class, Mr. Anderson, the teacher, looked at the late note, then put it on his desk. He looked at Andi, who was waiting for him to give his approval, and said, "What are you waiting for, Ms. Carillo? Have a seat."

Clearly, *everyone* had heard the news about the outcome in court.

Jeff was waiting for Andi when she came out of sixth-period history. He knew she was headed for the locker room and the bus to Bryn Mawr Tech.

"I heard you were *great!*" he said, giving her a hug. Then, embarrassed, he said, "Sorry, didn't mean to get too excited."

Andi laughed. "No worries," she said. "Who told you I was great?"

"Your dad texted my dad. He texted me."

That made sense.

Jeff was on a roll now. "Some of the guys were thinking about asking Coach C to kick Arlow off the team because of what he said about you on TV."

"I doubt Coach C will do that," she said.

Jeff grinned. "Yeah, maybe he'll get *so* mad he'll quit. Then Coach Dunphy could coach *both* teams."

Andi laughed at the joke and said, "Leave him alone. He's ours. Gotta go."

Normally, Coach C walked into the locker room on the stroke of 3:30 p.m. If anyone wasn't there on time, he noticed. Which is why it was a surprise when 3:30 came and went with no sign of either coach. There was also no sign of Arlow. Then came 3:35. Finally, at 3:40, the two coaches and Arlow walked in together. Everyone else was dressed and ready to go. The game was scheduled to start in twenty minutes.

"Sorry we're late," Coach C said. "Ron has something to say."

Arlow stood in front of his teammates, arms folded. His voice was uncharacteristically soft, almost to the point where it was difficult to hear him.

"I talked to the coaches and they've explained to me how upset everyone was—including all of you—with what I said about Andi Carillo on television last night. It was wrong. I guess I'm still a little upset she got all the glory in soccer season."

Jeff started to say something. Arlow noticed. "Sorry, Michaels," he said. "Didn't mean it that way. I was wrong to say what I said. The entire girls' team signed that petition to remove Coach Josephson. I'm going to apologize to her and I'm apologizing to all of you guys now because I embarrassed *our* team by saying what I said."

He paused for a moment and Jeff thought he was finished. But he wasn't. "I've also told Coach C and Coach B that, given what I did, I shouldn't be cocaptain of the team anymore. I want to be part of this team and help us win. But Michaels should be the captain."

Now he was done. Jeff wasn't sure how sincere he was, but he'd made the effort.

Coach C jumped in. "Anyone have any objection to Michaels being our captain the rest of the way?"

There was silence.

"Okay, Jeff, get 'em in. We need to get warmed up in a hurry."

Jeff stepped to the middle of the locker room and said, "'Beat the Techies'—on three."

They all joined him—including Arlow—and then they headed out the door and up to the court.

36

FORTUNATELY FOR MERION, BRYN MAWR TECH'S STRENGTHS
were science and math, not sports. It was the weakest
team in the league. It was known to one and all as "the
nerd school."

It showed.

Jeff started at point guard and Arlow started on the
bench. By the end of the first quarter, it was 19–6 and
Coach C brought in five new players—Arlow among
them. It really didn't matter who played; the lead
continued to build all afternoon. The final was 49–22.
Coach C ordered five passes before taking a shot in the
fourth quarter to keep the score down. That helped,
but Bryn Mawr simply couldn't score.

"It'll be tougher Friday when we got to Radnor, I
promise you that," Coach C said in the locker room
after the game. "We have to keep winning because

Haverford's not going to lose anytime soon since Jordan's healthy again."

Jeff had checked the schedule and had seen that the rematch with Haverford—it was one of the four teams Merion played twice—was in the last game of the season. They would almost certainly need to go undefeated between now and then and hope Jordan missed another game along the way if they were going to have a chance to even tie for the conference title. For now, he was happy to be 4–2—especially after the events of the last few days.

As he and Danny walked out of the locker room, Danny commented, "No media, huh? That's a switch."

Jeff laughed. "We're playing sixth-grade basketball and we're surprised there's no media waiting for us after a game. Something's wrong with this picture."

Danny laughed. "Maybe," he said, "we've finally got it right."

Andi felt like she was dreaming. For the first time all year, she was playing with a group of girls she felt completely comfortable with and a coach who had no ax to grind with her—or anyone else.

The Bryn Mawr Tech girls weren't any better than the Bryn Mawr Tech boys. By halftime, Merion led

31–9 and Andi had scored fifteen points. Coach Dunphy got everyone playing time in the second half, putting his players in a passive zone defense to give Bryn Mawr a chance to score and telling his players not to shoot any threes.

"No need to embarrass them," he said softly during a time-out.

The final score was 53–25. It could have been far worse than that. This was one game that Andi suspected Merion could have won with Coach Josephson still in charge.

Maybe.

The bus ride back to school was unlike any other she had experienced in soccer or basketball. It was loud and celebratory and included some singing. When Coach Dunphy said he couldn't stand one more Jonas Brothers song, they challenged him to come up with one of his own. He promptly launched into Billy Joel's "Piano Man" and impressed them all with his ability to carry the tune.

Jeff had texted Andi to say that everyone had played, Ron Arlow had stepped down as captain after apologizing for attacking Andi in his TV interview, and they had also won easily. Maybe Andi *was* dreaming. It all seemed too good to be true.

Her mom was waiting for her when the bus pulled up to school.

"Quite a day," she said. "Your dad said you did great in the courtroom."

"Well," Andi said, "let's put it this way: I did better than Ms. Josephson."

"So I heard," her mother said. "So I heard."

There was plenty of media coverage the next couple of days of what had happened in court. Andi was glad there had been no TV cameras allowed into the hearing because she had no need to see Ms. Josephson's meltdown again. She did find *The Caine Mutiny* on Netflix and watched it on Saturday afternoon from beginning to end. Her father's comparison of Ms. Josephson to Captain Queeg fit almost perfectly. She could almost see her rolling the steel balls in her hand.

Jeff called Saturday morning to see if she wanted to go out for a celebratory pizza. There was, he pointed out, lots to celebrate. She asked for a rain check until the following Saturday. She was exhausted from the events of the week—even though everything had turned out well. Better than well.

All of a sudden, they had gone from their season appearing to be over to feeling as if they could beat anyone they might play in the conference. They were now 4–2 with six games left and trailed just two teams—Haverford and Radnor. They would play Haverford to end the season and they had just beaten Radnor at home on Friday. A lost season had become a promising season.

Even more important, it had become fun.

Coach Dunphy had changed the lineup to start the five best players and make sure they got the most minutes, but he had managed to keep everyone involved. Those who had been starters and were now coming in off the bench didn't mind. They were still getting playing time and the team was winning.

What's more, the better they played, the more they proved that they had been right about Coach Josephson—certainly on the court. Of course, it was unfair to compare a sixth-grade gym teacher to a possible future Hall of Fame coach. Still, the changes he'd made weren't that complicated and he had seen his team practice exactly once before making those changes.

Andi wasn't surprised that she had played better once she wasn't looking over her shoulder constantly, but she *was* a little surprised at how good a player Lisa Carmichael was now that she too was getting to play more minutes. Lisa had long arms and was very quick getting off her feet. She was actually a better rebounder than Eleanor, even though Eleanor was a couple of inches taller than she was.

Maria Medley was much more effective at point

guard, because when her quickness forced a double-team, she had multiple choices on where to go with the ball. No longer was Eleanor the only consistent scorer on the court.

Jamie Bronson, freed of the need to try to be a second scorer, was a natural at doing the little things that needed doing: guarding the other team's best inside player to help keep Eleanor out of foul trouble; keeping the ball alive on the boards so that Lisa or Eleanor could get to it; setting hard screens that were almost impossible to get around.

There was no doubt the seven bench players weren't as good as the first five, but Coach Dunphy was able to spot them into the game, almost always keeping at least three starters on the floor. That way the team might dip a little bit on offense, but very little on defense. He was also a master of changing defenses. He spent almost an entire practice one day teaching the girls the art of the zone trap. That meant Merion could play man-to-man, straight zone, or trap—full-court or half-court. It became almost impossible for an opponent to get into any kind of offensive rhythm.

What had been a bad team in December became a very good team as the calendar turned to February. Andi went from dreading practice every day to looking forward to it. Basketball practice wasn't just fun, it was a learning experience.

As they walked off the court one afternoon, Jamie threw an arm around Andi. "You know, we all owe you, Carillo," she said. "If not for you, I think—I know— we'd have all just suffered our way through the season with Coach Josephson and figured there was nothing we could do about it. No matter how we finish up, this has been *fun*. Winning makes everything more fun, but it's all been fun."

She paused and her voice choked just a little when she said, "Thank you for that."

Andi gave her a hug. It was amazing how far they had come since those first practices.

When she told Jeff what had happened, he laughed and said, "You could write a book about your year in the sixth grade."

Andi nodded. "I could write two," she answered.

"Yeah," he said. "And just think, the basketball's season's not even over yet."

37

THE WINNING STREAK THAT THE MERION SIXTH-GRADE GIRLS' team began when Fran Dunphy became the coach was easy to understand. The winning streak the boys started at the same time was harder to explain.

Except that, somehow, Ron Arlow's outburst on TV seemed to have a calming effect on the entire team. Arlow losing his captaincy seemed to make everyone feel better about what was going on in the locker room. And Coach C's decision to bench him, starting Jeff at the point and then bringing Arlow in for brief spurts, at either the point—when Jeff was rested—or at the shooting guard spot next to Jeff, clearly worked well.

Jeff knew that Arlow couldn't stand the new setup: he was accustomed to being the star and the captain, not a sixth man—a valuable one, but still a sixth man. The stars of the team now were Jeff, Tavon

Washington, and Danny Diskin. With Arlow's minutes limited and Jeff controlling the offense most of the time, Washington and Diskin were seeing the ball a lot more and were taking full advantage.

What's more, Merion was a much better defensive team with Arlow not playing. After Jeff's buzzer-beating shot against King of Prussia, they had gotten on a run, reeling off six more wins to get to 9–2 in the conference with one game to play. The girls had done the exact same thing. In fact, they were 7–0 under Coach Dunphy and also 9–2 in the conference with one game to play.

Both would finish their seasons against Haverford: the boys at home, the girls on the road. The girls were one game behind the Squirrels, but the winner of the finale would win the conference title, since Merion had beaten Haverford early in the season and would have the tiebreaker by virtue of sweeping the two games between the schools. The boys were also one game behind and needed to win to tie for the conference title. The tiebreakers were more complicated on their side, since the two schools would split if Merion won the rematch.

What made things even more difficult, though, was Michael Jordan.

Jordan was the reason that, after Merion had traveled to Narberth and won easily to get to 9–2 and set up the showdown with Haverford, Coach C began practice the next day by asking his players not to go through shooting drills, but to sit on the bleachers.

A little puzzled, they all complied.

"We have a decision to make," he said. "And I do mean *we*, because Coach B and I have talked about this and we agree this is something all of you need to be on board with, if we're going to do it."

Jeff was completely puzzled.

"Look, fellas, we all saw Jordan play six weeks ago," he said. "I think all the attention and publicity he's been receiving is ridiculous—unfair to him, really, because to heap all of that on a twelve-year-old is just not right. He can be the greatest kid in the world and it's going to impact him. It has to.

"My guess is, if you guys play basketball all through college, you probably won't face someone as talented as he is. Calling a twelve-year-old a 'can't miss' player is stupid. Heck, he might not grow another inch. He might get hurt or all the attention might go to his head. But he's about as close to 'can't miss' at this age as anyone I've ever seen, and I have a close friend who saw the real Michael Jordan in high school and reminded me that he didn't make varsity as a sopho-more."

Jeff had read about that, how getting sent to the JV

team had fueled Jordan throughout his career. It did not appear as if that would be a problem for Little MJ.

"I know I'm not telling you guys anything you don't already know. So here's my question: We played them about as straight-up as we possibly could have the first time and, as we all agreed afterward, we had no chance.

"We can do that again. We're a better team now than we were then and maybe we can slow Jordan down just enough to have a chance to steal the game. I've talked to some other coaches and they say the best thing about him is if you try to double-team him or triple-team him, he's happy to set up his teammates. That's why he's averaging a triple-double—points, rebounds, assists playing about twenty minutes a game.

"I don't think they're unbeatable, I really don't. But I'm wondering if we shouldn't try something different, something that might throw him—and them—off-balance."

He looked around for a moment as if waiting for someone to say something. Someone did: Danny Diskin. "What have you got in mind, Coach?"

"Hold the ball," Coach C said. "There's no shot clock at our level. We can spend the next two days working on a spread offense. I actually talked to Coach Dunphy about this over the weekend. We're good passers and good ball handlers, especially when we have Michaels and Arlow on the court together, which I know we haven't done much lately. But we have to be ready for them to trap—especially Jordan. He loves to float in the passing lanes looking for steals. And if we get behind, we have to scrap the idea and play straight-up as best we can."

"Coach, isn't that kind of a cowardly way to try to play?"

It was Arlow.

"Not an unreasonable question, Arlow. How many of you here have heard of Dean Smith?"

About half the hands went up—Jeff's being one of them; Arlow's not.

"Dean Smith coached at North Carolina for thirty-six years—won eight hundred and seventy-nine games. Coached the real Michael Jordan, as a matter of fact. He was famous for an offense called 'the Four Corners,' where he put one player in the middle and had him dribble the ball until double-teamed and then pass to the open player to kill the clock when he had a lead.

"This was before there was a shot clock. He even tried it at the *start* of a game against Duke once, held the ball for fifteen minutes with his team down two to zero."

"What happened?" Tavon Washington asked.

"They were down seven zip at the half and lost. But he was willing to try it because he thought it was the best way to win the game."

"Bet he never did it when Jordan played for him," Arlow said.

Coach C grinned. "I was hoping you'd say that, Arlow," he said. "As a matter of fact, he did: ACC Championship game in 1982. UNC was up two early in the second half and Virginia was playing a zone with Ralph Sampson, who was seven-four, at the back of it. UNC held the ball for fifteen minutes trying to pull Virginia out of the zone."

"Who won?" Russ Ramsey asked.

"North Carolina—by two. People still point to that game as the one that convinced people it was time for a shot clock. So, if a team with Michael Jordan was willing to hold the ball like that, is there anything wrong with a team playing *against* Michael Jordan holding it?"

Jeff stood up. He was, after all, the team captain. "I say we try it," he said.

Danny Diskin raised his hand. "Agree." A chorus of voices followed him, all agreeing.

Coach C turned to Arlow. "Ron, you'll be an important part of this, but if you're uncomfortable with it, you don't have to play. It's your call."

"I'm good with it, Coach," Arlow said. Jeff was pretty

sure Coach C saying he'd be an important part of it helped Arlow make his decision.

"Okay," Coach C said. "Let's get going. We've got a lot of work to do the next two days."

Andi couldn't help but notice that the boys' team was running some funny kind of offense when she came into the gym a few minutes before the end of their practice to be ready when it was the girls' turn to take the court.

Jeff was handling the ball in the middle of the court, almost as if he were putting on some kind of dribbling exhibition. The other four players were standing in what looked like a box formation around the court. As soon as one player left his man to double-team Jeff, he would pick the ball up and throw it to the open man. Then he would race in the direction of the player with the ball, get it back, and start the dribbling exhibition again.

It was weird.

As the boys came off the court, Jeff jogged past her and said, "I'll tell you later." She saw Coach Crist stop to talk to Coach Dunphy for a moment. Coach Dunphy was doing most of the talking.

Andi had been baffled initially when Haverford began plowing through teams as the conference season unfolded. The Squirrels had been, without doubt, the worst team they had faced before winter recess. Merion had beaten them badly even with Coach Josephson still playing her silly games with the lineup.

What she hadn't known was that Haverford's two best players had been injured at the time. According to Maria, who seemed to know someone on every team in the city, their center, Helen Bjorn, and their point guard, Alana Faroh-Wantu, had recovered from their injuries during winter recess. They had beaten Bryn Mawr Tech before Christmas and hadn't lost since their two stars had returned, meaning they were 10–1 and in first place, one game ahead of Merion.

"Imagine us without Eleanor and me," Maria had said in explaining how good Bjorn and Faroh-Wantu were. "They were both born overseas—Bjorn in Denmark, Faroh-Wantu in Ghana. Bjorn is about six feet tall; Faroh-Wantu is about my size. I'm told they can both *play*."

Andi knew worrying about how good Haverford might be was a waste of time. The only thing that was important was beating them. If they could do that, win the title and make the playoffs, she'd be happy. Beyond happy. If not, well, she was still happy because the last few weeks had been so much fun. She just didn't want to be *too* happy.

They still had one game left that they needed to win.

38

BEFORE THEY ENTERED THE GYM AT HAVERFORD TO WARM up, Coach Dunphy stood in front of his players.

"This may or may not be the last time we're together as a team," he said. "I just wanted to tell you all—win or lose today—how much I've enjoyed these last few weeks. I started out doing this as a favor to an old friend and to help you guys out because I thought you deserved it. It's ended up being one of the more enjoyable experiences of my career. That's because of all of you."

Jamie stood up and said, "Coach, how about taking over the varsity teams next year?"

They all laughed and Coach Dunphy said, "You've got a great varsity coach."

"Maybe you could be her assistant?" Andi asked.

Coach Dunphy smiled. "Now, that might be a possibility."

They all had smiles on their faces when they went out to warm up. That good feeling lasted right until tip-off, when Bjorn out-leaped Eleanor for the tip and directed the ball right into the hands of a streaking Faroh-Wantu in what was clearly a set play. Faroh-Wantu was past Maria before Maria could take a step and went in for an uncontested layup.

Fun time was over.

It was 8–0 before Coach Dunphy called time to settle his team down. "Hey, we knew they were going to be good," he said. He looked Eleanor in the eye. "Do you think the Bjorn kid is better than you, Eleanor?"

"No, sir, I don't."

"Fine, then quit playing like you're scared of her."

He looked at Maria. "How about you, Maria? Is that little point guard better than you are?"

"No, sir, she's not."

"Same thing: Play like it."

Finally, he pointed at Andi.

"You've had two open shots and passed them up, Carillo. You afraid to shoot?"

"No, sir."

"Fine. Then shoot. You're the best shooter out there

on either team. Funny thing, though, you can't score if you don't shoot."

He stared around the huddle as the horn sounded and one of the officials poked her head into the huddle. "Gotta get 'em out, coach."

Coach Dunphy put his hand into the middle of the huddle and everyone jumped to put their hands in, too.

"Play like champions!" he said, and they all repeated the three words.

It was the first time that Coach Dunphy had really gone after the players since he'd taken over. Of course, it was the first time he'd really needed to go after them.

Maria brought the ball down, raced behind a high-ball screen from Jamie Bronson and, as the defense came to her, quickly reversed the ball to Andi, who was wide-open. She was practically into her shooting motion as she caught the ball. It swished—for three—and Merion was on the board.

"Here we go," Andi said as she backtracked to set up on defense. "Here we go."

Coach Dunphy's words clearly calmed the Mustangs down, and they began playing like the team that had won seven straight games—most easily—since his arrival. The Squirrels' lead was down to 14–10 at the end of the first quarter. Both coaches gave their starters a rest in the second quarter because the pace of the game was fast and the intensity was building. The Haverford gym was packed—a lot of fans had come up from Merion, and there had been some Temple fans following the Mustangs since Coach Dunphy's arrival—so it was loud. Also, hot. The weather outside was unseasonably warm for late February—midfifties. It was 25–22, Haverford still up at halftime.

"This is exactly the kind of game we expected, isn't it?" Coach Dunphy asked during the break. "We don't need to do anything fancy, just keep doing what we've been doing since it was 8–0. Any questions?"

There were none. The season had come down to twelve minutes of basketball. You couldn't ask for much more than that.

The second half began with Eleanor pitching the ball to Andi out of a double-team and Andi drilling her third three of the game to tie the score at 25–25. Then, after a Haverford miss, Maria found Lisa on a sweet backdoor cut, and for the first time all day, Merion led. It was 27–25.

It was the Haverford coach's turn to call time to calm her players. It worked. A three by Faroh-Wantu put the Squirrels back in the lead at 28–27. The game seesawed. Neither coach went to the bench to start the fourth quarter. This wasn't the time to rest. There would be plenty of time for that after the game—especially for the losers.

An offensive rebound by Jamie set up a Maria three with 1:44 left, tying the game again at 49–all. It was the kind of play no one on the Merion team would have even thought about early in the season. Jamie grabbed the ball, quickly recognized she had two defenders in front of her, and turned and got the ball back to Maria as she stepped into her shot.

Coach Dunphy had told them not long after taking over that Mike Krzyzewski—who he had played with on an all-army team after college—had once told him the most demoralizing play in basketball was a three-pointer that came after a missed shot and an offensive rebound.

Haverford came down and was clearly in no rush to take a shot. Their players looked tired, but the Mustangs were tired, too. Finally, when the clock got to thirty-five seconds, Haverford called time.

"We can't just let them run the clock down and take a shot at the buzzer," Coach Dunphy said. "We have to attack defensively. Even if they score, we get the ball back with a chance to tie or win. I would rather give up a layup right now than a three. So, let's attack the perimeter. And don't worry about fouling. Let them have to make two and we'll still get the ball again."

They all nodded.

"One more thing: Don't call time when we get the ball. I don't want them to set up their defense. Just run the clock to ten and then"—he paused to look at Maria—"you create something."

Maria nodded.

Haverford inbounded and Faroh-Wantu stood near midcourt to dribble the clock down. Maria and Andi double-teamed her. She picked the ball up and passed quickly to Bjorn, who had come out to take the pass. Bjorn fed Faroh-Wantu, who went to the basket. With Eleanor having come out to guard Bjorn, the lane was wide open. Faroh-Wantu laid the ball in with the clock ticking under twenty.

Bronson grabbed the ball and inbounded quickly to Maria so Haverford wouldn't have a chance to call time. She raced into the frontcourt, then pulled up. Everyone ran to their regular positions in the offense. Maria dribbled the clock down and, at twelve, started toward the key. Faroh-Wantu backpedaled, keeping her in front of her, willing to give up a three but not a drive into the lane. Jamie came to screen, and her defender went with her to switch and get over the screen.

Maria picked the ball up and ball-faked as if to pass inside to Eleanor. Andi's defender, seeing the fake, dove in the direction of the lane. Maria saw her move and instantly swung a pass to Andi. Andi took one quick dribble and shot from just outside the three-point line.

Swish. It was 52–51, Merion. Andi saw the clock melting from three seconds to two. Behind her, Andi could hear Coach Dunphy screaming from the bench for time out. "Time!" he screamed. "Time!"

No one heard him. Bjorn had grabbed the ball out of the basket and flung a pass to Faroh-Wantu just short of midcourt. She took one dribble and shot—either just as the buzzer went off or just after it went off. Andi wasn't sure. The ball arced through the air, hit the backboard—and dropped through.

One ref was running downcourt, arms in the air to indicate the shot counted. The other—Andi made a point of looking—made no signal.

The Haverford players were celebrating. Coach Dunphy charged at the official who hadn't given any signal and said: "The shot was after the buzzer *and* you should have given me time out. You *can't* count that basket!"

The official put her arms up defensively. "Hang on, Coach. Let us sort this out."

There was, of course, no replay, and there were no tenths on the clock. The two officials went to the scorer's table and talked to the clock operator for a moment. Then, with two security guards having magically appeared to stand in front of them, they retreated to midcourt to talk. Everyone milled around waiting for a decision.

Finally, the official who Coach Dunphy had tried to talk to nodded her head, walked in the direction of the scorer's table, and put her arms in the air in the touchdown signal, meaning the shot—obviously a three-pointer—was good.

There was no way to argue or plead the point. There was no replay.

Final score: Haverford 54, Merion 52.

The season was over.

39

FOR A HALF, COACH C'S "FOUR CORNERS" STRATEGY WORKED to perfection. Almost.

After Michael Jordan had won the opening tap, one of his teammates missed a jump shot, and Eric Billings rebounded and quickly got the ball to Jeff.

Even with Jordan double-teaming and chasing, Merion was able to kill the clock, until Jeff found a wide-open Danny for a layup that made it 2–0 with 1:04 left in the first quarter. Jordan scored quickly to tie the game, but Ron Arlow hit a shot to beat the buzzer for a 4–2 lead after one quarter.

Haverford led 7–6 at the half, after Jeff started what should have been the last play too soon and Jordan rebounded a Tavon Washington miss and went coast-to-coast for a buzzer-beating layup. Jeff was kicking himself coming off the court. Every mistake, he knew, was crucial in a game like this.

"Anyone want to change our strategy?" Coach C said in the locker room. The shouts of "no way" were unanimous—including Arlow's.

"We were almost perfect—and that's why we're down one. We'll have to be perfect this half—maybe a little better than perfect. But we've got a chance, guys. We've definitely got a chance."

It was 10–10 after three quarters, and you could see the frustration in the eyes of the Haverford players.

It was Merion's ball to start the fourth quarter. The Mustangs dribbled and passed, the Squirrels chased.

When the clock went under three minutes, Haverford's coach decided it was time for a change in strategy. He ordered his players to start fouling. Quickly, they committed three fouls. That meant the next one— the fourth of the quarter—would put Merion on the foul line to shoot one-and-one: make the first, you shoot a second. Miss and you don't.

Coach C called time after the third foul. The clock was at 2:02. "I want the ball in Jeff's hands and Ron's hands," he said. "If one of you other three"—he looked at Diskin, Washington, and Ramsey—"have to touch the ball, you get it back to Michaels or Arlow *right away*. Everyone understand?"

They all nodded. Jeff and Arlow were easily the team's best free-throw shooters.

Haverford let some time slip off the clock, hoping to foul one of Merion's frontcourt players. Finally, with the clock at 1:13, Jordan went for a steal and fouled Jeff.

Haverford's coach called time right away—no doubt to let Jeff think about the free throws. It didn't work. Jeff made both to make it 12–10.

Haverford came down and, with surprising patience, worked the ball around. Finally, Jordan caught the ball at the top of the key, faked as if to drive, and floated a three-pointer at the basket. Jeff actually thought it was a break for Merion that he hadn't just driven by everyone. But the shot went in with twenty-six seconds to go. Haverford led 13–12.

This time, Coach C called time. "We're playing for the last shot," he said. "I know that goes against basketball protocol when you're behind, but we just can't give Jordan a chance to beat us if we score."

Everyone understood. "Jeff, Ron, I want you to take turns with the ball out front. Then, whoever has it with ten seconds left, run one-four like we do in the end game."

"Coach, I think Jeff should have the ball," Arlow said. "He's our best creator."

Coach C smiled. "I think you're right, Ron, let's do that."

They walked back on court. Everyone in the packed gym was on their feet. Jeff was nervous, but unafraid. They'd come this far, why couldn't they make one more play? And, even if they didn't, who would have thought they'd be in this position when the day started?

Arlow inbounded to Jeff. As soon as he came across half-court, Haverford jumped into a double-team, trying to surprise him. He recognized it, though, and quickly passed the ball to Diskin at the top of the key. Haverford dropped back into man-to-man with Jordan at the top of the key guarding Jeff—but giving him some space.

Jeff waited until the clock went under ten. Jordan was on him, long arms extended. Jeff made a fake as if to shoot and, to his surprise, Jordan bought it for a split second. That gave him a half-step, and he charged into the lane with the clock under five seconds.

The defense closed on him and he sensed Jordan coming at him from behind. He remembered reading something the great Jim Valvano had said once about being wary of a defender you've just gone by. "He's not leaving to go get a pizza. He's going to try to poke the ball loose from behind."

Jeff picked the ball up just before Jordan lunged

for it. Arlow was on the wing. His man had left him to try to cut Jeff off. Without a second thought, Jeff pitched the ball to Arlow, who took one dribble and, as the clock hit one second, released a jumper from the corner.

Jeff knew it was in as soon as it left Arlow's hand, and he was charging at Arlow when he saw the ball hit the net and heard the buzzer go off. There was no debating that the shot counted. Coach C's strategy had worked. They had pulled off the miracle. Final: Merion 14, Haverford 13. It sounded like a football game decided by a missed extra point. Only it wasn't.

They all piled on top of Arlow, who kept saying, "Jeff made the pass, Jeff made the pass." It was a little bit like Jeff trying to give Danny credit on his game-winner in another lifetime. Somehow, Jeff knew he meant it. Remarkably, he meant it all.

They went to shake hands with the Haverford players. Jordan was completely gracious. "You played a different game," he said. "But you outplayed us. You deserved it."

They charged into the locker room and were surprised their coach wasn't there. A moment later he walked in and held up his hands for quiet.

"Guys, that was a win you'll remember the rest of your lives. I couldn't be more proud of you. That said, I just found out that Ardmore beat Main Line. That means Haverford goes to the playoffs on the tie-breaker."

There was a moment of complete silence.

Then Jeff said: "Could there be a more perfect way to finish a season?"

They all screamed their approval and formed a huddle with Jeff and Arlow in the middle. "The best!" Jeff yelled. And they all put their hands in and yelled, "The best."

It *was*, Jeff thought, absolutely perfect.

"At least you missed out on the playoffs fair and square," Andi was saying. "And everyone will remember that you beat Michael Jordan."

It had been a while since they'd been to Andy's for pizza, but they were there at eleven thirty Saturday morning, sharing a pizza and details of what had happened on Friday.

"Anybody have a video of the last play?" Jeff asked.

"A couple people had it on their cell phones, but you can't really tell. I swear, Jeff, I heard the buzzer before she shot. And, anyway, they should have given Coach Dunphy time-out."

"What'd he say afterward?"

"That he'd never enjoyed coaching a team more,

that he was proud of everything we'd done. We all had a pretty good cry together."

"Nice to be part of a game and a season worth crying over."

She nodded. "Yeah, it was."

Then she smiled. "You know I hear Coach Jensen is going to retire at the end of the school year. Leaves the boys' varsity job open."

Jeff had heard that, too. "Yeah, maybe they'll promote Coach C. I wouldn't mind playing for him again."

In fact, he loved the idea of playing for him again.

Then he had another thought: "Maybe we could get Coach Dunphy to coach us."

"I think his days as a middle school coach are over," Andi said. "But it's a nice thought."

They talked some more about how amazing both the fall and winter had been.

"I don't even want to think about the spring," Andi said.

"Well, we're due at least one peaceful season," Jeff said.

"Wanna bet?" Andi said.

"No," Jeff said firmly. "Absolutely not."

They finished their pizza and walked to the entrance, where they were each being picked up. Andi's mom was taking her to Maria Medley's birthday party. Jeff's dad was taking him to see Penn play Harvard in the Palestra.

While they walked, Jeff decided to take a risk. Not a big one, but a risk nevertheless. "Andi, you wanna come over tomorrow afternoon to study?"

She looked over at him with an expression he couldn't read. After a moment, she smiled and said, "Sure. Sounds like a plan."

As they reached the doors, Andi said: "You know, Jeffrey Daniel Michaels, we're a pretty great team, even when we're not on the same team."

He was thinking of an answer when, without warning, she leaned over and planted a quick kiss on his lips.

She smiled, turned, and walked away. He stood staring after her for a minute, then realized he couldn't stand there all day. He walked through the doors to the parking lot. Except for one thing: He was convinced his feet never touched the ground.